HARVEST AMERICAN
Writing

UNORGANIZED TERRITORY

Missouri R.

MISSOURI

St. Louis

Mississippi R.

Waynesville

Jackson
Cape Girardeau

Springfield

Fort Gibson ✗

Fayetteville

INDIAN TERRITORY

ARKANSAS

Arkansas R.

Memphis

Little Rock

Mississippi R.

The Trail of Tears
1838 ~ 1839

The Northern Route of
Cherokee Removal

MISSISSIPPI

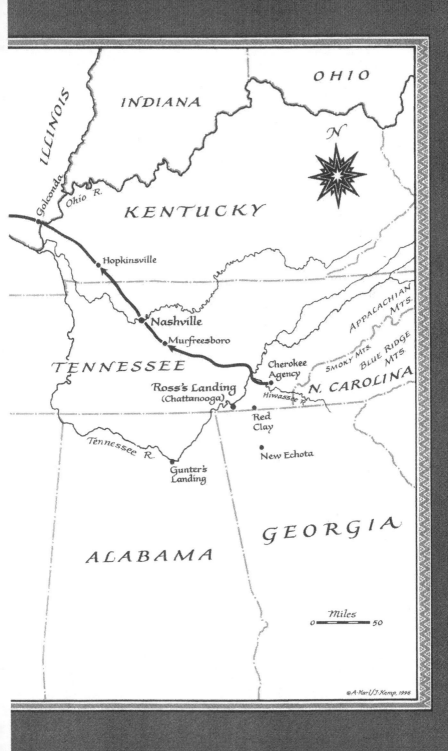

DIANE GLANCY

Pushing The Bear

A Novel of the Trail of Tears

A HARVEST BOOK · HARCOURT, INC.

San Diego   New York   London

Requests for permission to make copies of any part of the work
should be mailed to the following address: Permissions Department, Harcourt, Inc.,
6277 Sea Harbor Drive, Orlando, Florida 32887-6777.

Interior art: "Cherokee Eagle Dance Wand," photograph by Lynton Gardiner,
courtesy of Department of Library Services, American Museum of Natural History.

Library of Congress Cataloging-in-Publication Data
Glancy, Diane.
Pushing the bear: a novel of the Trail of Tears / Diane Glancy.—1st ed.
p.   cm.
ISBN 0-15-100225-8
ISBN 0-15-600544-1 (pbk.)
1. Cherokee Indians—History—19th century—Fiction.
2. Cherokee Indians—Relocation—Fiction.
3. Trail of Tears, 1838—Fiction.   I. Title
PS3557.L294P87   1996
813'.54—dc20   95-51020

Text set in Dante
Map illustration by Anita Karl and Jim Kemp
Designed by Linda Lockowitz
Printed in the United States of America
First edition

H J L M K I

For David Lewis Hall, my brother,
Lewis Hall, my father,
Orvezene Lewis Hall, my grandmother,
and Woods Lewis, my great-grandfather,
born in 1843 near Sallisaw
in Indian Territory (Oklahoma)

From October 1838 through February 1839 some eleven to thirteen thousand Cherokee walked nine hundred miles in bitter cold from the southeast to Indian Territory. One fourth died or disappeared along the way.

Contents

North Carolina

LATE SEPTEMBER, 1838

MARITOLE

"Maritole!" I heard my husband from the field. I sat on the cabin step helping the baby stand. "Maritole," Knobowtee called again. I started to get up, but the baby wobbled at my knees.

Dust swarmed over the dried cornstalks in the field by the cabin. Horses were coming. For a moment the woods beyond the cornfield whirled. Knobowtee walked between mounted soldiers into our small clearing. I stood at the cabin step, and the baby sat on the ground.

I had seen white men when they came to trade. Sometimes they rode by the farm not seeing our path. Now soldiers were in the clearing with their rifles and bayonets. I heard their quick words, but I didn't know what they said. They seemed invisible inside their dark clothes.

ᏬᏐ, I groaned.

We heard that soldiers had rounded up Cherokee in Georgia and Tennessee, but we thought the soldiers would keep riding past the settlements near us: Du'stayalun'yi and Egwanulti. Now the soldiers had found us. I stepped on an apple core that fell from my lap. The sun had burned away the morning fog, and the light and the dust blurred the men. I had to wash the baby's clothes. I was going to take the corn to the mill. A basket of apples and peaches from our trees waited by the wagon.

The soldiers talked fast. In our language, my husband told me to carry the crying baby. We were going to a stockade in Tennessee.

"ᎢᏍᏗᎥᎯᏍᏗᎥ," I told him.

"We'll march," Knobowtee answered. "Chief John Ross hoped we could keep our land. But Ridge and Boudinot, the leaders in Georgia, signed the treaty that took our land away."

"I won't," I said again to Knobowtee.

A soldier with white eyes spoke and gestured to me to take the baby. He dismounted, put his bayonet to my side, and poked. Knobowtee turned and walked ahead of me. I couldn't leave the farm. The cabin in the yellow leaves. My grandmother's spinning wheel and cotton cards. Her copper thimble. I felt my knees fold. The baby screamed and Knobowtee picked her up. The soldier lifted me to my feet, and I knew he said, "March."

They couldn't remove us. Didn't the soldiers know we were the land? The cornstalks were our grandmothers. In our story of corn, a woman named Selu had been murdered by her sons. Where her blood fell, the corn grew. The cornstalks waved their arms trying to hold us. Their voices were the long tassels reaching the air. Our spirits clung to them. Our roots entwined.

My feet would not walk, and the soldier held me up by my arm. I walked sideways and fell into the cornstalks at the side of the road. A bird's chirp filled my ears. I wanted to hold the air and the sound of the land. The soldier poked at me with his bayonet. I thought for a moment his face was blue. I tried to get up, but my knees wouldn't hold. I still had the apple core in my hand.

"Wagon." The soldier pointed and pulled me out of the cornstalks. I had heard their language from the white minister in church. He read scriptures in English, then one of our holy men would translate: ᎣᎦᏬᏓᏅ, ᏪᏍᎢ. The words spoke of hope but now there was no hope.

KNOBOWTEE

Chief John Ross had gone to Washington from Red Clay, Tennessee, to argue against the removal, but the Ridge and Boudinot faction in Georgia knew we had no chance to keep our land and signed the Treaty of New Echota in secret.

The white men were still angry that we had joined the British during the Revolutionary War. Then gold was discovered in northern Georgia near Dalonagah, and the white men wanted it. They also wanted our farms.

Chief John Ross sent runners to tell us about the men's angry voices in council. They knew Andrew Jackson wouldn't uphold the agreement that kept Cherokee land for Cherokee. Already, Georgia had made Indian meetings illegal other than to sign treaties.

I looked at Maritole as she stumbled on the path. I told her again we didn't have a chance.

After the Treaty of New Echota passed by one vote in Congress, Ross had gone to Washington to negotiate for us to oversee our own removal. His brother, Lewis Ross, would furnish supplies.

MARITOLE

I tried to follow Knobowtee, but the road kept going sideways. I walked like I was my grandmother before she died, when her knees wouldn't hold. I heard the soldiers laugh.

"Walk straight." Knobowtee carried the baby and looked at me. "We don't have any choice. There'll be a wagon ahead. You and the baby can ride."

I looked back at the cabin, but we had passed the first bend in the wagon ruts. My grandmother's scissors and her bone hairpin and shell beads were on my dresser. The bed my father helped Knobowtee make. The nutting stone and pestles he gave us when we married. Sometimes I still heard my grandmother's voice in the cabin. I couldn't leave. The sky passed before my eyes, and I felt myself hit the hard ground.

THE SOLDIERS

"Corporal, there's another cabin in the trees."

"Don't let 'em get out the back."

"Harder to stop than horses running loose."

GELEST

You soldiers. I knew you were coming. Ha. You didn't startle me. The baby who was born talking said you were coming. It was a Choolaskey. Conjurers. As soon as the baby's head was out, it sang its own birth song. It said its own secret name. ᎠᏇᎯᏍᏴᎢᎫᎭ. It said it was afraid of winter because it didn't want to be one-of-those-who-walked.

The holy men, ᎫᏓᎢᎠ-ᎤᏍᏴᎩ, made stick-crosses for the four directions, and the crosses fell to the west.

Even the birds are quiet. I would run from you, but my legs are stiff as the willow strips I soak in the creek. I hear your horses on the road. I know you stop at my cabin. I hear nothing but my heart beating in my ears. Maybe you are standing still thinking what to do. I could hear your footsteps if you walked to the creek.

If I were an animal, the soldiers could not find me. If I hold still I can become a deer. I lean over the creek and lap with my tongue. I feel under my skirt for the hooves. The soft deer tail. ᏁᎬᎤᎷᏃᎢᏆᏍᎤᎷ. My nostrils widen. I smell the wind. I look into the creek and see the downy ears on my head. I lift my head and step through the woods. My deer leavings are all of me you get.

THE SOLDIERS

"I think we lost as many as we rounded up."

"The corporal don't need to know."

"We got more than you think."

"Keep your eye on 'em. We're still losing some of 'em."

QUATY LEWIS

Of all the trees who spoke it was the pine who said we would go, covering its needles with its hands. The ground seemed to rumble loose our hold. "A whole nation would move," my husband said, sweating though it was no longer hot. Since the 1835 New Echota Treaty, the U.S. government had been trying to push the Cherokee to the new territory. A few had gone, but the rest of us wouldn't leave. Last summer, the soldiers began internment in stockades, but the heat sickened the Cherokee, and we knew they would wait until fall. Each day I looked for soldiers on the road.

MARITOLE

The rumble of the wagon startled me from blackness. I sat up. Knobowtee walked beside the wagon. "Some of the Cherokee have already gone west," I heard the men say. "How many trails have there been?"

I saw that Anna Sco-so-tah held my baby. "You can't take up the whole wagon." She pushed my feet with hers. The wagon was crowded, and I tried to make room for the others. Kee-un-e-ca and the widow Teehee of the Blue clan. Lacey Woodard of the Long Hair clan. Quaty Lewis, Wolf clan. Mrs. Young Turkey, Blind Savannah clan. The wheels jolted over the ground, and I held to the side.

The wagon rattled loose someone's voice. Was it Mrs. Young Turkey? "I seen a bug in the crock. It walk around. Around. It couldn't get out. Har. That's us now. That bug. The trees grow up like sides of a crock. Taller than us. Umgh. Soldiers make us walk in the circle in our heads. We're not getting out."

I looked at Knobowtee as he walked beside the wagon. He seemed a stranger to me.

ANNA SCO-SO-TAH

The birds called to me across the trees. Even the water spoke. "ᎤᏛᏅᎥᎤᏛᏅᎥ," I told the women bitterly in the wagon. The soldiers came down the road and told me to leave. My legs wouldn't walk. The soldiers grabbed my arms and held me up. The sky was brown as the hen blood on my boots. I tried to call to my neighbor, but my voice cackled. For a moment I thought I was a hen. I flopped on the ground. My brown feathers in the dust.

The soldiers let me stop at a stream to drink. "Maybe she'll stop cackling," they said.

MARITOLE

I took the baby from Anna Sco-so-tah and held her on my lap. I wanted to ask Knobowtee what stockade we were going to, but I knew he would not want his wife talking.

The wagon stopped along the road and was joined by other wagons and columns of men on foot in the thick woods of pine and yellow oak. The soldiers seemed nervous, and some twitched when a woman sobbed or a child cried out. Other soldiers were hard.

"Their eyes cut through us like bayonets." The widow Teehee talked under her breath.

"My legs trembled and I couldn't stand," Anna Sco-so-tah said to her as we waited in the wagon. "I sat on the ground in front of my cabin. They told me to *get up.* I tried, but my legs wouldn't stand."

The wagon started again with a jerk. Lacey Woodard cried out. Mrs. Young Turkey hushed her.

" 'Up,' the soldiers said." Anna continued twisting the hem of her cotton dress in her hands. "Their voices had vines in them. When they told me to walk, I could feel them pulling me to the wagon. My hands fluttered like they weren't mine. Somewhere the thunder growled."

Quaty Lewis had heard that the soldiers separated parents from their children in their hurry. Her voice choked. The men who walked near the wagon looked at the ground. Knobowtee told us all to be quiet. Some of the women cried to themselves. They held their faces in their hands.

Listen to that old woman.
She yell over ever bump.
Shud up. Woman.
Umgh.

When we joined another wagon on the main road, a Cherokee called out to a friend. A soldier rode over to him. I knew he'd hit him with his whip. I started to get out of the wagon, but Knobowtee yelled at me. I screamed at the Cherokee who had called. Knobowtee knocked me back into the wagon with his arm. Anna Sco-so-tah held me in her lap. I could hear the soldier hit the man. I could smell the dust from the cornfields on Anna's apron. I could feel her hands clawing my face.

There was musket shot, and another soldier ordered the one with the whip to stop. Behind us, a horse reared up and a soldier rushed to hold it. A principal soldier ordered the wagons to start moving, and we leaped forward again with another jerk. The men and women groaned and sobbed. I held the baby so close she fussed.

Knobowtee's face was dark with fear.

"Where are we going?" I asked him. He didn't answer at first.

"I don't know, Maritole. Probably the Hiwassee River."

"In Tennessee?" I asked, but he didn't answer. I put my head in Anna's lap and covered my face with her apron. Lights sparked the darkness of Anna's apron when I pushed my fingers into my eyes. The Hiwassee was several days away.

Hey you tree, you going like us?

I had been to Red Clay, Tennessee, when I was a girl. I visited relatives and went to a green corn festival. My great-grandfather came from the old Cherokee capital, Chota, Tennessee. He moved to New Echota, Georgia, and then to North Carolina. Red Clay was now the Cherokee capital. The white men had divided our land among their states and called most of our places by English names.

I felt sick in the darkness of Anna's apron and sat up.

My mother had wanted to go to Red Clay, but my father was angry with Chief John Ross there. He thought Ross was a dreamer. My father said we would stay in North Carolina and face the loss of our land and whatever came afterward with dignity.

Knobowtee kept his dignity. Why didn't he spit on the soldiers? Why didn't everyone stand up to them and say we weren't going? The baby crawled over my lap and struggled to get away, but I held her as the wagon jolted over the road. Knobowtee frowned at me as though there was something I could do to keep her still.

I knew the soldiers were rounding up Cherokee all through the woods. Every time we joined another wagon, I looked for my mother and father and Tanner, my older brother, his wife, and two small boys.

Behind me, someone was trying to calm a fretting dog, who turned one way, then another, making small, sharp cries.

I thought of the birds and geese. The raccoon that came to the cabin step. The curl of wood smoke and the chirp of bugs from the woods. The trees were ancestors. Their roots reached into the creek banks. I wanted to hear the buzz of a fly around me on the cabin step. We were made from the soil we farmed. Now the dust road seemed to flare like cooking fires. I thought once I heard thunder. I looked at the soldiers, their boots dusty from the road, their uniforms like bruises.

The wagons passed easier over some pine needles on the road. The baby slept for a moment on my lap but soon woke at a toss of the wagon. I thought of the butter not yet made. Knobowtee was cutting the dried cornstalks for fodder when the soldiers came. Did he leave the horse hitched to the plow? What would happen to it? The Cherokee men walked in their turbans and tunics. The autumn sun shone on our heads, lighting the black hair and eyes that were dark and strained.

QUATY LEWIS

The soldiers beat an old man on the road. He bowed under the weight of the bundle on his back. His turban fell. His legs wobbled as he tried to stand but couldn't. The soldiers beat him harder with the whip to make him get up. The women cried, but the Cherokee men looked away. The soldiers didn't stop hitting him. No one could do anything. The old man struggled once more to get up but fell back to the ground. The soldiers told the Cherokee to walk around him and pushed the Cherokee with their bayonets.

In the wagon I heard the old man's voice moaning. I put my hand to my neck and felt it stir. I didn't know if it was his voice or my own throat talking.

ANNA SCO-SO-TAH

"They got Kinchow, too," I said when I saw my neighbor.

Kinchow came to the wagon. "I heard Anna cackle. I knew the soldiers was coming anyway." He looked at the women. I saw the scratches on his face, but he hadn't gotten away through the woods. "I seen Anna, too," he told the women as we waited on the road. "In a dream. I was in my cabin and she came to the window. Her arms were short. They was covered with feathers."

"He talks all the time," I said.

"She a witch," Kinchow said. "That's all I can say."

"He's a sorcerer," I told the others. "The chickens cluck when he comes. Sorcerers are night-travelers. Chickens don't like them."

"Huh?" Kinchow said. "She only got three chickens. If she eat a chicken one day, I see it walking around again the next. She a witch, I tell you. That's all I can tell."

"My chickens would peck him if I didn't chase them with a stick."

"Huh?" Kinchow grunted, as the soldiers hurried us on.

"That's how I know he's a sorcerer," I said, riding beside him. "The chickens don't like him."

MARITOLE

The campfires spoke through the dark woods like stars. I heard Anna's voice. Kinchow's. Quaty Lewis. The widow Teehee. Others. Their voices made a low hum that would rise at times like wind. I think the trees were calling. The baby cried with me. Neither Knobowtee nor the other men could stop us. "What are we going to cook with? Where is our bedding?" We wanted our cabins and belongings.

If I slept it was only until the horror stirred me. I woke crying with the others into the dark air.

The soldiers ordered us to be quiet with words we didn't always know. They walked among us and poked with bayonets. Some Cherokee men hit their women. It had been agreed in council: We would bear our fate if the removal came.

But how could we go without pots to cook with, blankets to sleep in? How could we be quiet when we were being torn away from everything we'd known?

Children had been separated from their parents by accident. Wives could not find their husbands. I could not find my own parents in camp. Where was Thomas, my younger brother? Tanner and his family? But I saw no one from my family.

Knobowtee looked for his relatives, too. His brother. His mother and sister.

In the night a woman cried out. I woke suddenly and listened. I thought I had imagined it, but then I heard another woman scream. A man's angry voice rose above the woman's.

"The soldiers killed someone," Knobowtee said, and put his hand over my mouth. He held my head to his chest. The baby was in a sleep of exhaustion. Her small chest jerked in my arms as she dreamed. Soldiers rushed past. After some muffled voices, a hush folded the camp in its darkness.

In the morning a soldier was sentenced to ten lashes. He had stabbed the woman with his bayonet.

"He lost his head trying to keep order," a soldier told our men. We could hear the whip against his uniform.

"But we want our bedding," the women said. The pain of what we lost was worse than the fear of the soldiers. "How can we sleep on the ground? The nights will get cold." The women pleaded with the soldiers, and I cried with them: "We want our cooking pots. How can we eat the army rations? We're sick from salt pork. How can the soldiers feed us along the trails? Our children starve."

We kept after the soldiers into the morning. They heard what we said. A ᎫᏃᎠᎥᎧᎥᎩᎢᎩᎩ, a holy man, told them what we said.

The holy men and even the white ministers prayed for our loss. They prayed for the return of our land and belongings.

ᏔᎫᏏᏍᏫᏌ
ᎠᏳᎡ-ᎧᎥᎩᎩ

They even prayed against the insects that bit us.

Ꮻ	now
ᏆᏍᎥᎠᏍ	insects
ᎣᏝᎫᎩ	ha then
ᎠᎥᎫᎠᎥᎥ°	wood place just
ᎠᎫᎫᎥ	residers
ᎢᏝᎦᎢ	they certainly being

(Insects are in the woods, but we ask them to stay in their place and not bite us.)

One of the principal soldiers talked to the other soldiers. He came to the group of Cherokee, where I stood with Knobowtee. I started to ask Knobowtee what he said, but he put his hand against my mouth.

"They'll let the women go back for blankets and cooking pots," he said in a hush.

"The men?" I asked.

"No, we're under guard. Get ready, Maritole. Go quickly to one of the wagons when the soldiers order. Get the bags of seed-corn. Get my musket and the blankets."

The thought of my garden last summer with beans, peas, squash, melon, pumpkin, and potatoes gnawed at my stomach when Knobowtee spoke of corn. I could see my cabin, the bones of dried clay between the logs, the cluttered garden beside the cabin, the cornfields that crowded the garden, the narrow trail through the field, the cabin like a heart, the rows of corn like ribs in the chest of the woods.

The soldiers turned the wagons around. The Indians who spoke both languages said a few of the women could go back for whatever belongings they could carry. There was a stampede toward the wagons, then a gunshot in the air. The soldiers pointed their rifles at us. Not all could go. Too many had escaped already. They rode among us and poked at who could go. They seemed to choose at random. Women who were left behind fell to their knees wailing. The soldier with light eyes rode past me and touched my shoulder with his bayonet. He said something that sounded like Cherokee, but I couldn't understand.

"Get whatever will help." Knobowtee held the baby and pushed his hand against my back. I raced for one of the wagons and stood in line panting, thinking of things I would retrieve. A soldier wrote our names. It took him a long time to understand what we said.

We rattled back toward our cabins in the dawn. I would have my bowls and the bone-handled forks. My grandmother's bone-carved hairpin I had admired since I was a girl. Her scissors. The feather-edge dishes. I thought of Knobowtee's musket and shot pouch and his bullet molds. The bags of seed-corn. Animal traps. Ax. Cooking ladles. My iron pots and kettles. Quilts. Blankets. My garden beside the cabin bordered with blue columbine. The peach and apple trees. The fields and sky. My head scurried like a nest of field mice I had uncovered in the corn.

I gripped the side of the wagon so hard my fingers throbbed. I felt my shoulders tighten as if by holding my body stiff the wagon would go faster. I chewed on the sleeves of my blouse. When the wagon stopped, a woman got out and ran to her cabin to grab what she could. The soldiers did not help. The women came tugging their kettles up the wagon ruts. I helped pull things over the sides. The widow Teehee cried when she tumbled back in the wagon empty-handed. Kee-un-e-ca also returned with nothing. Her cabin had burned. Everything was gone. Others said the white men had already auctioned off their farms. Wails filled the sky.

I jumped frantically when the wagon came to our path. I raced down the road. Wood smoke was coming from my chimney. I threw back the door and found white people at my table.

I screamed at them. Oⁿⱽ ſˢ iℒ. They froze in horror. I pulled the cooking pot out of the hearth with my hands, and it spilled on the floor. *"Mine!"* I screamed at them in Cherokee. My plates and forks. I turned the table over. The children screamed and danced with terror to their mother. The man got his musket. He aimed it at my head, but the shot went past me. I kicked over a chair in my rage. He loaded his musket again, and the soldier rode his horse nearly into the cabin.

"This cabin is mine!" The words spit from my mouth. My body was stiff as a beam. The soldier grabbed me and threw me outside the door. I heard the soldier yell at the people in the cabin. There was a struggle, and he came out with the cooking pot and blankets he ripped from the bed. "The musket," I told him. "My forks and ladles. The quilts my grandmother made. Our corn!"

He yelled at me, but I didn't understand his words. He shot into the air, and another soldier came riding up the wagon ruts.

He picked me up and tried to get me on his horse, but I kicked and nearly pulled us both to the ground. It was the same soldier who had tapped my shoulder to let me come. He took his bayonet and held it to my chest. With the point against me, he pushed me away from the cabin. "No!" I held out my arms to the place where I had come as the new wife of Knobowtee. My grandmother's cabin before she died. My baby was born there. It was built near the old Db, the sweat house and storage cellar built after my family came from Georgia. It was my farm! We had not even cleared all the fields yet. Who is the white man to drive us from our land? I spit at the soldier's feet. He stuck me with his bayonet. The sharp point against my breastbone quivered my knees. He turned me away from the cabin and marched me up the road. My legs wobbled and I fell to the ground.

I was in the wagon bumping my face against the bed of it. My hands throbbed from the heated handle of the kettle I pulled off the fire. I saw the burn marks. I looked at the sky. It was as though the yellow leaves marched with us, too. The cooking pot next to me was on its side. The blankets thrown in it stained with the white woman's food. I sobbed with the thought of them in my cabin. I retched, but only a thin stream of water came from my stomach. The same soldier rode beside the wagon. I watched him blur into the trees. A streak of blood stained my blouse where his bayonet had stuck me. When he returned he gave me a rag to wrap around my hands.

It was as if a bear sat on my chest all the way to camp. I felt air would not come into my lungs. It was a heavy grief I couldn't push away.

Knobowtee was waiting with my mother and father when we returned. I couldn't say anything at first. My throat closed with sobs. My mother took me in her arms. My father prayed for my blistered hands. Others chanted Cherokee prayers for our wounds. I heard them through the woods.

"They have our cabin," I choked to my parents and Knobowtee. "They were eating supper. I couldn't get anything. The soldier pulled the cooking pot and blankets out of the cabin. Otherwise I would have returned even without them."

I saw Knobowtee's face turn solemn. He could hardly understand what I said. The thought of white men in our cabin made him stare into the trees. "The musket," he said. "The corn, Maritole. What will we plant?"

"I couldn't get them." I tossed the air with my hand, and he walked past me not seeing anything. "Knobowtee," I said, but he was gone. I hit my arms against a tree until my father held me. I waited for Knobowtee to come back and say something to me, but there was nothing he could say. My chest heaved with spasms. The whole sky seemed to suck into my lungs. My parents held me between them until my throat stopped jerking in my head.

I asked about Tanner, my older brother, and Luthy, his wife. I asked about their boys, Mark and Ephum. But my father hadn't seen them.

My mother held the baby, and I cried again about the white men in our cabins. I cried for the Cherokee who had lost everything. Hiccups rocked my body. I scratched at myself with my burned hands. I felt like I'd been picking corn from the tall stalks that always made me itch.

"ᎢᏛᎥ ᎦᎠᎰᏓᎦᎠ ᎠᏚᏈᎵ," I told my mother, and buried my head against the bright print of my father's tunic. I felt his chest heave against me. His eyes were like puddles in the wagon ruts of the roads when it rained.

"And where's Thomas?" I asked.

"Don't speak, Maritole," he said, and walked away from us, too.

My mother and I sat on the ground with the baby as long shadows stretched across the sky. We would wash the blankets in a stream somewhere. And what of the booger mask dances? The green corn and new fire dances? What would become of our celebrations? The stickball games? Would we take them with us? Would *going to the water* ever be the same? Already the ministers called it "baptism."

We had known trouble since the white man came. Even the Cherokee newspaper, the *Phoenix*, was named for the bird that rises from ashes. Our villages had been burned so often by white settlers it seemed the right name. Yet we always rebuilt.

In the clearing I saw that some of the people had food. Others sank with weariness near the trees where we sat. The evening air was cool against my shoulders.

I remembered my parents sitting at our cabin window at night, afraid our fields would be set fire. Sometimes Thomas and I sat in the platform at the edge of the field in daylight. Sometimes I sat with Grandma screeching at the crows to keep them from eating seed when it was first planted.

ᎣᎥᎶᎱᎥ. Mother petted her hands.

Dawn was coming across the field. The sun stirred the fog. I remembered waking in the night, and felt groggy.

"What's happening?" I asked when I heard the soldiers yell, but mother held the baby and said nothing. She didn't even cry out when the soldier shot his musket over us.

Shivering, I put my arms around her and the baby. "They're telling us to get up, Mother," I said. The dew steamed from our bodies. Mother's face was swollen with tiredness, and we moved awkwardly.

The soldiers were in a hurry. They rode past us impatiently, whipping us to our feet along with the horses and mules we called ᎦᎳᎫ ᎯᎠᏍᏫᎾᎭᏞ (long-eared horse). Their words sounded like wind hissing in the trees.

My father joined us. "We're moving to a stockade near Rattlesnake Springs, a few miles south of the Hiwassee River near Charleston, Tennessee." He used the soldiers' names for our land.

Knobowtee's family was in a group that joined our camp in the night. I saw him talking to his brother as the fog lifted behind the horses. His mother and sister were somewhere else. They always stayed together. The men probably were talking about the trips the chief and other leaders had made to Washington to plead for Cherokee land. But nothing they said would change the removal.

The soldier told Mother and me to ride in the wagon. My

father and I helped her up. The wagon was already moving. I got in after Mother, and my father handed me the baby. I sat looking into my lap as the wagon rolled over the North Carolina soil early on a hard October morning.

KNOBOWTEE

Why was I standing in the field the day the soldiers came to the cabin? I knew the removal was coming. The runners had told us about the stockades.

Maritole had reacted first. Now she seemed quiet, her head bowed in the wagon. But I, who had been calm when the soldiers came, suddenly felt the jolt of removal.

Some of the men wanted to fight. We talked of it under our breath as we walked, but the wives said we would be killed.

"There was an old magician, a conjurer," one of the men said. "We asked him how long we were going to live in the East. The magician found a piece of rotten tree trunk. He set fire to one end and it burned slowly to the other."

"What'd it mean?" another asked.

"The conjurer said he didn't know."

Some of the men laughed low as we walked.

"I know what that burned wood meant," another man said. "Strangers would come and bad things would happen. It was just like them other signs."

I felt weak in my legs like I had plowed all day. But I wasn't a farmer any longer. Why hadn't Maritole been able to get anything when she returned to the cabin? It seemed simple enough. I wanted to strike out at something.

MARITOLE'S FATHER

"The first people the Great Spirit made were wooden sticks," I said, "but they didn't live. Then he made the clay people next. We could bend our knees and lift our feet. The Great Spirit knew we had a trail to walk. He knew we had to speak to survive."

Some said if it was going to happen, we might as well get started.

Someone else said, "They told their friends they were going to see the new land, and no one ever saw them again."

I wondered if anyone would see us again. How many years had our leaders gone to Washington to plead our case? It made the young men bitter. It made the women turn pale with fear. What would happen? Just walk and taste defeat? It felt sour in my mouth. How would my wife survive? My grandchildren?

I had made a trap to protect our cabin. I removed the brain of a yellow mockingbird, the magic ᎱᎱ, put it into a hollowed gourd, buried it in front of the door. But the soldiers came anyway. Now we were walking.

I could hear the ancestors murmuring beside us as we walked. Were they making snares to catch other mockingbirds? Would it change our removal? No. Something bigger was happening here. I knew it now. Even the ancestors had no power. They could only walk unseen beside us.

My wife cried for Tanner, our older son, and his family. She cried for Thomas, our younger son. "We'll find them in the stockade," I told her when we stopped.

The soldiers gave us something to eat, but I couldn't swallow. I heard an old man talking. "Some men buried part of a log hit by lightning in front of their door. They say that Thunder himself guarded their house. But I see them on the trail behind me."

Now I held my wife's head against me so she couldn't see people fall. I sang my stand-up song so she couldn't hear their cries. I sang as if the wind or rain had beat down the corn and I was telling it to stand. I sang to the people like I sang to the corn.

ᎠᏯ	here, right
ᏧᎾᏅᎾ	where they have sat down alive
ᏗᏕᏙᏕ	over there it stands
ᎤᏬᎯᏳᎠ	he believes

Yes, I turned four times and sang to the directions.

ᎠᏯ
ᏧᎾᏅᎾ

ᏍᎨ.

(The corn may get beat down, but it is able to stand up again because the words of my song tell it to, or give it power to.)

I was singing and didn't hear the soldier behind me. His whip hit my back. My wife cried with fright. "It doesn't matter," I told her. "Hush." I held her head to my chest.

"I still sing where they cannot hear," I said as we walked in the line of people.

How much of our songs are mostly thought? Maybe the magic is not in the words, but in the thought that is wrapped in the sound. Yes, I could make my songs, and the soldiers would never hear.

KNOBOWTEE

"Chief Justice John Marshall's three decisions got us in trouble and left the door open, too." I listened to O-ga-na-ya, my brother, when we rested that afternoon. "When Johnson purchased land from a chief and Mackintosh bought the same land in the claims office, who do you think owned the land?"

Why was O-ga-na-ya talking about court decisions? Did he think we were in the council house back in New Echota, Georgia? What did it matter now?

"Mackintosh," a friend of mine answered.

"Yo," my brother agreed. "Because Marshall in the Supreme Court went back to the beginning. He talked about the doctrine of discovery. U.S. discovery and conquest. Then the government is sovereign. Indians can only sell to the government."

"So what do you do with Indians living on that discovered land?" I asked bitterly, looking at one man already asleep under a wagon.

"They called us savages without rights of our own."

Some of the men eyed the woods as we talked. But how far could we run? How could our families follow?

"Call us unchristian so it's even easier to take our land," a friend offered.

"How else could Marshall have settled it?" O-ga-na-ya wiped his face with the hem of his shirt. "If he argued for the Indian, the government would be undermined. Marshall knew it opposed natural right, yet he did it anyway."

"Yo."

I listened to my brother, but I would rather hear the corn talk. I looked into the trees high above me. O-ga-na-ya had always listened to what the men had to say. Now I listened also. How long had we been walking? Sometimes I thought the corn walked with us. I could almost feel its hands.

"Then the second decision. Eighteen thirty-one."

"What good does it do to talk?" I snapped at O-ga-na-ya.

"Then the second decision," repeated my brother. *"The Cherokee Nation versus Georgia."* O-ga-na-ya had talked with some men who'd been in New Echota and had heard the council. "Chief John Ross and other leaders had gone to the Supreme Court because Georgia was about to outlaw the tribal legislature and divide Cherokee land. We claimed the Supreme Court had original jurisdiction. The Cherokee nation is a foreign nation and the Court can intercede. But the Court ruled against us. Marshall said we were in a state of pupilage and were not a foreign country inside Georgia."

"The chief justice declared us a domestic, dependent nation." I sputtered at the insult of the word *dependent.* "Our relation to the U.S. is a ward to his guardian."

"Then does Georgia have the right to assert its laws over the Cherokee?" O-ga-na-ya asked the question he wanted to answer. "No. Third decision. *Worcester versus Georgia.* Georgia had a statute requiring permission to enter Cherokee territory. But two ministers, Samuel Worcester and Elizur Butler, had refused to ask permission when they entered and were sentenced to four years hard labor. The state law ignored the federal Trade Act in which only the U.S. government had the right to regulate travel in Indian country. The federal court said that the Cherokee are a distinct community within the state and that the statute requiring permission to enter Cherokee territory isn't legal. In other words, Georgia can't regulate who can and can't enter our land."

"So Marshall came down on the side of U.S. supremacy over the states," I remembered.

"Maybe he provided space for us." My friend was hopeful.

"Not yet anyway. We're on our way out, aren't we?" I asked.

Silence followed. I saw a girl trying to cover her feet with her skirts. She should have a husband to rub her feet against his chest.

We rested on the ground, surrounded by the crying women and children. We sat with our heads bowed as we talked. If we didn't have farming, what was left? What could we do? Maritole's father had his musket, and maybe we could make knives. But how could we fight against the soldiers' bayonets and guns? We would only provoke more cruelty from them.

Besides, weren't we marching on our own? After the attempt at removal in Georgia and Tennessee in the spring, Chief John Ross had procured money. The Cherokee would be responsible for our own removal. The soldiers were only forcing us to the stockades. Soon most of the soldiers would be gone.

The wives were right. For now, all we could do was think of our corn and walk toward the stockade near the Hiwassee in Tennessee.

BIRD DOUBLEHEAD

The ministers say we go. They say their different ways. Presbyterian. Moravian. Methodist. Baptist. How many gods does the white man have? They can't agree on anything. But wasn't He *three*, a many-voiced God? *All voices tell the same story though,* one man says. No they don't. He-three's a god with many mouths to say because there's many ways to say.

CHIEF JOHN ROSS

There were white men in Washington arguing for the Cherokee to stay on their land. There were Cherokee cooperating with the government to remove the Indians. None of the boundaries were clear. There were fractures and inconsistencies everywhere I turned.

I tried to explain the complications, but President Jackson sat at his desk thumbing through a newspaper. Jackson didn't want to hear. Sometimes the government would not recognize me. John Ross! The principal chief of the Cherokee nation. An educated man with the same responsibility for governing my people as Jackson had.

In the end, I asked for funds for removal.

In the end, I argued for anything that would get my people out of the stockades before they died there.

How many voices were there making nothing clear?

WILLIAM HOLLAND

I thought the trees by my trading post were soldiers. Their shadows stood in my door. Okonoluftee. Listen to that name. Was it a river? A town? I couldn't remember. It drove me crazy to hear the name over and over in my head. *Woouh*. The trees were breathing. The chest of the woods moved as the trees breathe. The woods were taking the Cherokee into its hands. Ripping our bones apart. I could hear the bones snap like twigs on the path. I felt myself in the mouth of the woods. Its teeth grinding me. The shadows that wouldn't stop coming.

CHIEF JOHN ROSS

The United States in account with the Cherokee nation, for expenses incurred under an agreement, with Major General Scott, for the removal of the Cherokee.

Detachment No. 3

For compensation to Jesse Bushyhead, conductor, from 3rd September 1838 to 27th February 1839, inclusive, making 178 days, at $5 per day $890.00

For compensation to assistant conductor, for same time, at $3 a day $534.00

For compensation to attending physician, from 1st September, 180 days, at $5, $900; allowance for returning $120 $1,020.00

For compensation to interpreter for physician, for same time, at $2.50 per day $450.00

For compensation to commissary and wagon master, from 3rd September 1838 to 27th February 1839, inclusive, 178 days, at $2.50 each $890.00

For compensation to assistant commissary and assistant wagon master, for same time, at $2 per day each $712.00

For hire of 48 wagons and teams, for 950 persons, for same time, at $5 per day each, $42,720; allowance of 40 days each for returning, at $7 per day, including traveling expenses, $13,440 $56,160.00

For forage for 430 wagons and riding horses, from 16th of October 1838 to 27th February 1839, inclusive, making 135 days and 58,050 forage rations, at 40 cents $23,220.00

For subsistence for 950 persons, for same time, making 128,250 rations, at 16 cents $20,520.00

For allowance of three pounds of soap to each 100 rations, making 3,847   pounds at 15 cents $577.12

For allowance for turnpikage, ferriage, &c, at the rate of $1,000 for each detachment of 1,000 persons $950.00
                                                        $105,923.12

I certify that the above account is accurate and just.

JOHN ROSS, Principal Chief,
and Sup'g Agent of the Cherokee nation
for Cherokee removal

REVEREND BUSHYHEAD

I felt a sudden wind as I walked with the men. I was going to be the conductor of a detachment. Who had chosen me? Why? When I heard the voices of the Cherokee men, I didn't know what to do. I was used to feeling powerless around them. The holy men and conjurers scoffed openly at times. I was one of the Cherokee converted to Christianity. I preached after Worcester and Butler were imprisoned. I wasn't a minister the way they were. I hadn't been to their school. But I had something to say. I consoled the widow Teehee and Kee-un-e-ca after they returned to camp with nothing from their farms. I knew Quaty Lewis's white husband had stayed behind on her farm and let her go to the new territory with nothing.

"We aren't spared by the harvest of our hands but by the

blood of Jesus." My words seemed to fly back in my face as I talked to the men. "Something will happen to change what's happening. Something will—"

The wind seemed to pick up the corners of the afternoon and turn it into dark as we finished our walking that day. The voices high in the trees hissed. I thought I heard my cabin door slam. Sometimes the trees seemed to pound themselves against the ground in a fit of anger. If only the soldiers could hear the woods speak.

Someone called. A Cherokee had shot himself in the head. I went to the group that surrounded the man. I told some of them to gather the wood they needed for supper and for fires that night. I told others to help bury the man. Then I read a scripture at the mound of dirt by the new grave.

Was it only a few nights ago I woke in my bed and felt doubt lapping my faith? Now I made camp along the edge of the dark woods as Knobowtee helped two women struggling with a tarp in the wind.

I had a pregnant wife and a young daughter. My widowed sister, Nancy, walked with us. I could feel my heart the size of a corncrib in my chest.

WAR CLUB

"Yop. I hear Bushyhead," I remarked. "I don't believe no god. The white men. *mehpush*. They come. Take the land. Say we don't have the truth. Well, put their god on a cross. Leave him there."

THE WIDOW TEEHEE

We walk through North Carolina toward Tennessee. We walk through the trees. Wait by the road. Someone fixes a wagon. I see a man die. But he's not gone. We knew it before we had ministers. We go on living. Not here, but in the next world. We come back and speak to those who live after us. One of the conjurers say we're born again and again. That's a lie, too. We're born once on earth. Isn't that enough? Death is leaving the cabin and going outside. Then the afterlife. Hardly a ripple. I knew it the night my husband got up. I thought he was standing at the window or maybe outside. Sometimes he worried about the field and animals. When renegades burn the farms so often, sometimes you think you hear a rider on the road and it's only the wind. Anyway, I turned to look at the window, but he was still in bed. I felt his chest and he was dead. It was his spirit that had gotten up, left the cabin. I wouldn't want him to know we had to leave the corn. We walk. Camp. Walk.

KINCHOW,
ANNA SCO-SO-TAH'S NEIGHBOR

"My dogs sleep with me at night. I want my dogs. *yafp*," I said as we camped that night in the woods.

"My chickens wouldn't go near my neighbor's cabin," Anna told the others.

"Huh?" I said.

Anna moved closer to me in the dark. She knew I wanted to feel someone next to me. "They wouldn't cross his yard," Anna said to the others. "You ought to see Kinchow's place," she said. "It ain't no cabin. It's a hovel. Fit for dogs and sorcerers."

"Is that true?" Quaty Lewis asked.

"Huh?" I said.

"Quiet!" someone said.

"I built my own place," I said.

"No floors. Just dirt," Anna told Quaty. "No windows. Just lets the door hang open for light."

"Huh?"

"Flies? You'd think it was corn day on the town square!"

"If I had my dogs here I could sleep. *yafp*. My dogs tell me stories. That's all I can say."

MARITOLE

In the dark night, Indian fires looked like burning stars on the ground. My stomach ached from the salt pork. My father had his musket in the bundle he carried on his back. He sang his hunting song. "ᎢᎦᎾᏞᎢᎣᏝᏙᏩᎠ ᎣᏝᏀᎩᏴᎷᏞ."

Knobowtee walked with his mother and brother, his sister

who never said anything. I saw him before dark. I rocked the baby on my lap, covering her with one of my mother's quilts.

I woke once shivering and saw the fires gone out. I looked up into the huge black sky. I had dreamed it was white and wet as the inside of an apple. The stars were black as apple seeds. Maybe I only imagined instead of dreamed. The earth was strange to me now. There was something over us. Some dark animal we pushed against. I could almost hear it breathe.

TANNER

At night I heard the half-breed who'd gone mad. The one who'd had a trading post on the North Carolina Turnpike. Soldiers restrained him with rope, letting him howl in one of the wagons until they cut him loose and took him to the woods to disappear.

MARITOLE

We traveled several days to get to Rattlesnake Springs near the Hiwassee River. Along the way, I heard someone say we had crossed into Tennessee. I rode in the wagon with the other women, the baby sucking and fretting. My legs and back were sore from the ride. My hands were blistered from the burns.

"I heard my cat talking in a dream," Kee-un-e-ca said. "She was confused and not her usual self. She said she brought me a field mouse, but when I looked, it was just a dried cornhusk. One of her eyes wobbled as she talked. One of her ears had grown rounded." Kee-un-e-ca cried quietly while the rest of us talked.

"My hominy pestle moved around in the cabin," Mrs. Young Turkey said. "I would find it in one place then it would be in another. I should have known the soldiers were coming."

"We all knew it would happen," Quaty Lewis said.

"I don't think anyone knew," I said.

The Stockade

EARLY OCTOBER, 1838

MARITOLE

The stockade at Rattlesnake Springs was open under the sky. Inside the gates the seven clans of the Cherokee were crowded together row after row like corn in a field. I couldn't see the end of the people. No one spoke. If a child cried, its voice cut the air like a whippoorwill at dawn. Goats, chickens, and dogs made their noises. The stockade smelled of urine and fear.

We stood at the gates until the soldiers led us to a place along the front wall. I didn't want to follow, but one of the soldiers took my arm and pulled me until I walked behind my father and mother. My parents were carrying my cooking pot between them.

"Some of the people have been here since last summer," my father said.

"I saw the graves outside the stockade," my mother added.

"We came from farthest away," my father told us as we stepped over feet and belongings.

"And the soldiers let us go back for a few things," I said.

I saw that other people had more bundles than we did. One woman had a loom. Some of the rich Cherokee had their slaves. There were even a few pack dogs. Why did they have so much while I had nothing but a cooking pot and blankets?

KNOBOWTEE

We knew when the Georgia, Alabama, and Tennessee Cherokee were rounded up in stockades. Many had been loaded on flatboats at Chattanooga and traveled down the Tennessee River, to the Ohio, to the Mississippi, and up the Arkansas on their way to Indian Territory. But a drought had lowered the rivers, and the people had to walk or take baggage cars on trains in the heat. Many were sick with fever and dysentery and were returned to the stockades to wait for cooler weather. A few of us were just now arriving from our farms.

There were stockades all over the Cherokee nation. You couldn't count them on two hands. A man named Gu-nun-a-ku said the white men who called themselves commissioners of Indian property had demanded his horses. When he refused, he was driven into a pen with his wife and children. The horses were taken by force and sold to the highest bidder for almost nothing.

MARITOLE

Suddenly I heard my older brother, Tanner. He had come to the stockade before us. He rushed to my father with relief. His two boys, Mark and Ephum, came running after him. They hugged my mother and father.

I saw Luthy then, too, my brother's wife. She wore her turkey-bone beads around her neck and was wrapped in a shawl as though she were going to church. I hugged them all and felt the people around us. Luthy took the baby from me. For a moment the sky came together in a circle above us, and we were the center again.

"Where's Thomas?" my father asked.

"I haven't seen him since soldiers came into the cabin," Tanner said. "I was sitting there cleaning my musket. Luthy was tying Ephum's shoe, telling him to sit still. I can still see"—Tanner's voice quivered—"a crack between the logs I was going to fill. Then soldiers were there. The dogs bark when anyone comes. I don't remember the dogs barking. But Thomas was gone in an instant."

My mother stood with her hands to her face.

"Maybe he's still there," Luthy said.

"He's probably hiding in the woods," I told her, "with the others who managed to stay behind."

"He was bitter about the removal," Luthy said.

"Who isn't?" I asked.

"He said he wasn't going to Indian Territory."

"I said that, too," I told them. "But I'm here."

"Up the road there was a woman with three small children," Luthy started, and I knew she was going to make herself cry. "One of the children was on her back," Luthy went on, "the other two clung to her, crying. Suddenly she fell on the road. Dead! Her heart must have given out. The soldiers put the three screaming children in the wagon. They left her body by the road." Luthy cried against Tanner.

"Someone buried her, Luthy," Tanner said.

"They left her by the road," Luthy said again. The boys cried when they saw their mother crying. "I don't know what happened to the children." Luthy held my baby as the boys crowded around her.

Even my father cried, and I turned away from them. Just awhile ago I danced the green corn dance. The thought of food brought a pain to my jaw. I longed for my cabin, for the taste of new corn, for the whole earth under my feet.

I could imagine Thomas running back into the hills. He would stay in the woods near Du'stayalun'yi. We would march the trail to the new land. Even the holy men said it. There was nothing we could do. But a part of our lives would remain in the old territory.

"Where's Knobowtee?" Luthy asked me suddenly.

"I don't know. He must be off talking to someone." I took the baby from her.

"Maybe Thomas will show up," Luthy said. She put her arms around my mother, who was still crying, but I knew he was gone.

The sight of Mother crying made me cry also. I jerked the blanket from the cooking pot and spread it on the ground. I was going to walk away from them, but I sat down on the dirty blanket instead. It was as though I had net sinkers on my feet. I slumped on the blanket in a fit of exhaustion and fell into a black sleep.

J. H. HETZEL, PHYSICIAN
AT RATTLESNAKE SPRINGS

I sent a note home to Pennsylvania: "The main spring flows from near George Moore's house just east of Dry Valley Road three and seven-tenths miles north of its junction with the Tasso Road."

I spend my days tending measles, whooping cough, pleurisy, bilious fevers. There's upward of several thousand Cherokee in the stockade and one physician.

JAMES MOONEY

The soldiers gathered the Cherokee in "stockade forts" built on their own land: in North Carolina, Fort Lindsay, on the south side of the Tennessee River at the junction of Nantahala, in Swain county; Fort Scott, at Aquone, farther up Nantahala river, in Macon county; Fort Montgomery, at Robbinsville, in Graham county; Fort Hembrie, at Hayesville, in Clay county; Fort Delaney at Valleytown, in Cherokee county; Fort Butler, at Murphy, in the same county; in Georgia, Fort Scudder, on Frogtown creek, north of Dahlonega, in Lumpkin county; Fort Gilmer, near Ellijay in Gilmer county; Fort Coosawatee, in Murray county; Fort Talking-rock near Jasper, in Pickens county; Fort Buffington, near Canton, in Cherokee county; in Tennessee, Fort Cass, at Calhoun, on the Hiwassee River, in McMinn county; Old Agency, on the Hiwassee River, near Rattlesnake Springs; Ross's Landing, near the present Chattanooga; and in Alabama, Fort Turkeytown, on Coosa river, at Center, in Cherokee county; Gunter's Landing, at the present Guntersville.

MARITOLE

I must have slept a long time. When my mother touched my arm, I didn't know where I was.

"Maritole, you need to eat," she said.

"No," I answered, and I knew I was not on my farm.

"If you miss these rations, there'll be none until morning."

I remembered then that I was in the stockade in Tennessee surrounded by hundreds of Cherokee. I saw the soldier stand above me, but I couldn't lift my arm. It had gone to sleep under me. The baby clawed at my blouse. I wanted to hit her away. I opened my hand for the salt pork and piece of bread the soldier handed me.

"Water," I said.

The bucket and dipper were coming. I felt like I could eat the tin dipper. I remembered rain collected in the nutting stone. The baby had splashed it with her fingers. I grabbed for the dipper handle again when the soldier took it from me, but he jerked the bucket away and passed the water to others.

"My milk is disappearing," I told my mother.

"The baby is nearly old enough to eat now," she said.

"Eat what?" I asked. "The soldiers' rations? Is there anything but hunger and thirst?"

"We have our lives, Maritole," my mother said.

"Is that enough?" I snapped at her. "We're the DhB⊖ᴔ, the principal people. We live in the center of the earth. Where is my farm and cabin? Where are my grandmother's things?"

"We're together," Mother said. "If we had Thomas."

"And where's Knobowtee?" I asked her.

"Your father is looking for him."

"I need my father to look for my husband? Why isn't he here on his own?"

"It's hard on all of us, Maritole," my mother said.

REVEREND EVAN JONES

In the midst of much anxiety and urgent haste in the preparations for removal, it is a matter for sincere and humble gratitude that the gospel is making advances altogether unprecedented in the Christian history of the Cherokees. The pressure of their political troubles appears to be overruled to the spiritual advantage of the people. The sentiment of the poet is happily realized to them:

Behind a frowning providence
He hides a smiling face.

We had, yesterday, such a display of the triumphs of grace as will doubtless fill many hearts of the people of God with holy joy. For several days, the brethren had been hearing the relations of candidates for the sacred ordinance of baptism, and a considerable number had been approved. Yesterday, at the conclusion of the forenoon services, the members of the church met again, and several more candidates were received; after which, br. Bushyhead and myself baptized fifty-six hopeful believers in the Lord Jesus Christ, in the presence of an immense concourse of serious and attentive spectators. Twenty-four were males and thirty-one females—Cherokees, of all ages, and one white woman.

We afterward united in the commemoration of the death of the Savior; perhaps for the last time in this country. It was sunset when the exercises of the day were concluded, and no opportunity was afforded to invite inquirers to come forward for prayer, who were anxious to be so privileged. In fact, the work of at least three days was, from necessity, crowded into one. But I trust eternity will afford ample opportunity to contemplate, in all its bearing, the glorious work of grace carried on among the Cherokees in this time of their afflictions.

I have also to record, to the honor of divine grace, the happy death of a faithful brother in the Lord. His name was Astooeestee. He had, for several years, been a humble and consistent follower of the Lord Jesus. He was a very useful member of the church and an acceptable preacher in his own vicinity, viz. Dseyohee. He enjoyed, during a short and severe illness, a hope full of immortality; and, from a humble shed in the camp of the captives, his happy spirit took its flight up the "glorious hill of God"—the "font of life, the eternal throne and presence chamber of the King of kings," where all the prisoners' bands are loosed and their captivity forever at an end.

MARITOLE

Sometimes fear pierced sharper than the soldier's bayonet. Sometimes tears ran down my cheeks as I nursed the baby, feeding her my thin milk and the salt water from my face. Some people sat with their heads bowed not knowing what else to do. They grieved for the farms and families they were leaving and the ancestral burial grounds. I thought of my grandparents alone in their graves while we marched off. Some of the children ran and played as if nothing had happened. I remembered how I chased Thomas through the cornstalks long ago. The men stood in groups talking to one another. Women sat on their blankets, some staring into the air, others trying to fix something for their families to eat. I saw a soldier motion to another. They stood talking, and soon I saw them carry an old woman out of the stockade. I heard the weeping of her family. Then someone argued with one of the soldiers about something, probably the old woman's burial. I heard shouts and screaming. A warning shot was fired, but the men couldn't hold their anger. There were more shots and screams. I was frantic, but my father held me.

"Many die," my mother said rocking my baby.

"And many of us live," I told her as my father let me go. "I've heard talk of it for years. The territory west of the Mississippi where the Indian can live without harm." I mocked the white men. "They only want our farms."

KNOBOWTEE

The men were going to have a council meeting. I watched them beyond the open gate of the stockade, but the removal had been determined. Chief John Ross was not among them. He was as much white as Indian. Ross was preparing to leave on the steamboat *Victoria* with some of the sick and elderly. Ross wouldn't walk the trail with us.

I saw the Cherokee clan leaders gather. Fly Smith. White Path. They had been war chiefs and peace chiefs, or descendants of them. There were also twelve members of John Ross's council. There were elected chiefs, or mayors, and leaders from many districts. There were holy men, orators, and other spiritual leaders. But they were all from Tennessee. None of the North

Carolina or Georgia Cherokee were included. The white soldiers squatted at the gate. A few sat by the trees beyond the group of Indians. ᎤᏗᏁᏍ. ᏍᏯᎵᏋ! I spit on the ground.

The voices of the Cherokee men were subdued. The sound of the wind in the trees drowned their words. Yellow leaves blew down upon the stockade. The whole earth seemed to grumble. Once in a while an angry voice would lift from the council. I heard them curse Ridge and Boudinot because of the treaty. They had already gone to Indian Territory, leaving the Georgia Cherokee to carry the blame.

MARITOLE

In the stockade, I felt the sound of ᏍᏣᎵ, a rattling gourd. I saw the camp as if ᏍᏕᏣᎶ, wild hemp. The women who had just arrived wore print dresses, some of them not yet faded from washings. The men were in their tunics and turbans. I saw ᎦᏴᎠ, the red paint. ᎦᏞᎷM, the red-brown moth that flies around blossoming tobacco in the evening. ᎤᏲᏂᎦᏫ, the corn tassel. A settlement of all of them.

I heard my father's voice and stood up to look for him. I saw him talking to Knobowtee. My heart pounded a moment at the sight of my husband. My father was angry at him. He took Knobowtee's arm to pull him to our place along the wall. No! My father can't drag him against his will. Knobowtee tried to get away, but my father kept talking to him. I saw him jerk his arm from my father. *No!* I thought. Not in front of everyone. I wouldn't let them see my father drag my husband back to me. I wanted out. They couldn't hold me here. I ran toward the gate, past makeshift tents and baggage, jumping over bundles and baskets and legs of people and playing children. I ran past the soldiers and council. I would run past the graves. I would run past everything back to my cabin near Du'stayalun'yi in the place they called North Carolina. No. Back farther than that. Back to the field where I chased Thomas, knowing where he was by the movement in the corn tassels. The trees ran with me. Their voices shouted. Their yellow leaves like the cornmeal I hungered for.

I heard my mother call at me from inside the wall. I heard the soldiers yell. But I kept running. Soon one of them caught me and spoke to me in Cherokee. He told me to get back into the stockade. I couldn't move. I wanted to crawl into the earth with the old woman who died. I wanted to be back on my farm. I felt the heat come up from my body and sting my face. "Go back to your place in the stockade," he said again.

Everyone must be looking. I could see nothing clearly. Streaks of red and blue flashed by my eyes like on market days when Thomas and I ran through the crowd. "Thomas!" I called. The dirt roads and wooden buildings moved toward one another. I thought I heard him answer. My legs wobbled.

The soldier carried me over his shoulder back to my mother and baby in the stockade. Back to my father and Knobowtee, who waited for me.

I sat against the stockade wall and hid my face in a blanket. My mother put her arms around me. "I want to go back to Du'stayalun'yi," I said.

My father pulled my mother away from me. She took the baby, and they walked away from our place, leaving me with Knobowtee. He said nothing at first. I could hardly feel his presence, though he stood there next to me. I trembled with embarrassment. He didn't want to be with me. I had made it harder for him by running. Everyone had seen me. No wonder my husband didn't want to be with me. I didn't want Knobowtee to comfort me. I didn't want him to say anything because it would come from the distance between us. What had happened? I sat with him on the blanket surrounded by the crowd of people probably listening to us, watching us. He touched my shoulder, but it felt like the soldier's bayonet.

When we had married, he'd given me venison to say he would provide, and I gave him an ear of corn to promise I would make bread for the family. My mother and father had stood behind us. They were of the Bird and the Paint clans. Behind them had been Knobowtee's family, who were of the Blind Savannah clan. Thomas, Tanner, Luthy, and the boys also had stood with us when we married.

Where were the friends who had been with us? The girl

Thomas danced with after the ceremony? There had been a feast in the churchyard. The leaves had shined above me like stars. Later a baby was born. Knobowtee hunted and worked in the fields. I tended the cabin and the crops. Now there was not even that between us. Maybe Knobowtee still longed for his first wife, who died. Maybe he wanted one of the other girls for his wife. Maybe it was the musket I couldn't get from our cabin or the seed-corn from its storage house.

ANNA SCO-SO-TAH

"Listen, Maritole," I said in the dark. "What do you hear?"

"Nothing, Anna."

"What else?"

"The babies crying."

"Listen again," I whispered.

"What's there?" Maritole asked.

"You tell me."

"Someone's sick."

"Listen again."

"Some soldiers talking to a girl?"

"No, not that," I said.

"The river?"

"Yes. The Hiwassee," I answered. "What does it say?"

"Yep, Anna. I hear it now. The river talking to the trees. Saying we're moving now, too."

TANNER

What kind of God was this who had some of his men talk of loaves and fish while others took the land and beat an old man to get him to walk? Women and children cried. Luthy. Mark and Ephum. My sister. I cried also when it was dark. Afraid and hungry, I remembered the land, the stover I left in the field. The soldiers had brought new voices to the land. It made the land grumpy. Maritole called them soldiers and principal soldiers without distinguishing their rank. I chuckled to myself. Maybe they should be lumped together. Colonel. Major. Captain. Lieutenant. Sergeant. Corporal. Private. There also were soldiers who acted as government teamsters and contractors. The Light Horse Guard also moved the march along. The Cherokee men talked about all of them. I watched the sergeant who carried Maritole back into the stockade when she ran. The one with eyes so pale they looked white. There was something about him.

But some of the soldiers took girls into the woods at night.

Worse was John Schermerhorn, President Andrew Jackson's commissioner to the Cherokee. Schermerhorn worked behind the backs of the Tennessee Cherokee and John Ross. His offer to Ridge and Boudinot, the Georgia leaders, to buy all Cherokee lands, divided them. Chicken Snake Jackson and the Devil's Horn. I chuckled again, but it was something more like my wife's sobs that shook my shoulders.

Five years ago, in 1833, there'd been a meteor shower. We had stood in the clearing in our fields and watched the meteors like sparks from a hearth fire thrown across the sky. The holy men said it was an omen. Schermerhorn and all the white men in Washington could not be trusted.

The next year there was an eclipse of the sun. A holy man, ᏗᏓᏥ-ᎾᏍᎩᎩ, and a more-holy man, ᎠᏂᎶᏍᏗᎥ, said the eclipse, too, was an omen. The conjurers beat their drums. A great frog was trying to swallow the sun, and they had to beat their drums to scare the frog away. But a frog like Schermerhorn didn't leave. He just stood on the town square and made speeches, giving away blankets so people would come.

The Christian ministers tried to explain how the moon got in the way of the sun. I listened to the ministers as they spoke to people. Who would I choose to hear?

I could hear Luthy praying for me sometimes as she cried. I could hear Knobowtee talking to his brother. I could hear many voices, each one trying to speak a place on which to stand.

In the stockade in the night, I heard the ministers and soldiers above the crying of Maritole's baby. I heard my wife. I heard the conjurers. I heard the voices of the ancestors and grandfathers. I heard the elders and spirit beings who camped around the stockade. Getting into their detachments, saying their clans:

DhⱧⱤ∿Ⱦ	Bird
DhⱫ℉h	Blue
Dhℚℚ	Deer
DhƳ𝒢Ᏺ	Long Hair
DhℰℐⱢ	Paint
DhℚᎦ	Wolf
DhⱯℐⱤℚ	Blind Savannah

THE SOLDIERS

"Get that Chereky back on his blanket."

"They think they can walk anywhere." A soldier kicked a man and hit another with the flat side of his bayonet. The Indian cried out.

"General Scott said no more injuries."

"General Scott ain't around. He just wants us to keep the Indians in line."

"They'll soon be marching on their own."

The soldiers were pulled between their fear and hatred of the Indians, and the sense of power from having them under arms.

"Just think what they've done."

"Massacred our people—"

"Owned slaves—"

"Listen to them conjurers. Spooks, I tell you."

"My daddy used to scare us with Injun stories."

"Look at them now. Don't look too scary."

"Smell the stink of this place."

"Most of 'em look sick."

"Ain't as bad as last summer."

"Bice couldn't take it. Just walked off through the woods. Ain't seen him since."

"All the graves out there—"

"They're known for war." A soldier spit.

"They are?"

"But we got 'em."

The soldiers knelt by the fire.

"Greasy Indians."

"Just keep giving 'em whiskey."

KNOBOWTEE

I saw my wife bend over the baby. There was no moss in the stockade for a diaper. There was no dried moss for a fire to keep the insects away. I should be able to comfort my wife, but I sat with my mother and Aneh, my sister. If I got near, Maritole would bite me with her words. Didn't I know hurt? Hadn't I lost my father? Hadn't I heard my mother cry? Maybe I should think of Maritole. Even if I missed my first wife sometimes. Even if I'd rather walk with my brother. O-ga-na-ya doesn't glare at me like Tanner and Maritole's father. I worked the fields that Maritole's father and grandfather had cleared. Because I'd married Maritole. But none of us could plow the fields any longer.

Shouldn't I look after Maritole as she tried to comfort the baby? Even if I'd rather watch the young girls' legs when the doctors wrapped them?

I don't trust the soldiers, especially the one who looks like he has no eyes. Maybe I should stay with my wife.

MARITOLE'S FATHER

Even the woods had a clan. We heard it voice its feelings. We didn't say anything but looked at one another.

Even the sleep of the Cherokee spoke. At night our moans were night crawlers under the weight of the removal.

MARITOLE

"ᏍᎦ," I cursed.

What's this white dust the soldiers gave us when they passed out rations? It had to be mixed with water from the Hiwassee. Knobowtee brought the bucket to me. I drank water greedily and sprinkled a few drops over the flour. It was white and pasty. What good was it?

"Bread," my mother said.

"Not like the meal we make from corn. Not the flour we get from Brainard's mill when our corn is ground."

The family was quiet as Mother and I tried to mix the white paste and mold it into bread. "If we had a skillet or pan," I said, "but I have nothing but the kettle I pulled from the cabin!"

I longed to pound corn in my wooden bucket. Sift the ground meal in my basket Grandmother made of white oak splints. Wrap the bread in green corn blades and boil it. That's how bread is made!

Quaty Lewis talked as we tried to cook in the crowded stockade. "I remember going over the mountains to Georgia. Grandpa took his ax to a chestnut tree and peeled off a piece of bark wide enough to cook dough on. My granny carried ᎤᏘᏆᏔ, the parched cornmeal, with her. Sometimes she put beans or pumpkin in it. We'd get to the creek, and she'd spoon water in the meal and lay it on the strip of bark. She stood the bark in front of the fire and when one side baked, she turned it over and browned the other." Quaty kept talking. More to herself than us.

My mother sat with her head resting against her hands. I saw how chapped they were. Soon she spoke. "Grandmother had a dream before she died, Maritole." She spoke as though trying to remember. "She knew something was going to happen. I can't think exactly what she said. But she was glad to be returning to the Great Spirit."

Quaty tried to eat her bread, which was raw dough or covered with flakes of black crust.

"I want to stay here and see this new land we're going to," I said watching Quaty, "this favor from the white man."

"Where's the squirrel meat? The corn bread to soak up the grease?" I asked.

"Hush, Maritole," Knobowtee said. "None of us are better for looking back."

"It's all I can do."

"Are Luthy and Tanner coming?" Mother asked.

"The soldiers said we have to stay in our places in the stockade. We'll be with them when we march."

I gagged on the white bread we spooned from the pan.

Hunger made my mouth wet, but I couldn't eat. The white lumps looked like the scent sacks we cleaned from squirrels. Or the white phlegm of their eyeballs.

LACEY WOODARD

"All night I hear the animals talk." War Club talked as I tried to sleep. "They don't know what to do with us. Men are bad to them. We let them die slowly. Kill too many. Don't we know they want life, too?" War Club sat in the stockade with an old animal skin on his head. A badger or raccoon.

"Let's poison the men, the animals said." War Club kept telling the story to himself.

"Let's make them sick, another animal agreed."

I looked at War Club now and then. Maybe it was the badger talking. Or the raccoon. Maybe War Club was possessed by an animal spirit. Look at that disgusting pelt on his head. It must be older than him.

"No. Here comes the white man, the animals said." War Club scratched himself and chewed on his story. "The white man'll keep the Indians crowded together in the stockades. That'll kill them. They'll make 'em walk. See the long trail over the mountain? See the trail the Indians'll walk?"

War Club took a breath and saw me frowning.

"Yeah. But what'll we do with the white man? the animals ask."

ANNA SCO-SO-TAH

"*umph*. War Club's telling the animals' story," I said. "Why doesn't he shut up? That old man's always talking."

"Huh? What'd War Club say?" my neighbor asked. "I didn't hear. What'd his story say?"

"All I hear is people sick," Quaty Lewis said. "I hear them gag."

"AAAAHHHHGGG. AAAAAHHHHGGGGGGG. All night," Kinchow said.

"I hear them cry," Lacey Woodard added.

"SSSSGGGG," Kinchow grunted in his throat.
"Stop it." I hit him.
"GGGGGGG."
"Stop." I hit.

KNOBOWTEE

"VMoᏝ. It's true. We saw it coming." We sat before the fire in the stockade, not looking at one another again. We knew the soldiers and the Cherokee leaders were outside the wall, lining up the wagons for the march. We could hear the wagon hitches. I watched Maritole as she listened to us talk until her weariness pulled her into the blackness outside the fire.

"We're moving west of the Mississippi now. Horses, oxen, mules, slaves, wagons. Where the sky bends down to the earth. Across Tennessee, Kentucky, Illinois, Missouri, Arkansas, to Indian Territory, in time to plant spring crops. The small corn farmers as well as the rich landowners. And most of them from Georgia."

"Ha," I said. "But the Georgia and North Carolina Cherokee are left out of council meetings."

"Yop," O-ga-na-ya agreed.

"John Ross did what he could," Maritole's father said. "He arranged for some of our old and sick ones to remain. He got the Cherokee prisoners released from the jails. He even got General Winfield Scott to let him lead the removal."

"ᏬᎵᏈ." One of the men repeated the Indian name for Scott.

There'd been a proclamation from General John Wool, commander of the removal before Scott.

> May 10, 1838. Cherokees! The president of the United States has sent me with a powerful army to cause you by the Treaty of 1835 to join the pact of your people who are already established in prosperity on the other side of the Mississippi. Make preparations for emigration. Hasten to Calhoun, where you will be received in kindness by officers selected for this purpose. You will find food, clothing, and will in comfort be transported to your new homes.

And so we would march. A mix of diverse peoples. Agreeing on little. Our seven clans divided between three white peace clans and three red war clans, with the neutral Long Hair clan to break up disagreements. Small farmers, many of us illiterate. Plantation owners. Slaves. Half-breeds. Whites who'd intermarried. Conjurers. Christians. Some had been spokesmen in Washington. Then there were soldiers. Government teamsters.

It felt brutal to be marched in a haphazard way, not by the seven clans, nor ᏚᏏᎩ, which were our townships, but in several groups, here and there, some led by Christian ministers, some led by local chiefs—the Dh ᏙᎾ ᎠᏟᎯ, the smooth men—feeling broken and apart.

Tennessee

OCTOBER 16, 1838

MARITOLE

At dawn there was a shot. A few women cried out, the baby startled at my side. I sat up.

Knobowtee stood behind me. "It's the march—" Others roused with a groan.

The sky was hard and gray. Drizzle began to rustle the trees. The Tennessee hills were so quiet I could hear a dog bark from a distant field. The soldiers passed out rations of flour and bacon. We had to cook our breakfast and prepare one meal to carry with us.

My father brought tinder for the fire. He and Knobowtee held the blanket over us while mother and I cooked the bacon. She tried again to make a lump of bread from the white flour. A wave of nausea came over me as I watched her. I felt like I had when I first knew I would have the baby. But there was not another baby. Not now anyway.

Reverend Mackenzie led the camp in prayer. His voice carried over the stockade the way rain hisses over the hills when a storm comes. He asked forgiveness for the Georgia Cherokee in the hearts of the Tennessee Cherokee, who felt they signed away the land. Another minister, who was the leader of our group, Reverend Bushyhead, prayed also for the Great Spirit's blessing in getting us to the new land.

"Can't you carry the cooking pot?" I snapped at Knobowtee. The baby screamed wildly as I grabbed her off the blanket and followed my mother.

The men loaded the wagons. Luthy and Tanner and their two sons found us among the crowd of people trying to get out of the stockade and into a line forming on the road.

"We're in Reverend Bushyhead's detachment," I heard Tanner say to my father.

The rain soaked through the blanket I had over my head. I shivered and held the baby against me. It wailed until I asked Knobowtee to find me a woman with milk.

"How can I do that?" he said, pulling his tunic around him.

"I'm sure there's a woman with more milk than her baby can use. I remember squirting mine into the fire when my breasts were full."

Knobowtee looked hopelessly up the road.

"Ask a soldier if there's milk anywhere. Anything to stop the baby from crying."

We started walking slowly. Soldiers rode back and forth. Their voices were confusing. Our own people also were telling us to march. Women cried and the men were silent. Knobowtee passed me once still looking for a woman who could nurse the baby. Luthy's calmness irritated me. Her boys were old enough that they could be talked to. For them it was a trip as though we were going to the green corn dance.

"When a baby cries that hard its spirit goes far away," Quaty Lewis told me. "You got to call it back."

Old women rode in the wagons. I saw the widow Teehee and Anna Sco-so-tah. A soldier pointed to my mother to get in the wagon also, but she refused. I held to her arm as we started to walk. I heard the soldiers whistle at the horses. The Cherokee men slapped their haunches to get them to move. The whole column started with the creak of axles and wagon wheels and the huff of the horses and mules and oxen who pulled the wagons.

I slipped in the mud in my moccasins. The wet leaves were slick as bear grease. Rain dripped on us from the heavy foliage. The baby squirmed in my arms. My mother offered to carry her, but I wanted my mother to take care of herself. Her face looked drawn and her eyes hollow.

I shivered as the wagon train moved. The wetness soaked through the blanket around my shoulders and ran down my neck. My ribs quivered under my dress. I held the baby with one arm and held on to the wagon with my other hand to keep from slipping. I said the baby's name under my breath, trying to call her spirit back.

"*Gruumph.*" My mother fell facedown in the mud beside me. I called my father. He was walking behind the wagon and saw her fall as soon as I did.

The soldier rode up beside us and said something in his own language. I couldn't always understand.

"He said to lift her into the wagon," my father told me. My mother didn't want to get into the wagon, but my father said, "You have to." He and Luthy helped her into the wagon.

I handed the baby to my mother. Its nose was stopped up, and it had to stop crying to suck air into its lungs. My mother held it to her and cried. Anna Sco-so-tah sat beside her.

When Knobowtee came back to the wagon where we walked, he said there was a woman about a quarter mile back who would feed the baby when we stopped. He looked at my mother, who wiped the mud from her face with a wet corner of the blanket. Soon he fell in with the men who followed the wagon: my father, Tanner, the boys, some neighbors, and a Cherokee man who was a friend of my father's. Lacey Woodard helped Kee-un-e-ca walk. Someone helped Mrs. Young Turkey into a wagon. Quaty Lewis followed.

All along the road I heard the growl of wagons, the drip of rain on the yellow leaves, and the late October morning full of the groans of the people.

We were nearly at the head of the wagon train because we had been near the front of the stockade. I wondered how far back the line went. How many other groups of Cherokee would we meet? The news of other stockades being cleared along the Hiwassee reached us as we parted Rattlesnake Springs.

"Snattle-rake," one of Tanner's boys said. I watched the rain dripping from his ears.

Mother rocked the baby though the wagon tossed them around. When we stopped at the Hiwassee River, she told Knobowtee to get the woman who had milk. The baby couldn't wait.

"How will we cross the river?" I asked Tanner, who chased after his smaller son.

"You'll be like one of the children who can't find his parents if you don't stay with us," Luthy said, trying to scare Ephum.

Tanner acted like a lost child wailing for his parents, and Ephum saw how he would look if he got lost.

I heard a shout and turned to see a soldier push a man into the water. The Hiwassee surged before us. I had heard its voice from the stockade in the night. Now we stood at its bank. We would walk across!

Reverend Bushyhead stepped into the water. "Take your moccasins off," he called in Cherokee as though it were a prayer. "Walk into the river. Cross to the other side." He started chanting. His sister and his pregnant wife holding his young daughter followed.

"Get in the wagon," the soldier who rode beside me said. I looked up into his face. He was the soldier who let me go back to the cabin. The soldier who carried me into the stockade when I ran. He was an older man, probably thirty-five. There was gray in his hair. His eyes were light as the sky on a mid-July noon. He poked at me with the bayonet and pointed to the wagon. I climbed the wheel spokes and got in beside my mother. Luthy followed. When I saw the baby I cried. My mother had it against her breast. I looked at the wet face. The closed eyes. The small nose that bubbled its raspy breath.

"Knobowtee," I called, but the wagon went into the river. Soldiers pushed the men and women. Some of them fell into the cold water.

My mother looked to the sky.

The soldiers spoke angrily to the men and women who hesitated to step into the river. The cold water swirled around their legs and waists. I could see the grimace on their faces. The contorted face of my baby. But the river covered the rasp of its breath. Wagons moved downstream with the current. People held on to ropes to cross. Reverend Bushyhead and his wife walked awkwardly. They stumbled at times trying to help their daughter. I heard the cries of agony from the people. Kee-un-e-ca beat her arms like wings at the water. The children in wagons cried for their parents. My own heart banged at the sky, hating the white men who drove us from our cabins into the dark river in the cold.

MRS. YOUNG TURKEY

I held to the wagon as it jolted across the Hiwassee. The women screamed and knocked my hands loose as I jostled in the wagon. I heard the soldiers' whips on the horses. I thought the wagon would turn over and I'd drown. A low growl escaped my throat as my body tossed in the wagon. I was leaving my cabin and land. I went inside myself to remember a story so I could walk to the afterlife. It was Selu, DSⱭⱰW, I thought of, who gave the Cherokee corn. She let her two sons, the Thunder Boys, kill her. She now lived up in the Sky World with her husband. The Ghost World is off there. I saw the sky from where I'd fallen helpless in the wagon. Selu watched me coming. Selu gave me life but took back my spirit after death. "Selu!" I called. I thought I could see CⱲⱭℽθ, the Land of the Ghosts.

KNOBOWTEE

I heard my wife call my name, but I was helping an old man across the Hiwassee. The rush of cold water around his legs and hips paralyzed him. The man's turban had fallen off, but I had a hold of his tunic, pulling him, trying to keep his head out of the water. The old man started to choke. I loosened my hold on him. Maybe the animal stories were true, that someday men would suffer the cruelty we had done to them. A horse swam past me, its ears thrown back, its eye wide as a dark, full moon, the bit jerked in its mouth by someone trying to get the wagon to move against the current. The women screamed. I saw my brother with my mother and my frantic, silent sister in the water. The soldiers yelled orders. I kept my hold on the old man.

LACEY WOODARD

The baby who was born talking said we would walk. The Christian ministers say Jesus is stronger than omens, but our holy men don't believe it. Yet Reverend Mackenzie and even Reverend Bushyhead say there's a Christian God. Surely he has power. Otherwise why would Mackenzie walk with us? Look at him stumble out of the water. Look at the fear on his face. His wet clothes.

But look at the other white men who believe in Jesus. See how they push the people into the water? See how they beat a screaming animal to pull a heavy wagon it cannot?

The people struggled to walk or swim through the uneven river. What have we done?

Our grandfathers followed a stick to northern Georgia. It was an old migration. The Great Spirit led us here. How can the soldiers drive us from our land? Maybe it was because we worshiped the earth instead of God, Reverend Mackenzie preached. Maybe it was because some of us had black slaves, Reverend Bushyhead said. Maybe it was because of gold and our cornfields, the men said.

Maybe the Great Spirit just calls us to the beyond where he lives. Maybe he's going to show us another world.

But who wants another world?

And look what happened to Jesus when he came to earth. What kind of God would let some of his men be soldiers and kill his son? But the Christian God had the power to know what would happen, Reverend Mackenzie said. He knew the tree in the form of a cross would save men from their sickness.

The Great Spirit knew the way. Did not the Cherokee follow a stick to where we were? Did not Israel follow a pillar of fire? Reverend Bushyhead asked. There would be a sign for the Cherokee from this God whose healing medicine was blood.

Just think of it, Lacey, I said to myself.

A wind stirred the camp we made on the other side of the river. I sat among the women drying their feet and clothing and slapping the bugs.

I wouldn't be frightened when a baby was born talking. I wouldn't look away when I saw an animal flailing on the ground and foaming at the mouth from exhaustion.

The evil spirits tried to frighten me so I'd do something stupid. So I would forget that Jesus protected the ground I stood on because I drank his blood

WAR CLUB

"Yop. We follow a stick to the new land." I leaned over and spat near Lacey. "The stick of the soldiers' guns."

KEHTOHIH

I held my blanket to my face on the other side of the Hiwassee. In my head a whole cornfield walked. The leaves waving. Ahead there was a divided path. Some stalks walked to the clouds. Some went into a hole in the ground. The ones who went into the ground were swallowed by an animal. They walked into the long tunnel of the entrails. There was only darkness ahead. The stalks who went above. Well. Their feet lost the ground. They could walk on air. They spirit-walked here. They spirit-walked there. Saying ᎤᏩ to the stars. Shaking their hands. Acting like they were old friends. Like they always had lived in this place. They had circles coiling around their heads. They were all full of light. What did it matter that soldiers came down the road? I went with the cornstalks to the sky. The weight lifted from my back. I was floating then. The way clouds floated over the clearing in my field at evening. Who was that ahead of me? I thought for a moment of my husband who was dead. I thought to call his name.

MARITOLE

We crossed to the north side of the Hiwassee River at a ferry above Gunstocker Creek. As soon as we got to the other side, I jumped out of the wagon and drank. My mother wet her finger and put it in the baby's mouth. The holy men prayed for her, and I thought she seemed better.

We traveled along the river, dazed, with the sick and aged and children. The rest were on foot or on horses. Even the pack dogs seemed to stumble. There were only a few blankets, cooking pots, and belongings. What was too heavy to be carried on our backs or hung under the wagons was soon left behind. The wagons had to carry people.

We looked like the white man's army marching, regiment

after regiment. The wagons and a few of the officers were flanked by horses and men. Soon we met with other groups of wagons and helpless-looking Cherokee from other stockades. Our trail lengthened beyond what I could see. Knobowtee had heard soldiers say we would cross the Cumberland Mountains then walk north through Pikesville, McMinnville, and eventually on to Nashville. He didn't know where we'd go beyond that. My father said we would make about ten or fifteen miles a day. He didn't sing his song against the insects anymore. They disappeared suddenly as the afternoon turned cold.

Rain splattered all evening on the wagons. My toes hurt from the cold. I cried when I saw my people in wet moccasins. Some of them were without any covering on their feet. The rain plastered our hair to our heads. One man walked without a shirt, his thin shoulders hunched.

Leaves fell from the trees. They were like yellow moccasins on the trail to the new territory.

ᏩᎷ.

Sometimes I didn't know if it was really happening or not. Maybe it was a ghost dream. But I knew we pushed against the bear that resisted us. It stood before us each step we took on the trail. We were marching west toward darkness, toward death. The sick ones groaned in the wagons when they jumped over the uneven road. I had gotten out to make room for others. My mother held the baby under a tarp the soldier had thrown over them. The baby was quiet. When we stopped, the woman came and gave the baby her nipple but the baby didn't suck. The woman squeezed a few drops of milk on the baby's mouth and it swallowed. Knobowtee couldn't bear to watch. He went off through the people to walk someplace else. Often I looked for him, but I saw only the suffering faces. The tree trunks blackened with wetness. The cold sat upon my bones. It was as though I had no clothing. It was as though I had no skin. I was nothing but a bare skeleton walking the path. I felt anger at the soldiers. I felt anger at the people in my cabin. They were using my plates and bowls. Sleeping under my quilts! I cursed them. There was something dark and terrible in the white man.

KINCHOW

"I'm going to tell you this one," I said that night with the fire-light on my face.

"He heard it from his dogs." Anna rubbed her hands.

"Ꭶ. Them fish-and-loaves stories Bushyhead's running telling everyone ain't nothing."

"Ꭶ." Quaty tried to sound like me.

"Once a hunter went hunting," I said.

"There was a river and a deer standing in it.

"The hunter shot the deer.

"His arrow went through the deer and stuck him to a tree.

"The hunter said it looked like he would have to take off his boots and get into the water.

"The hunter took off his boots.

"Well, there was a rabbit's leg sticking out from underneath him.

"Well, he'd sat on a rabbit.

"He struck it on the ground where a family of quail were sleeping and they were all killed, too.

"When he walked to the deer stuck to the tree, he felt something in his boots and he took off his boots, and there was a pile of perch inside them."

"I thought you said he took off his boots before he went in the water," Anna said, moving when the smoke from the camp-fire burned her eyes.

"Huh?"

"Yes, you did," Quaty agreed with Anna.

"Well, he had his boots on in the water because they were full of perch.

"And when he pulled the arrow out of the tree, honey came out."

Anna chuckled.

"He gathered up his fish and rabbit and quail and deer."

"And honey," Anna finished.

"Ꭶ. That's all I got to tell."

MARITOLE

I took the baby to the woman with milk. She was of the Paint clan. The baby was able to suck for a while. I called the baby's name under my breath. I think her spirit had gone to Du'stay-alun'yi. I called it back. Tanner called also. In the Cherokee way, an uncle's responsibility was the same as the father's.

ANNA SCO-SO-TAH

Kinchow kept talking, even after the campfire fizzed in the rain. I was so cold I moved toward Quaty Lewis, but Quaty's cold legs made me move again. How my neighbor talked. He talked to make himself forget the cold. He used to make up reasons to come to my cabin, and I'd fed him corn bread. He'd fix the chickens' fence. He'd pet me under my skirts sometimes. I chuckled when I remembered. I was so cold I felt giddy. The small pebbles on the ground cut into my hip. I moved closer to my neighbor. We shivered under his thin blanket. I put my hand over my neighbor's mouth to keep him quiet when I heard a soldier on guard. Probably the nervous clucking of his bayonet against a canteen. I kept my hand over Kinchow's mouth. His teeth moved as if he chewed my corn bread.

KNOBOWTEE

I remembered when the news of the Removal Act came from New Echota. Hardly more than two years ago. I'd ridden the horse from the farm, Maritole holding on behind me. We weren't even married yet, but I worked with Maritole's father and brothers to repair the fields. Maritole's grandparents hadn't been able to keep up the farm. I'd decided I'd marry Maritole. She had the farm. She wanted to marry me. I didn't tell her about the Removal Act, but on the way back she told me she'd heard about it in Du'stayalun'yi.

Maritole's father was always looking at me. I could sit with Maritole's family while her father led them in morning prayer at dawn, but I wasn't part of them. Her family didn't have conjurers in their background. My father could catch a bird with his words. He only had to call to the birds in their flight, and they'd fall into his trap.

"You could act like you were with us for Maritole's sake," Tanner said to me as we put out the fire and prepared to march for the day. "You chose to marry her."

I didn't say anything. I wanted to be with my brother, my mother, and sister in their circle. I didn't feel separate from them. I wanted to remember how I'd hid in the bushes while my father caught birds with nothing more than his voice.

Tanner put his hand on my arm just as Maritole's father had done. I pulled away from him. My shoulders ached because I hunched them in the cold.

"You got my grandmother's cabin," Tanner told me as we walked that day. "My wife didn't have any fields."

"Well, mine did and I plowed them."

"I helped you in the field after dark many nights."

"When your fields were burned, I cleared them with you," I returned, looking at Tanner under the scattered trees. We had started the day's walk, stiff and groaning. The woods were growing thinner. Soon we'd be in the open clearing. What would it be without the hills of North Carolina? What would it be without the voices of the trees to help us walk?

"You're a farmer," I told Tanner. "My father was a hunter. But I can farm, too."

"You're always looking at the groups of men talking," Tanner said while Quaty Lewis listened. "There's more to a farm than plowing. You got an eye for what's in it for you. I think sometimes you don't see Maritole but for the fields and cabin she offered you."

"You can't see beyond the end of your horse," I said.

"You follow whatever passes. You don't have a voice to guide you. You tag along with us, but you don't believe. You're not really with us."

"That's your feeling."

"Yes, that's mine."

Quaty nodded as she stood with us.

I wanted to hit Tanner. Knock him to the ground. Show him the self-righteous brother-in-law he was. I had something to say. I just didn't know how yet.

I looked at the long line of walking people behind me like kernels on a cob of corn. For a moment, I could almost believe we were walking a holy walk. As a unit. A people. One kernel following another. Our voices united. If we could be one in our walking, we would make it to the new territory. All of us had a part. And if some were silent, it would be like a cob with kernels missing.

"I know you never liked me." I didn't want to argue with Tanner.

"If you'd prove yourself other than someone after an opportunity."

"Does it make any difference now who the fields belonged to?"

LUTHY

I was asleep that night when I heard my mother's voice. She was praying and beyond her voice, I heard my father making the tobacco offering. I was glad to hear my parents again. My father had died after my mother. It happened when I was still almost a girl.

I listened to the sound of the campfire and smelled the smoke. There was a holy man making the offering of Ꮎ-ᏮᏒꭲ, the power that heals, because my mother was sick.

Other people there knew me. I think some of them were ancestors. Had they known my mother wouldn't heal? Had they come to walk with her to the next world?

Now it was the green corn dance and it was summer. I circled with the women, only my stomach was big with Tanner's and my first son.

They had taken my mother to the creek long ago. The holy man had washed my mother's face by dipping his hand in the water and wiping her face. But my mother had died. The Ꮎꭵꮑꭶ, the evil medicine, destroyed the power that heals. It happened sometimes.

I wanted my mother. We had bought tea and a cat-lidded teapot from a trader. My mother and I had been the first to drink tea in the Cherokee village in North Carolina.

Now we danced in a circle again, but I didn't dance. The booger men in their masks made me laugh, and my laughter was causing the baby to push out of me upside down and head-first into the dirt circle.

Now I was hungry for deer meat. I put my fingers in my mouth to have something to taste. I moved with the older women now. *Mamma*, I thought. The small shells sewn to my skirt said, *shh-sh*. My uncle of the Deer clan with antlers on his head led the hunters to the white-tailed herd. In the woods the wind hummed, *hoom-hoom*. I carried the oval of the sky in my basket. *Fill it, Great Spirit, with deer meat*. I had picked berries and hazelnuts. The hush of women was a bundle of bird skins. I grazed the dirt circle with my feet. The click of deer-knuckle bones in my hands.

MARITOLE

We stopped before the Cumberland Mountains several miles north of the Hiwassee River near Charleston, Tennessee. Knobowtee and I held the hands of Mark and Ephum. Luthy held my baby under her blanket. We had been given a small tent in which my mother, Luthy, the boys, my baby, and I shivered together those first black nights. Luthy and I tried to keep the boys between us, but they fussed and complained that we were smothering them. They cried that they were cold and they cried for the bed in their cabin. Mother and I tried to keep the baby warm. Sometimes I had a little milk for her. I thought several times she would not make it until dawn. No matter how hard I tried to close my eyes and forget the cold, my eyes opened to the dark that surrounded us.

For a while the men left us. They sat outside a circle of men in council, angry because they were not included. The council determined again we would endure our hardships and not fight the removal any longer. They determined we would keep our constitution and laws both on the trail and in the new territory, where the soldiers were leading us. Otherwise we'd become the uncivilized men they called us. Otherwise we'd become like them.

Once our leaders were holy men and chiefs. Now I heard the voices of traders and landowners, especially the half-breeds who sold deerskins to the Panton & Leslie Company. "Fifty-four thousand last year." I heard the men talking as they mourned what we were leaving. Sometimes their voices faded into one another. Other times I'd hear someone I knew. Sometimes I heard my father's songs through the dark and the cold.

ᏴᎡᎤᎵᎬᏆ°Ꮧ (hair white able to live with he she).

It was a song for us to live long enough to have white hair. I listened to his voice and felt the cold tears come to my face. I would be able to live with white hair. If I lived through this night, then nothing would bother me again. I felt my mother jerk with a stifled sob. I reached my hand to her, and we cried to ourselves as we listened to my father's voice.

Farther away, the men talked. Could they have done something different? Was the Treaty of New Echota legal? Could something else have been said to Chief Justice Marshall or President Andrew Jackson?

In the small world of our tent, it was my mother's hand that mattered. She had helped me plant my first corn. The orators who had come to bless the corn-planting cheered us as they walked through the fields, chanting and beating an earthen pot covered with deerskin. Grandmother sat on her perch screeching the crows out of the grain.

Luthy's parents were already dead, and I felt pity for her with no one to cry against. There was no room for Tanner in the tent.

After a while all I heard was the silence of the cold night outside. Maybe the men slept. Maybe they just stood under the hard sky waiting for the light.

Before dawn, I knew I had been dreaming. "I saw the umbrella I ordered from Atlanta," I told my mother. ᏪᏟᏏ. Mother held the baby against her chest. Her voice cracked as we crawled from the tent and got in the wagon. I watched my father fold the tent with Tanner and hang it over the end of the wagon. He moved slowly and I knew his body was stiff. Mine was also. Soon I couldn't watch him any longer because of the tears.

"Why didn't we go earlier when we had a chance?" Mrs. Young Turkey asked, chewing on her rations. "We could have sold our cabins and started again in Indian Territory."

"You heard rumors of the men who returned from the West. Some of them didn't get paid for their land. It was just another empty agreement." I listened to Anna Sco-so-tah.

"How could I leave my family?" Quaty Lewis argued. "The farm we worked for since we were married?" Quaty grew quiet thinking of her white husband, who had stayed behind.

"But we could have taken what we had," Mrs. Young Turkey insisted, chewing her ration of jerky. "We could have sold our cabins and started again in Indian Territory."

"If they hadn't burned our cabins," Kee-un-e-ca cried.

The soldiers called for us to start, and soon the wagon lurched forward with a jerk.

"Where's Grandma's orange quilt with the yellow moons in the corners?"

"Hush, Mother," I said.

She felt for the quilt with her hands, and I thought she must be out of her head.

"We'll be all right," I assured her.

ᏢᎩ ᏎᎢᏏ. I heard Luthy cry out. A soldier was beating an old Indian to get him to move. The bundle on the old man's back was nearly as big as he was. Others behind us cried in protest, and Tanner started toward the soldier. My father tried to stop him, but another soldier rode past me and pushed the first soldier away from the old man before Tanner got into trouble. It was the same soldier who let me go back to the cabin. He looked at me and I watched him ride away.

A rich woman, a trader's wife, with her baby, followed behind the wagon in her own carriage when we started again. She sobbed just like the others.

A man named J. Powell, who was the doctor, gave me some goat's milk he'd gotten from a farm we passed. But each time I tried to feed my baby, she choked or whimpered almost silently. She didn't have the strength to cry.

Mark and Ephum rode in the wagon. Sometimes Tanner carried one of the boys on his back.

The Cumberland Mountains ahead of us were like huge burial mounds.

O-ga-na-ya, Knobowtee's brother, came from behind the wagon. "Eyes-for-the-white-soldier" he called me.

ᎯᏓᏍᎤᎠ. I stared at O-ga-na-ya for speaking to me.

For the rest of the afternoon we made almost no progress. We'd started the ascent, but the horses and mules and oxen weren't used to the added pull of the wagons. The soldier ordered us to make camp early.

LUTHY

An old woman had died during the day. We kept her body in one of the wagons until we could bury her. For now the ground was too rocky and there was no coffin.

MARITOLE

When I woke the next morning, a drizzling rain fell on the wagons and soaked through my quilt. I sat up and saw the line of wagons down the side of the mountain in the gray dawn. There was not even an outhouse for privacy. The soldiers rode here and there. "Get up. Pack your belongings. We're starting out again. Get some broth in the line and stand at the wagon if you need to eat." The soldier rode by and spoke to us. The one who was always there. He looked strangely at my mother before he rode on.

The campfires sputtered in the rain and would not even cook our bacon. My mother didn't seem to know what she was doing anyway. She couldn't see this unreal land we started through.

No. I will not walk, I remembered saying. Now I pushed the wagon up the hill. The Cumberlands were a barrier to the new land. The soldiers beat the animals to get them to pull the wagons up the steep land. Luthy and I couldn't bear it and got out of the wagon. It took a long time to push the wagons a few feet. One horse fell and broke its leg. A soldier shot it. One less animal to pull the weight of the wagons. Tears burst out without warning, and nothing could stop them. Kee-un-e-ca cried continually for her cabin that burned to the ground. My own chest heaved with grief. My mother and baby were dying. It was only a matter of who would go first.

"Why aren't we going by flatboats?" Mrs. Young Turkey asked.

"Because this removal is by wagon," someone answered.

Reverend Bushyhead passed our wagon and stopped at the head of the train. He led us in prayer because the task of getting over the mountain seemed impossible. Soldiers rode up to see the wagons bogged in mud, the sick and old ones trying to walk with bundles on their backs. When the wagons finally started to move again, it felt like we had pulled off a scab.

It rained again the next morning. Breath steamed from our mouths. "We're together," I said to my father standing by the wagon where Mother sat with the baby, "if only for now."

"We don't have Thomas," my mother said.

"He's hiding in the hills, Mother. Part of our family will not be driven away."

"We may never see him again," she answered me quickly and held her blanket to her face.

My father wiped his hand over his face.

"I haven't seen Luthy and Tanner this morning," I said.

"They're behind this group of wagons," he said, the rain dripping from his nose.

The wagon rattled slowly up the sloppy ground that morning, bump after bump. Sometimes I held on to it so I wouldn't slip in the mud. Nothing I did kept the rain from my skin. I felt it run through my eyebrows, into my ears, and down my neck. Sometimes I shivered so much that I could hardly walk. Mother had her arm around the baby, but none of us kept warm. I heard teeth rattling together.

A great dark cloud hung over us. We marched as though we weren't in our own bodies. As though something would happen to jar us back to the way we had been. Then I heard the growl of thunder like a bear, and I knew it was happening to us. As we neared the top of the mountain, I turned and looked back and saw the enormous line of Cherokee. "Ten miles long," my father said.

When we reached the top of the Cumberlands, I looked back again and wailed with the others. I waved to the North Carolina woods already far behind. Du'stayalun'yi! It was no longer ours. Even with Thomas hiding there. The loss and sorrow was so jumbled I could hardly walk.

The soldier rode beside me for a moment. He leaned toward me as though he wanted to help me. The men walked with their heads down. I looked for Knobowtee among the men but didn't see him. Then I turned back toward the way we marched and buried my head in the quilt I held around me, not watching where we were going, only walking beside the wagon step by step.

We traveled slowly across the mountain all day, holding on to one another, slipping and falling and getting up to walk again. Children cried and refused to walk. Their legs went limp under them. Their parents carried them or they were put in wagons.

The men walked solemnly behind the wagons, finally catching up with their families when they helped pull the last of the wagons in our group up the mountain. I fell a little behind and found Knobowtee. He looked at me, and we said nothing but walked together. I tried to take his hand, but he pulled it away from me.

"The baby is dying, Knobowtee. I want you to know it will happen."

"The better for her," he said.

Only late in the afternoon as it sleeted did I take his hand again. I looked to the ground to keep the sleet out of my face and used his hand for a guide. My ribs hurt from constant shivering. The cold drove us away from each other into ourselves. The rain on the tarp raged like a burning campfire.

We didn't know where we were walking, but we walked silently, following the ones before us.

I felt I had shriveled into a corner of my shoulder, or into my fingers, which held the quilt close to my chest. *What had we done? Why were we hated?* I kept thinking over and over as we walked the mountain piece by piece. The whole endless groaning wagon train like a long snake was winding up the mountain. Maybe it was Uk'ten' following us to the new territory.

By evening I could stay awake no longer and fell asleep against a tree. When I woke I saw Luthy and Tanner crying and knew what had happened. Tanner and the soldier were already digging a grave. I heard their shovels in the rocky earth. "On top of the mountain," the soldier said to me when I walked toward the wagon. They would remain on top of the Cumberland Mountains, nearer to the North Carolina woods than if they'd have gone to the new territory. Tanner pulled the blanket down, and I saw my mother's gray face. Her eyes were closed and her mouth was open in a tiny *o*. The baby was in the crook of her arm. Its eyes were open, looking toward my mother's shoulder. I looked southward, too, in the hard dawn but couldn't see anything. Maybe they could see it with their new eyes. Maybe they were no longer here and the memory of the trail had washed from their heads. Maybe my mother's spirit had just gotten up in the night with the baby, and they went back.

VOICES AS THEY WALKED

"They saw him lying there in the water."

"In the lake."

"Yes. That's the way they saw him."

"Uk'ten'."

"Yes."

"They tried to pull his head above the water."

"How?"

"They had a rope, and they caught him by the horns."

"Because he had horns."

"Yes, and rattles like a rattlesnake."

"And they pulled him up by the horns."

"The oxen pulled."

"He was spotted."

"Yes, and very huge."

"That's the way he looked."

"In the old days the Cherokee wanted to kill him."

"They were after his scales."

"Yes, the snake with scales."

"The scales helped the Cherokee in war."

"They chased away the enemy."

"The scales might be somewhere in the wagons."

"Yes."

"The scales might be."

THE SOLDIERS

"Some dumb ox ate poison ivy." The soldiers passed the halt signal along the line.

"It was more than one."

"We got to stop," the captain said.

"Those Indians need a rest."

"They ain't started walking yet."

"Look at that old bastard who can hardly stand."

"He'll be in the meat wagon by tonight."

"Why don't we just kill 'em all right here?"

"Do the country a favor."

"We'll have time to finish the burying."

"I'm tired myself."

"This ain't no easy march—beating them Indians and horses so they walk."

"Ain't for the pay we're getting either."

"Nor army rations."

"Where the hell we going?"

"Indian Territory."

"How can we push them off the end of the earth?"

"That old one there just talks about his dogs."

REVEREND BUSHYHEAD

Sequatchie Valley, Tennessee, Oct. 21st, 1838

Sir:

I am under the necessity of troubling you with a communication asking further and more explicit instructions as to the points and manner that the contractors are bound to forage our detachment. From the extract furnished me saying that the contractor "agrees to furnish forage & substance at such points on the road as may be required," I take it for granted that each place of encampment is the point at which such requirement shall be made. And especially so, until we shall have made our way across the mountains—or the result will be that the detachment stops, and a portion of the waggons employed, first in hawling forage to the place designated, and then returning for the people and loading assigned each. We have a large number of sick and very many extremely aged and infirm persons in our detachment, that must of necessity be conveyed in the waggons. Our detachment now consists of about 968 or 970 Cherokee. There is forty-nine waggons—so that you will see the impracticability of hawling forage from place to place to serve the convenience of the contractors. Aside from the subsistence rations, it will require twelve waggons to hawl the three days forage rations between this and McMinnville, Tennessee.

It is also proper to state that we have been required to draw rations of sugar, coffee, salt, and soap at Blythes ferry to supply the detachment to Readyville or Nashville, which amounts to some six barrels sugar, 4 of coffee &c. The fact is the detachment cannot progress under such circumstances. We have now to double many of the teams in ascending the mountains. There is about one hundred and fifty loose horses aside from the teams & oxen. It does seem to me that if the conductors are authorized to require of the contractors that forage should be delivered at any point between the Agency East—and Fort Gibson (Indian Territory) that on Waldens Ridge & Cumberland Mountain should be the place.

You will perceive the difficulty has occurred between the Agent of the contractors and myself upon this subject. And I now submit the final adjustment of the matter to yourself.

I would also ask your advice as to purchasing a waggon and team for the exclusive purpose of conveying the very old and infirm of the detachment.

I think your letter will perhaps make all things right with our friend Hog. Very Respectfully,

Jesse Bushyhead
by J Powell

KNOBOWTEE

The men looked worn already. Most of our turbans were gone, and our tunics were torn and dirty. I could hear the dead sometimes. My ear aches. How did I hurt my hand? The skin on my knuckles is gray and swollen as a rotten peach. Maybe Tanner was right. Women had the property, and that helped me decide to marry her. But I can farm. Yes, except I have no farm. I have nothing, again

MARITOLE'S MOTHER

The Great Spirit covered a turtle's back with mud so the land would form. So we wouldn't drown in the waters all around us. Don't you see the mud swirls on the turtle's back? The patterns of earth when you look down at it. Like the edge of the field after the Coosawattee flooded.

The boys were little. Thomas and Tanner. I knelt on the ground with them. Maritole was on my back. Like I carry her baby now. Maritole wanted to see the turtle, too. I pulled her off my back. She pointed to the turtle and squealed. I still hear her voice. The dead go on talking whether anyone listens. Our words float from the drafty caves of our lungs. See the far line down there. *Tell stories*, I say to them at night. *Riding on your voices you can walk.*

WAH-KE-CHA

Look at all this white flour. More of it than we seen. "Snow," the soldiers say in English. What fire bakes it? People look up. It keeps coming. "The sky's fat," they say. Soon our heads get wet. People shiver worse. They stand around looking. The ground slips under 'em. People sit down. Wait and see what happens. The rest of the people are still crossing the mountain.

QUATY LEWIS

"Who's that old woman carrying a bundle, holding it to her?" I asked her clan. When we huddled together under a tarp, I saw the woman look into her bundle. What was in it? Rags. Twigs.

Leaves. Had she picked them up along the way so she'd have something to carry? Junk. Junk! All of it.

Now who is that loud woman talking about baskets? That other detachment catching up with us again? Who is that woman crying? Why don't they all just shut up? Luthy with her prissy shawl and little feet. Old War Club with his open mouth. Why, he's got no teeth!

The people are afraid of this much snow. The widow Tee-hee. Anna Sco-so-tah. Even Lacey Woodard. How many had seen the snow getting deep? We covered our heads under the blankets and tarps. We hid under the wagons. We talked to it. Should the conjurers chant? What would the snow do? Children cried or laughed at the white flour sifting from the sky. The soldiers laughed at the Cherokee who were superstitious.

Not ᏊᏆᏏᏔᏔ, our cornmeal bread. No, this white bread is nothing my granny would have touched.

WAR CLUB

Ɦmph. Even the snow is white.

MARITOLE

"My wife," he says, "my wife," and walks in line, his head bent, snow falling on his ears. I put a blanket over my father's head. ᏜhᏍA. I sing his corn-stand-up song. I lead him by the hand. If he stumbles, I tell him to walk. "See the boys holding on to Luthy and Tanner?" Behind us the rest of the line crosses the Cumberland Mountains. I try to look, but the wind and snow blow into my eyes. We know now how hard we're hit. Nothing but our feet walking west. The wagons slipping, people crying, soldiers hitting horses, some of them screeching under the whip.

TANNER

I planted my axes toward the four directions to break up thunderstorms over the fields. I heard the thunder when the soldiers drove us from North Carolina. Now it snows. It feels strange on my hand. The boys hold up their hands, too. Who is that crying with cold? Who is that sucking snot up their nose? The widow Teehee? That's what happens to a woman when her husband dies. She grows hollow. I'm glad Mother died first. I want to out- live Luthy so she won't have to be alone.

Anna Sco-so-tah wiped the spoon with a dirty cloth as it passed to Luthy. It turned my stomach, but I was hungry. The cramps would come later, but for now I ate.

LUTHY

Look at them trying to keep a featherbed on a horse. Blankets and children tied there, too, pots and pans rattling when we started to move again.

MARITOLE

Knobowtee made it harder to walk. He might have said, *I'm sorry the baby died. I'm sorry your mother died. Let me walk with you. It's not your fault the soldiers came down the road.* But he walked with his mother and brother and sister. He walked sepa- rate from me. He could have held my hands, where the cold hurt the scars from my burn. He could have rubbed my feet when we stopped to rest. He just stood against a tree and didn't look at me. He didn't say anything to heal. The way the sun cleared the fog that crept on the fields in the morning. The way clouds came over the cornfields and stuck their tongues into them. I wasn't anything he wanted to see. His eyes went far away. He didn't see me as his wife. I was something different from him. The stars bursting the night's borders. One star squeezing into the next space with nothing to stop it from slip- ping. I thought Knobowtee would walk with me. I thought he would say he was sorry we had to leave our land. His fields were gone, and he did not know who he was. We could still walk to- gether. There would be other fields someday.

I felt the trees as I walked. The insides of the bark. The tall and narrow place of the trunk. I felt my arms branch. The leaves hang from my arms and head. I opened my mouth in an O the way a knothole opens in the trunk of a tree. I looked at the groups of people with the *O* in my open mouth. I shuffled my arms like a tree. I could rip him into air.

TANNER

The men grumbled as they camped that night. "Thirty-five men signed away land that belonged to seventeen thousand Cherokee. All the petitions we signed and sent to Washington had no effect. John Ross didn't change anything."

"The white men, the Oᵨ⅃ᕲ." The men wouldn't stop. "We farmed to prove to them we were civilized, then they took our farms."

"We emulated the white man. Established a capital. Took power from the women. Made a two-party government."

I shivered and stomped my feet with Father for warmth.

"Yo. The Removal Act. We didn't believe it."

I held the boys' heads against my chest to keep them warm. The fire sputtered in the snow. The conjurers kept chanting. The fire keepers kept the fires going with their words. The boys heard the men's voices.

Nearly thirty years ago there had been a Cherokee ghost dance. Some remembered it. A prophet named Charley said to get rid of the white man's ways. Then hailstones would fall and kill the white man, and the Indian could farm his land unharmed again. Charley had even seen horses in the sky. He told the women to pound corn in the mortar rather than at the white man's mill. He told the women to give up their muslin dresses and dancing reels. He wanted the Cherokee to be the red clay people they were created to be.

"Maybe if we had listened—" someone said.

I laughed, *huumphh*.

White Path and Fly Smith also had led a rebellion against the white man's culture. But the two men were now in the line of the removal, and John Ross was the leader of the Cherokee.

Look at Ross. How he listed all his property. How he kept count. Now he rides on a steamboat to the New Territory.

Elias Boudinot had signed the New Echota Treaty because we were being killed by the white man. They gave us whiskey and disease. Their broken treaties broke us. Boudinot said in the *Phoenix* that we would be better off in the West. Then John Ross had returned from Washington last summer and found the Cherokee miserable in the stockades.

How many statesmen had spoken for the Cherokee? Henry Clay, David Crockett, Daniel Boone, Daniel Webster, Sam Houston.

What's happened to my farm now? The squeak of my shed door? The collards, cotton, peanuts, oats, tobacco, muskmelon? The soldiers laughed because I fenced the garden and let my animals roam.

The boys should know about Junaluska. No, about Tsali, who lived near the Cheowa River in North Carolina. They should understand. The men felt defeated. The men felt whipped. Driven from the land. Those-who-live-between-the-cabins had our farms. We had gotten up and walked away without a fight.

"But we have our heroes," I said as I put the boys under the tarp with Maritole and Luthy. "Tsali and his sons, Soquah, Tahlee, and Chahee. And Tsali's brother, Teetlunuchee."

"And Agiya, his wife," Maritole said.

"The white men taunted them." Luthy sat behind me. "The white soldiers came to their cabins to arrest Tsali's family. Tsali's sons wanted to fight, but Tsali wouldn't let them. They were obedient sons." I looked at the boys. "So Tsali let the soldiers take them to jail. But Tsali's wife was sick and lame. He asked for a stretcher for her to ride on, but the soldiers wouldn't listen. She got up anyway and walked because she didn't want her husband to fight. The soldier kept his bayonet poked in her side as they marched to the stockade. His sons said they wouldn't let the soldiers treat their wives that way. The time of great warriors was gone, and now it was the common man's time to act. Who were these white soldiers with their Manifest Destiny? And the idea that they were sent from God and could steal the land?"

"What kind of country could be built on stolen land?" Luthy asked. She knew it was my story to tell and she was quiet.

"Finally Tsali's wife died from the soldier's harsh treatment,"

I said. "And Tsali decided to take revenge. He told his sons they would attack the soldiers."

"And they did?" Ephum asked.

"Yes, they did," I answered my son. "Tsali, Soquah, Teetlunuchee, Chahee, and Tahlee made their war whoops. They jumped into the path and killed the white soldier that had taunted Agiya."

"What happened?"

"The men ran into the hills and hid."

"Is that where they are now?"

"Yes."

"Maybe they're with Uncle Thomas."

"Yes, maybe."

WAUSKULTA

1 round log house 14 × 14 board roof weighed on a small pole corncrib

7 acres bottomland cleared and fenced

18 very good peach trees

1 house round logs board roof wooden chimney

2 corncribs

1 round log stable board roof weighed on

SALLY BEE HUNTER

house 16 × 16, hewn logs, board roof, puncheon floor, wooden chimney

kitchen 12 × 12 round log board roof

3 corncribs

3 large hewn log bee shelters

16 acres on creek, 82 large peach trees

2 acres bottomland, 7 large, 1 small apple trees

1 fish trap on Long Swamp Creek

CHIEF JOHN ROSS

Dwelling house 70 by 20 two stories high, cellar, a basement story, ash single roof, weather-boarded & ceiled. Brick chimney, 4 fireplaces. Porch & shed the whole length, and

height on one side 10 ft. wide. 20 glass windows, some good worksmanship	$3,500.00
Kitchen 28 by 20 H[ewed] L[og] plank floor	50.00
Workhouse 18 by 20 H.L. [plank floor]	35.00
Smokehouse 18 by 16 puncheon flr	25.00
Negro house 18 by 16 puncheon flr	25.00
3 [Negro houses 18 by 16] each $20.00 pr	60.00
Stable old 24 by 24 loft	25.00
[Stable] new with loft 16 by 14	20.00
Crib 9 by 19 H. L.	20.00
2 [Cribs 9 by 19] R. L. $15.00 pr	30.00
Stable 18 by 20 H. L.	20.00
Smith Shot & waggon shed old	15.00
Outhouse 14 by 16 puncheon R. L.	25.00
Well 50 ft 20 ft through rock	100.00
Field 75 acres cleared, 85 under fence not cleared, river low ground $10.00	750.00
Field 56 acres cleared, 15 not cleared under fence, river land at $12.00	672.00
Field 5 acres upland @ $6.50 pr	32.50
Field S[outh] S[ide] Coosa [River] 20 acres cleared 10 acres not cleared under fence @ $12.00 pr	240.00
Field [at] fork [of] Hightower & Oostanaula [rivers] 14 acres cleared & [some] woodland under fence at $12.00 pr	168.00
5 small lots at $3.00 pr	15.00
Garden fence	10.00
170 Peach trees @ 80 cents pr	136.00
34 apples trees @ $2.50 pr	85.00
9 pear trees @ $2.50 pr	22.50
5 Quinces at [$2.50 pr]	12.50
5 damson Plumbs at 75 cents	3.50
Total	$6,097.00

Ferry net income $1,000 pr year. Mr. Ross was dispossessed in April 1833 and was dispossessed of the whole from the winter following under the laws of Georgia	4,000.00
Ferry valuation	10,000.00
Spoilation for rent	1,700.00
Total	$21,797.00

D, DNA, RG 75 Cherokee Register of Valuations; FC, DNA,
RG 75, M 574, Roll 8 (file 75), <u>Ross Papers</u>

TERRAPIN HEAD

Each day we walk. The animals. Wagons. People. Har. It snows
more. In my cabin I made shutters that closed and locked. Did I
think the soldiers wouldn't get me? $4o∤Ɵſ (across the rear
side). I made my bar-the-way dance.

But now my legs pump as if my heart was in them. My feet
slip in the snow. My hands pump. My head slarps. Har. I am Big-
heart-walking-all-over.

MARITOLE'S FATHER

Yo, soldiers. I lost my wife. I don't care. I will follow her. But
look at my grandsons. They need corn. I have a musket. I can
shoot game. But we have to have corn. Corn! That's what we
eat. We can't live without corn. It's our bodies. Our lives. We're
driven inside. The way loose snow blows across the ground. Our
faces change. Red. Hard. Cracked. Our eyes run like rabbits.
Burrow in our head. We shiver. How can the women have tears
to cry?

MARITOLE

Somewhere in Tennessee, north of the Cumberland Mountains,
the snow turned into a blizzard. We had been protected from
winter in North Carolina by the hills or by the Great Spirit himself. But now we looked into the driving sleet. We slipped as we
tried to walk across the fields all day. We slept in wagons or on
the ground without fire at night. No fire would have withstood
the wind of the storm. We huddled together shivering and
afraid. I heard the conjurers working their magic against the
storm. I heard Lacey Woodard pray.

In the cold white dawn I could see more people had died in
the night. The men carried their bodies to a wagon. The soldiers
wanted to leave the dead unburied beside the trail.

"No!"

"We can't carry dead bodies." I heard an argument behind the wagon.

"We bury our dead." It was Knobowtee's voice.

"Their spirits would wander without rest." It was Knobowtee's brother.

"I ain't got patience with your heathen superstitions—"

"I *ain't* got patience with you, either."

I started to get up, afraid for Knobowtee. He always looked ready to spring on anyone. I wanted to yell at him that it wouldn't do any good to fight, but I heard a shot ring out in the cold dawn as the principal soldier rode to our camp and pushed the other soldier away from Knobowtee and O-ga-na-ya.

"We'll take the dead with us. For now," he ordered.

The white minister Mackenzie rode back and forth between the groups of Cherokee. What made him walk the trail with us when he didn't have to? He stopped and preached from the Book of Acts. "There was a storm and a ship broke apart on some rocks." Reverend Bushyhead said the Apostle Paul told the people to hold on to the boards and broken pieces and they would make it to the shore.

"What's a ship?" Ephum asked.

"A wagon without wheels," Tanner told him.

"What's a shore?" someone else said under his blanket.

Knobowtee wouldn't listen to the rest of the sermon and walked away. War Club followed, spitting.

Later Reverend Mackenzie led the funeral services. He prayed with the others. Then the rich woman wailed the death wail for her baby. I didn't know why I couldn't wail for my baby and mother. I felt numb when I thought of them.

Luthy hobbled between my father and me, leaning on a stick for a cane. She had blisters on both feet but walked because the wagons were full of dying Cherokee suffering from fevers worse than blisters.

I felt there was a dark presence over us. The bear we pushed would not move away. Each day I felt his ragged fur. Sometimes I could smell his breath.

Reverend Bushyhead stopped to speak to my father. He had read some words from the Bible when my mother and baby were buried together. Why did he stop? Why didn't he just lead the detachment and not say anything? My father's shoulders jerked again with grief. Kee-un-e-ca and Mrs. Young Turkey sat under their blanket watching. Quaty Lewis just stood by the wagon.

Each morning it took us longer to get ready. We felt the soldiers' impatience, but it became harder to get ready and we were later and later. There was no reason to move. There were too many wagons full of moaning people. There were too many wagons full of the dead. But the ground was frozen, and we could find no place to bury them. We argued each day with the soldiers against leaving the bodies by the trail.

I felt like we were suspended in air. The salt pork always hurt my stomach, and I cried with cramps. My father hunted deer, and we ate chestnuts. At nights the white men sold some of our men whiskey, and they were sick with it the next morning.

A few men who tried to run off were fettered. The sores climbed their ankles above their blistered and bleeding feet. Knobowtee never mentioned his boots or coat or hat I couldn't get from the cabin. He didn't say anything to me anymore. One night I held one of the boys. "What have we done?" I said before I realized I spoke. Ephum looked at me as though he understood but didn't have the words to answer.

Because of our weariness, Reverend Bushyhead decided that we would not walk Sundays. The white soldiers wanted us to walk, but Bushyhead and some of the leaders of the other detachments said we would stop. We were responsible for our own march. We would not make it to the new territory if we didn't have a day to rest from the walk.

That night some woman gave her blanket to a child she saw shivering. She went back to her place in camp and sat against a tree in the cold. The next day, she died of pneumonia as my mother and baby had done.

It was easy to die. During a rest a woman beside me gurgled a moment. Her eyes were open and her mouth was also open, as though waiting for a bite of food. She just stopped her noise. My father tried to close her mouth, but it hung open. "Lay her down before she gets stiff. She wouldn't want to go to the after-life bent over."

Soon after that a man had convulsions. It was Anna Sco-so-tah's neighbor. He walked ahead of me on the trail. I heard Anna cry, but I wanted to laugh at his jerky movements. They worsened, and Kinchow fell to the ground and continued to jerk as if churning butter. He kept kicking with a frenzy. The men could do nothing. Anna Sco-so-tah tried to hold him. The doctor came, but he could not stop him, either. Gradually, after the spasms grew more severe, he stiffened in an outstretched position and didn't move again.

Why did the Great Spirit let the whites take our land and possessions? Not even a ᏗᏓᏅᏘᏅᎧᎩ could understand our suffering. We owned nothing now but a brutal march through the cold with needles of ice hitting our faces.

MARITOLE'S FATHER

"Corn, I tell you. We have to have corn."

"Kill them soldiers for it," said an old man who walked beside me.

"Kill John Ross for it." War Club spit. "He's got the government money."

"We won't kill anyone," I told them. "There's something stronger than soldiers and leaders. There's people of the families and the land. There's people of peace."

KEE-UN-E-CA

I saw the dirt floor of my cabin. The split-log bench. My quilts and blankets on the wall. My husband's shirt and tunic hanging there. But what gross place is this? My eyes feel swollen. Have I been crying? Why can't they be quiet? What strap is hitting an animal? I don't care. My head is cold. My throat is sore. I can't swallow. That's Maritole's voice. Or Luthy's. What liquid are they putting in my mouth? It makes me choke. Someone pushes me forward and bends me back. I hear the minister's voice. That's better. Now the tree puts its arms around me. I sit on a branch above the people. The wagons creak below me in the cold. The animals cry. There's my cat stepping out of the field, with a large cobweb hanging in her eyebrow. I puff my feathers and watch the cat. There's hardly a time the trees don't speak. I turn my head backward and blink my large eyes.

"Eat, Kee-un-e-ca, eat," Maritole told me.

"Whoooo."

"We can feel the corn move our bodies. We can get up. We can go on," Maritole's father said.

MARITOLE

When the weather cleared, General Winfield Scott determined we could make more than ten miles a day. At the present rate, the trip would take four months, maybe five, and he said there was no need to travel that slow. Under his orders, we hurried our fires in the mornings. I cooked not only the morning meal but also the day's provisions. No sooner had I lifted the bread off the coals than they threw a bucket of water on the fire. I set the scorching pan in the wagon and moved on, chewing a piece of salt pork for breakfast and drinking strong coffee.

The leaders soon found we couldn't march that far in a day, especially through the snowy fields or in the mud after a thaw. We rested three days after our short effort while the men repaired wagons and shod horses. Some of the sick in our group found shelter in a schoolhouse near a spring. We heard many were sick from river water or wild grapes. The doctor, whose name was J. Powell, treated us for dysentery, diarrhea, fever, toothaches, gonorrhea, constipation, and frostbite. Many children were dying of whooping cough and measles. We were also afraid of cholera. I felt my flesh shrivel when I heard the rattle of their breath.

Luthy rode most the time under a quilt in the wagon, shaken like milk in a churn. Once in a while she moaned or complained to one of the boys that he was squirming against her. She wouldn't let the children out of her sight. She'd wake from a bad dream in which death was pulling her boys away from her. She said she had a ringing in her ears that was a sign that someone from the dead was calling her.

"It's not true, Luthy," Tanner leaned over her. "Mark and Ephum are all right."

"Maybe the noise is your parents telling you to get strength to walk," I told her.

Luthy would look at the boys, relieved, and fall back into a restless sleep.

I sat by my father one evening as the doctor pulled the moccasins off his feet. Red blisters spotted his soles and heels. He flinched as the doctor applied salve. A squeamish feeling quivered in my chest when I looked at his feet. I got up and went back to the wagon where Luthy held the boys.

Often we stopped near towns for corn and bacon and flour. Fodder for the mules and horses and oxen was provided daily. When we made camp, we had to share cooking pots and utensils.

I pulled the blanket over my shoulders and leaned against the wagon wheel. No creek water could ever clean the blanket I brought from the cabin. Or my mother's quilt. They'd been soaked with rain and sleet and dried stiff so often they would always be stained.

Some of the soldiers, who Knobowtee said were called government teamsters, were sent in advance to find camp sights at intervals of about ten miles. Places with water and dry wood for our fires and grazing for the horses and oxen. Also, a water mill had to be found now and then for grinding the corn whenever the soldiers could get us corn. Sometimes I talked to the horses when they were tethered beside the wagons. I told them the Great Spirit would bless them in the hunting grounds for the hard work they had done. Once I woke with a dream of our own horse in North Carolina still hitched to the plow.

People continued to die every day, especially children and the old ones. Soldiers brought wood from towns we came to. Sometimes more than one was buried in the coffins our men made. Sometimes there were no coffins at all. The next day, more people had died, and more bodies were piled under a blanket in the wagons. It seemed we would never get them buried.

A GEORGIA CHEROKEE

That night men passed through camps with buckets to collect toll. "Them farmers want money for Indians walking through their land."

"What the shit?"

"We're on their fields, you know."

"Listen to them. Those lame North Carolina Cherokee don't have nothing to complain about. Last summer the Georgia militia got us from our farms. Held us up in stockades. We got sick. Threw up. The camps were full of diarrhea smell. We were put on rocky boats. Our legs quivered. Our mouths filled with water. We didn't know where we were. The rivers were low in drought. We walked on the shore. The trains took some. We got off. Ran back. The walk north in winter's not as bad."

LUTHY

When I tried to stand the next morning, a blackness filled my head. I didn't feel like a part of the earth. I prayed. I had to take care of my husband and two small boys. I wanted to survive the trail.

Look at them all in the line. How many families?

Oosasquawatoh. War Club. James. Willie. Deer Biter. Spoilt Person. Jefferson Cinrad. White Path. Rogers. Moses. Coming Deer. Ahchee. Oowasatte. Burnt Fence. Junaluska. David Again. Kinequeakee. Thompson. Gay Candy. Ross. Sequawyah. Woman Killer. Fly Smith. Landseller. Terrapin Head. Crow Mocker. Leaf. July. Oolathookee. Raccoon. Walter Hunter. Teesahtagskee. Dirt Pot. Pigeon Lifter. Wm. Griffith. Alotohee. Deer in the Water. Rattles. George. Push Him. Tannoswech. Kitto Wahleh. Crying Snake. Dance on Nothing. Isaac. Sweet Water. Choolaskey. Kuhlawoskee. Bushyhead. Joseph. Ned. Push Back. Horse on Her Back. Runner. Kakawe. Sequeechee. Hicks. Bee Hunter. Tune. Tah-se-kah-yah-kah. Kinner. Light Toter. Shovel. Dun Bean. Ah-ne-cah.

The line went on. Beyond what I could see. Beyond names I knew. My head felt dizzy. Worse than dizzy. There was a buzzing, a sucking momentum, a black energy in me. I wasn't sure if I was walking or riding in the wagon. I didn't always know if it was dark or light. And where was the screwing, grinding, torturing Schermerhorn, agent of the United States government? Why did all these pieces of thought turn in my head?

John Ross had called him "the Devil's Horn."

I laughed recalling that Schermerhorn had spoken at a town meeting for three hours and twenty minutes.

"What's wrong, Luthy?" Tanner asked.

"I was thinking what it would have been like in New Echota hearing a three-hour sermon." I laughed again. Maritole heard me and laughed also. Then Tanner and the boys. We laughed because nothing was funny. We laughed because we wanted to survive.

TANNER

All night I heard the prayers and hymns of the Cherokee Christians. All night I heard the conjurers. It was never quiet. If it wasn't the wind and the freezing rain, the moans and crying of the sick, it was the prayers. There were always two groups of Cherokee. The believers and those who worshiped in the old way. They called to the sun and moon. They called to the wolf, the blue jay, the mulberry.

Luthy laughed again. ᏛᏍᏗ (mulberries where they are). "I'm praying to the mulberries in the field by our cabin," she told me. "Maybe they will hear."

"Don't give up." I didn't know what else to say. The boys slept like raccoons, restless in their blankets. My father was crouched behind a wagon.

Behind us for a hundred miles stretched the trail of ghosts of our dead ones. All around us the Raven Mockers sucked the spirits of the dying.

The Christians' god ᏩᎭᎦ. It was the name I heard on Luthy's breath.

The conjurers called to the tortoise. The polecat. They prayed for a woman whose legs and feet were so swollen she could hardly walk. The soldiers had left her beside the trail that morning with her sick parents. They prayed for a woman in childbirth who asked for time to rest but was put in a wagon and driven over the hard ground until she could endure no more. I knew others they prayed for also had died in the wagon because I couldn't hear their voices any longer.

It's better that Luthy's out of her head again. In the morning I'll find a place in the wagon for her to ride. Her thoughts spin like dried bits of cornstalks in the dust of my field. Her legs still walk in the spasms of her delirium.

KNOBOWTEE

Those Georgia Cherokee would have to do something. Even the Tennessee Cherokee. The soldiers aren't our only problem.

"We should organize into our own group," I told Tanner. "Otherwise the Tennessee Cherokee will erase us as if we hadn't been." I talked with the men, but Tanner wouldn't listen.

"Why do you think you can speak?" Tanner asked me.

Walking with my brother, my mother, and sister was better than listening to Tanner. I would have something to say. It would come from inside. Something could birth it, yes, but I had to speak from my own voice. With the power of thought behind it. I had learned that from my father. And from Maritole's.

But what to say?

Tanner's voice made me feel even more silent. I wanted to pound him. I wanted to jerk the soldiers of the Light Horse Guard off their horses. I wanted to pull the Christian God out of his sky.

MARITOLE

"You hang on, Luthy," I said one evening as I spooned the broth to her mouth. Her fingers were like the sawtooth borders on Grandma's quilts with four yellow moons. "Your boys are alive. We've got a new land we're going to. Not the land of North Carolina with yellow leaves. But a new land. The old land won't leave us, Luthy. We carry it within us to wherever we're going."

She looked away and fingered the edge of her ragged shawl. A drop of broth ran out of her mouth. Her turkey-bone beads were gone. One of the boys must have pulled them off. "You have to imagine it, Luthy," I said. "Maybe there'll be peaches," I told her. "And apple orchards. We'll build our farms again. This time we can live closer together. I'll have a new spinning wheel. I'll find a copper thimble again. We'll make quilts."

ᎣᏏ.

I used to hate quilting. I hated weaving baskets. I cut my fingers. My baskets fell apart. Maybe now I would want to learn.

I patted the wet hair on Luthy's forehead. "You'll have a new cabin," I said. "Maybe a new baby." My voice stuck in my throat like a knife. I bent over as though I had a terrible pain. The heaving started in my stomach and rose to my chest. Soon it was in my throat, and I wailed for my baby and mother. Wailed for them in their graves on the Cumberland Mountains, their bones carried off by wolves.

KNOBOWTEE

I was eating some cornmeal my mother fried in the dark when I heard Tanner call. I ran to the wagon because of the sound of his voice. Maritole cried beyond what I'd seen anyone cry, and I held her.

She cried for her mother. For our baby. She cried for Thomas. She cried most of the night, and if she slept she woke again, her mouth open against the blanket I held around her.

The few times my ears weren't filled with Maritole, I heard Anna Sco-so-tah and the other old women talking to themselves. Talking to the sky.

TANNER

Maritole should not have married Knobowtee. His mother was part Creek, and there'd always been trouble between the Creek and Cherokee. But Maritole did what she wanted. Everyone knew that. Her heroine was Nancy Ward, ᏌᎦᏯᏍᏗ, a woman who'd fought in the war against the Creeks after her husband was killed. Maritole must have changed her mind about

Knobowtee. Often I saw the look on her face. But she wouldn't admit it. No. Knobowtee was strong-willed, also. And handsome. Other girls would have been his wife. He'd had two wives before Maritole. Who knew how many more he would have?

"You wouldn't have been on the town square ground when the treaty was signed," I said as Knobowtee held Maritole. "You think you're such a statesman."

"I wasn't in favor of the treaty."

"If you weren't there, it was assumed you were."

"You think I was for the treaty?" Knobowtee asked.

"Where were you?" I returned.

"Three years ago? I don't know, Tanner." Knobowtee looked at me. "I was plowing. We don't live in Georgia anyway."

"We were plowing my mother's field." O-ga-na-ya joined Knobowtee. He had come to see about Maritole. "Some of us had to farm—"

"All of you should have stayed on your farms," said someone neither of us knew. A Tennessee Cherokee by the sound of his voice. "But if you lived near New Echota, Georgia, and not in North Carolina, you would have been there, signing treaties."

"We were going to walk," I said. "Sooner or later."

"One way or another," O-ga-na-ya agreed.

LUTHY

Maritole tried to open her eyes. I knew she heard O-ga-na-ya's voice. There was a group of men— What was it? Maybe the white renegades who came to sell whiskey. Maritole called after Knobowtee, and I held her. The sky felt crooked. The men were going to fight. The renegades would hurt them. "Tanner, you can't," I begged. I heard the low voices of the men. The pleading of the women. I tried to cover Maritole's ears from hearing. Then soldiers rode up. Someone was fighting. There was a shot. Everyone was quiet. "Knobowtee!" Maritole called. But I put my hand over her mouth.

One of the Tennessee Cherokee had jumped a Georgia Cherokee. Someone had been shot.

"Keep them Indians busy digging their graves," I heard a soldier.

"Get back in line," a soldier told Tanner. Another soldier held his gun at Knobowtee and O-ga-na-ya.

"Get up," Knobowtee said. "I'll put Maritole in a wagon."

"Be quiet and walk," Tanner said, but I knew he was talking to himself. "That's what we do."

MARITOLE

After the baby was born. Yes. After that. I heard the stars click their teeth. It was after the baby had pushed her way through my body. My mother held my arms. My grandmother was there, too. Trying to give me the baby through the narrow space. The baby howling because she didn't want to come. My grandmother singing she had to.

ᏬᏆ.

While the light was still on the baby's face. Before it became dark and she forgot the sky where she shined. Just before she was born. We heard about it. The soldiers stockaded some of the Cherokee. Each day I watched for them on the road. But they didn't come into North Carolina. I was heavy with the baby and couldn't walk the trail anyway.

I had wanted Knobowtee to name the child after my grandmother. I felt her during the birth, though she had died a year before. And I had felt my grandfather out in the yard in his booger mask to scare the baby out. But Knobowtee was silent each time I asked. We would name her when it was time. I called her my grandmother's name under my breath and watched Knobowtee clean his musket by the fire. I had stirred the squirrel meat from time to time and smelled the corn bread. Once in a while Knobowtee looked out the window.

KNOBOWTEE

In the cold light of dawn my wife got out of the wagon. She would be all right. The sound of men hammering coffins reminded me of building cabins in the woods around North Carolina. I had helped with most of them. I remembered repairing the cabin of Maritole's grandparents and watching Maritole. But that wasn't my job now. It was digging graves. The Light Horse Guard bought shovels in the towns they passed. I tried to push the shovel into the cold ground when we camped. I tried to close my eyes and think I was hearing cabins taking root in the North Carolina soil. I could almost hear the conjurers chanting to the trees, thanking them for moving over and giving us a place. But soon I worked without listening. It hurt to dig. My hands blistered like my feet. My whole body ached. My brother groaned as he dug beside me. My anger drove the shovel into the ground. "Just enough to bury people under a thin cover of soil," the soldiers said. Just like the blankets we had on the trail. We put as many Cherokee into each coffin as it would hold. "They'll have companionship as they walk to the afterlife," the ministers said. The conjurers sang their magic. The women wailed. Their families sobbed. Then O-ga-na-ya and I covered the coffins in the ground.

Now the farmers along the way collect toll when the line passes through their land. They think we will steal their stock. They say the topsoil is disrupted. They want compensation. One Cherokee had been shot refusing to pay. I had no money. How could I have money? Maritole's father had to pay. I looked away when the bucket came along our line. My wife knew I couldn't pay. Her face turned ugly with red splotches from the cold. When will I ever have anything but blisters on my hands and the ache that hammers into my back?

MARITOLE

ᎭᏏ.

I stood by my father as he went through the few coins in the leather pouch from his pocket. The soldiers said that one detachment paid forty dollars at Waldens Ridge and the man finally agreed to let the others pass at half price. We were supposed to pay thirty-seven cents for four-wheeled wagons and six cents for oxen and horses.

"They fleece us," my father said. "I heard one farmer

wanted seventy-three cents a wagon and twelve cents a horse for us to pass through his land."

We slowed down so the wagons could get through the mud when it was not frozen. The sky dumped on us until I held my fist to it. Sometimes the soldier rode by me and watched me walk beside the wagon. He would stay with me for a while, then ride on.

The horses and oxen struggled to pull the wagons. Sometimes we halted so they could rest. Sometimes the sick had to wait before the doctor came. He had so much to do he couldn't take care of everyone. Tanner called angrily several times for help for Luthy, but all he could do was sit by her while she moaned and talked out of her head again.

My father sang a song for her the next morning.

Ꮒ	now
ᏀᏗᏞᏀᎣᎤᏗᎭ	provider you
ᎤᏉᏃᏢᏀ᷄	quickly very
ᏗᎣᎠᏢᏀ᷄Ꮎ	you uncover a healing
Ꮒ	now

The holy men prayed for her. They lit a few small pieces of cedar from their pouches and rubbed the smoke over her.

Finally the doctor bent over Luthy. "She worries that something has ahold of the boys," Tanner said.

"She shoos away the Raven Mockers," Quaty said. "Already she sees them."

I knew the doctor thought Luthy wouldn't live, but I thought she would. What had she lost? She was always happy and would be again. I made a grass mattress for her, but the grass packed together and she moaned until I removed the clumps.

"Sometimes she's all right," I told the soldier who rode beside me again. Quaty Lewis helped him understand what I said. Anna Sco-so-tah also talked between us. "Sometimes Luthy doesn't know where she is."

Then Ephum wouldn't eat for a while. He was fatigued and sat in a stupor. He couldn't chew the squirrel stew I made. "Open and close your mouth," I said. "The food goes down when you swallow." I touched his throat and made him swallow by tickling him.

"There's always someplace I hurt," I told my father as we walked. "I scraped the skin off my fingers starting a fire this morning. The burns on my hands are still tender. I dropped a log on my foot yesterday. My head aches and my legs cramp from walking. There are always blisters and my nose is raw. My shoulders hurt from the pack of some of Mother's things I carried on my back. I'm hungry." My legs gave out from under me again and I was facedown in the dirt, weighed down with the day's provisions bundled in a quilt on my back. My father tried to pull me up but he wasn't strong anymore.

The soldier got off his horse and pulled me up.

"You can ride my horse for a while."

"No." I shook my head. "I can't."

Now my father had strength, and he pulled me away from the soldier.

The soldier told my father he wanted me to ride his horse. I understood what he said. He told us his name. "Sergeant Williams."

I knew his name. I had known it since he had touched me to be one of the women who went back to their cabin. I had heard other soldiers call him.

My father said that I couldn't ride the horse. Certainly not a U.S. military horse. My father was angry. I stepped away from the soldier, pulling at my father's arm.

Knobowtee came from somewhere behind us in line.

O-ga-na-ya had probably called me a white woman in front of him. That's all Knobowtee cared about.

"Mind your own nose," I told him, and walked away.

Knobowtee grabbed my arm and was going to strike me, but the soldier grabbed him. Then there was a scuffle and a shout of the men. More soldiers rode into the scuffle and pulled Sergeant Williams away. There was a rifle shot into the air, and the Cherokee men stopped their fighting.

I walked to the wagon and sat under it by myself. I was ashamed. Soon Knobowtee walked up. I saw his feet by the rear wheel. I didn't say anything but waited for him to speak.

"You are no wife to me," he spit, "the way you talk to the white soldier."

I scratched the hard dirt with my fingers and crawled out from under the wagon. I knew everyone was listening. Sometimes far back in the wagons I would hear scuffling or someone crying out. I wanted to be in our own cabin.

"You belong to the enemy now," Knobowtee said. "I can put you away as though you were never my wife."

"What did you do for me while I was your wife?" I spat back at him. "Everyone is with their husband who has one, but I never know where you are. You stay with your mother and brother. Your sister. You stay with your friends rather than me. Our own baby died, and you never comforted me. My mother died, and you just stood there beside me like you hardly knew me. When have you been a help? I lost my farm and child and mother and now even my own husband."

Knobowtee raised his hand and hit me across the face because I had provoked him. I got up and crawled into the wagon with Luthy to get away from everyone's sight. She lifted the edge of the tarp and let me climb under it with her. She held her arm around me while I sobbed.

LACEY WOODARD

The wind growled high in the trees. Where were we? Still in Tennessee?

"Of course we're in Tennessee," Quaty said.

"Near Murfreesboro?"

"Maybe."

Hadn't Maritole said the morning sounded like a bear? I slit the belly of the earth with my knife. The bowels of rivers. The first light of the sun beating. The fields still steaming.

I listened to the wind before it came down to call the morning fog back to the sky. The wind reminded me of the Cherokee men in council. It reminded me of the Georgia Cherokee left out of the council. Arguing and murmuring over what should be done. I felt the fire between them. *Something will happen again, Lacey,* I said to myself. If not soon, then later.

The wind had a moan to it. It was like the stories of the old ones. The voice carried power. What was spoken came into being. Even Reverend Mackenzie talked of the Great Spirit creating the world with his voice. Was the white man just now finding that out? Hadn't the Cherokee always known the power of the word? The white man only got it out to read on Sunday. The Cherokee thought about it every day. Our church was not a house. It had no walls.

The wind seemed still for a moment. The energy flowed into my feet. This morning, the boys were still quiet. I heard the silence of the earth. It was speaking, too.

Words of hurt came from Knobowtee's mouth. He knew the voice made the path on which we walked. Why didn't he guard his words? Tanner didn't say those things. He talked angrily sometimes, but he didn't use words that destroyed.

Sometimes Luthy said things Tanner didn't want to hear. But the way she said them stopped Tanner from anger. Why didn't Maritole speak gently to Knobowtee? Why did she always stir him to anger until he spoke the words that would make the bad path?

"You just watch out, Maritole," Knobowtee said.

I put my hands to my ears in the early morning. Why didn't Tanner's children wake and give me something to do other than hear Knobowtee's anger? Why couldn't I move to another place in the line?

If Knobowtee left, I'd still hear the soldiers. Who were these white men who only saw things in their own way? Didn't they know the land was not bought and sold? Would they be arguing over the sun next? The stars? Didn't they know they belonged with the earth and animals to the Great Spirit? But didn't even the Cherokee own people? Some of the prosperous farmers had bought the black man to help with the work of farming.

No, the Cherokee wouldn't perish, Lacey, though it's what the soldiers wanted. The Cherokee would survive because we were the land. ᏒᎬᎦᎠ, home. I felt a rush of tears. Something terrible and shameful was in our journey. Yet something lifted, too. How could it be?

Once the Cherokee women had power. The women still owned the land that the men signed away. Didn't we tell them that? No, no bitter words. I still have power because my words are strong.

MARITOLE

The soldiers threw the bodies out of the wagon. Most of them were already stiff, but some of the arms jerked when they hit the ground. Women cried out, looked away.

"We don't have time," one soldier said. "What does an Indian matter to you?"

"They want them buried," another insisted.

Knobowtee, tight as a wagon spring, rushed at a soldier who threw a dead body to the ground. Luthy held the boys to her and wouldn't let them look from her blanket. Quaty Lewis and Anna Sco-so-tah yelled at Knobowtee not to hit the soldier. When Tanner tried to stop Knobowtee, the two began fighting. Their frustration and anger at the soldiers, and their own disagreements, fired them until they were on the ground pounding each other with their fists. The soldiers stood watching them, laughing.

"Our men fight among themselves?" My father tried to stop them, but he was powerless.

"What's going on?" the principal soldier asked. He fired a warning shot, and the soldiers pulled Knobowtee and Tanner apart.

The soldiers beat the horses and the men to move. I saw the whip strike Knobowtee. His mother and sister and O-ga-na-ya looked away, but I would not. For a moment I wanted to hold Knobowtee and not let him hurt, but I changed my mind. Let him know how it feels. I pulled the blanket around my head and walked away.

The wagons started with a jolt, and we began marching. Lacey prayed for the spirits of the dead to find their way to the afterlife without burial. Quaty spat at me for not mourning our dead.

KNOBOWTEE

There was a full moon that night, and the sky was clear for the first time in a long time. My shoulders stung from the soldier's whip, but not as much as the pain in my jaw from Tanner's fist. My hands were too swollen and stiff to rub together.

"We shoot them dead. *Phooo PHOOO,*" one of Tanner's boys said.

I watched two girls walk by.

The fields of snow were white under the moon, as bright as anything I've ever seen.

Maybe the Great Spirit threw his corn mush to the ground to protest the removal. Maybe the Great Spirit threw his milk bucket across the fields so the soldiers would know his disapproval.

MARITOLE

I heard the conjurers chanting. I looked out from under the tarp. The moon shone across the white fields of snow. It was almost like daylight. I could see Knobowtee against the tree. Everyone's face was eerie and white. Snow faces. Ghost faces. It was magic. I agreed with the conjurers. Mark and Ephum danced with laughter. "Daylight in the night," Luthy said. "*Whooop.*" They danced.

A whiteness on the fields seemed to dance of itself. I could see the whole world before me. I could see the world beyond. The spirits of the dead rolling up to heaven. I could see them jigging. Ceremonial dancing. It was the shore. That's what it was. They were the broken pieces of the ships. Rolling onward from this earth.

KNOBOWTEE

"Why'd you keep me from jumping that soldier?"

"I'm Maritole's brother," Tanner answered as we hitched the horses to a wagon that morning. "I'd have to take care of Maritole if you were gone."

I handed the bit to Tanner. We should have joined Tecumseh's rebellion against the U.S. government nearly thirty years ago. Look at what they did to the Cherokee.

The little regiment of women—Quaty Lewis, Lacey Woodard, Mrs. Young Turkey, Anna Sco-so-tah—were putting axle grease on the chapped faces of the sick, rubbing it on the broken lips of the children.

ALOTOHEE

The cold made the noises travel. Voices from across the field. If I open my mouth, sometimes the faraway sounds enter. I can chew the sounds. Swallow. The birds. The cattle. The animal sounds. The groans of the wagons far back in line. A snort of a horse or the oxen or mules. All of them in my belly.

Yes. The sound inside me. It brings the land inside, too. I see it when I close my eyes. I feel it in my chest. I carry the cornfields with me. The animals, too. My feet crunch in the snow. Sometimes they nudge the ground with their noses, searching for the grass.

O-GA-NA-YA

"In the early days, when we were in the old territory, a Cherokee man wasn't a warrior until he killed or took a prisoner. How many enemies have we conquered in our history? Catawba, Creek, Seneca."

"You sound like Chief Ross," Knobowtee said. "You know how he goes on—"

"He's a statesman; you're a farmer. A hill country farmer. No one wanted anything you had. They just wanted you gone."

"Ross is still more white than Cherokee. '*When I was in Washington*' is always a part of his speech," Knobowtee mocked.

"We'd be marching all the way under soldier's whips if it wasn't for Chief Ross."

" '*But now we have new enemies. We cannot be discouraged,*' " Knobowtee continued to taunt. " '*We've lost wives, mothers, children, husbands. Our dead are left by the trail to wander in their restlessness. We've lost our land.*' "

"Without Ross, we'd still be in the stockade." But Knobowtee could outtalk me.

"Let's not be discouraged," Quaty said under her breath.

Now Knobowtee had others talking like him.

" 'We must forgive each other, O-ga-na-ya. That's what we learn
on the trail. Anger is our enemy.' " Who was Knobowtee mocking
now in his North Carolina dialect?

Someone made a choking sound.

"We become human beings through our trials."

"We learn how to feel the soldiers' bayonets," Anna Sco-so-
tah said.

"We learn how to walk and walk," Mrs. Young Turkey said.

Shit. The whole detachment was on Knobowtee's side. But
no matter what Knobowtee said, he could never speak like Chief
Ross.

"We learn to walk." My mother sat beside Aneh, my sister.

"Yep," Knobowtee answered. "Walk."

KNOBOWTEE

"All this talk of the Tennessee Cherokee. The lives of the Georgia leaders who signed away the land—Boudinot, Watie, the
Ridges—then left for the new territory with others ahead of us
won't mean much."

"They leave us out of council," a Georgia Cherokee grumbled.

"We can't walk the trail divided," Bushyhead preached.

"Look at the soldiers. That new private come from somewhere. All of them, jackasses on their horses. They think they're
the war-stick himself."

O-ga-na-ya hit the side of a wagon with his fist.

I stopped him.

"I could peel their war-stick." O-ga-na-ya had the habit now
of digging at the ground as if looking for corn.

KNOBOWTEE'S MOTHER

"O-ga-na-ya, *umgh.* You're going to get in trouble if you don't
stop talking. You and Knobowtee. If you don't stop arguing with

those Tennessee and Georgia Cherokee. If you don't stop hating the soldiers. That new private's trouble. You hear me cough? Sometimes I think I can't walk. But I'm afraid to leave you alone. Who would warn you of yourself?"

I held to the rough side of the wagon, looking at the rags that wrapped my feet, the torn, caked hem of my dress. When someone died, I would get the next place in the wagon. The cold weather was part of me now. I could eat the trees, like Alotohee. My heart heats with the morning sun. I want the clouds again. Yes. The light on the bright snow cut into my eyes. I can see as far away as the grain of wood.

"You know how far we got to go? We're still in Tennessee. Not even Nashville. We got Kentucky, Illinois, Missouri, Arkansas, Indian Territory. You hear that, O-ga-na-ya? I go over them in my head. All the time. I walk with them in my head."

Can I die? With my sons ready to attack the soldiers, even our own people? With an unmarried daughter with no one to care for her? Why doesn't Aneh speak? I had scratched her tongue with the claw of the ᏕᎶᏫᎣᏴ, the noisy cricket, so she'd speak. But Aneh has always been quiet. Hiding behind the cabin. Sitting with her head bent to the ground.

MARITOLE

This is what bothers me about Knobowtee that I don't like to say. I see him look at other girls. When we're walking the trail. When we're camped. Sometimes he looks at me, remembering I notice. He did it at home. Once on the way back to our cabin, I wouldn't ride on the wagon seat with him and sat in the back of the wagon.

"Men are that way," Quaty said.

"Not my father," I answered. "Not Tanner."

Maybe it was because he was part Creek. Maybe the frustration of losing the farm was stronger than his respect. Maybe the sense of powerlessness.

"What am I supposed to do while you look?" I had asked Knobowtee once.

"I do what I want," he said. "It doesn't mean anything."

I could have put his blanket and tunic and musket out the door. I could have made him go away. But by then I was going to have the baby.

Sometimes I cried when Knobowtee was in the field. I remembered how I sat on the cabin step fat with the baby and fed the little raccoon that came out from under the cabin. I thought he'd lost his mother and that made me cry.

My mother said crying was a part of having a baby. But I saw the way my father looked at Knobowtee sometimes.

ANNA SCO-SO-TAH

The Cherokee were the Dhiθᐌ, the principal people. We lived in the hill country in the center of the world. "Now toot on that," I always told the Christians. Sometimes I wouldn't let the minister in the door. I'd send him to my neighbor's. Or I'd be sitting on the cabin doorstep and those Christians would pass on their way to church. If they tried to come up my path, I'd call one of the animals down from the One Above.

| ꝒꙨDꙅᏏᏂ | (his head is nearly always near the ground) |
| ᏏᏩᎥᏂᏔᏩᎬᏍᎶᎫ | (he smells something unpleasant [human beings] in his nose) |

The animal kept the Christians' minds off the path to my cabin. The animal turned them away.

MARITOLE

I heard thunder from the distant clouds and remembered my grandparents in their graves in North Carolina. I felt their bones stir and erupt from the ground. Maybe they walked north as wolves, searching for the bones of my mother and my baby. They gathered up the bones that were scattered across the mountain. One by one. They collected every bone and laid them beside their own bones in their graves in North Carolina. I felt all the bones lying down, resting with one another. The path our people had to take was nothing. The trail of a termite through wood. It would be a long time, but our family would be together again. I would see them in the afterlife. I'd see the ancestors and tell them what it was like to walk the trail. I'd tell Thomas and my great-great-grandchildren.

The Cherokee would come together as a nation again, no matter what Knobowtee said. No matter what turmoil came after the resettlement.

I held to the wagon as I walked that morning. There were large gray clouds on the horizon, rimmed with yellow, but in the middle of the sky where we were, the sun shined on the snow. How could it be bright and cold at the same time? I wanted the trees in North Carolina to cover us. Maybe the sky's where the bear came from. I held the blanket over my head to hide my eyes from the glare.

Sometimes I told Tanner's boys the clouds were a forest above us. It was frightening having the whole sky open on the land. I rubbed my eyes and looked from between my fingers as I walked.

It didn't matter how far we walked each day. It didn't matter where we were. The cold land hardly moved under us, and the bear was always before us. It was a terrible weight we pushed. *Oh hheee oh, move on, bear, move on.* He turned once and licked my face. I hit at him and yelled. *Get away, bear!* I still yelled and hit. Luthy tried to hold me.

I heard Tanner calling Knobowtee.

"No," I said. Knobowtee was walking with his brother, his mother, and sister. Didn't Tanner see how he held his head as he walked? Knobowtee was thinking of something other than losing the corn. He was thinking of something other than losing his wife.

When we stopped midday, I heard someone telling the story of the bear. After a while I slept in a yellow light, and when I woke, my mouth was open again against the blanket Knobowtee held around us.

"I dreamed of the sun coming up in North Carolina like a yellow bowl," I said.

"I would push it back down into darkness," Knobowtee answered. "I'd rather have night than the sun rising on us on this trail."

"No, anything is better than the dark," I told him. "I know my mother and baby are with my grandparents. I know . . ." I wanted to tell Knobowtee more, but I didn't know how to say it.

He tried to touch me, to comfort me, but I knew he did it because he thought he should.

"There's no bear," he told me.

"Yes. There is." It made me cry again. "You don't want to be with me, Knobowtee. You don't have to stay here."

"It was always your family that you cared for, not ours," he said, and walked away.

"You don't pace yourself, Maritole," my father said when we walked again that afternoon. "You walk with the wagon ahead of us, or the one behind. You talk to the soldier. You fight with Knobowtee or worry Luthy. You stare at the fire at night or talk until someone tells you to be quiet. Walk steadily," my father said, "and maybe you can forget you walk."

"I won't forget the trail." I thought bitterly of Knobowtee as I saw him talking to his brother. O-ga-na-ya's voice reached me once in a while like the squawk of a neighbor's goose. "I'm tired of hearing the wind howl over us," I said. "I don't want to see this white snow on the ground."

"This manna," Reverend Bushyhead said on Sunday. "It's a sign that God is leading us to the new land. Did not the children of Israel also grumble?" I saw agreement on the face of Bushyhead's pregnant wife as she held their small daughter.

I wanted to be in our own church. The men on one side, the women on the other. Our voices rising above theirs.

There was a song I heard along the trail. I don't know where it came from. It was just there. Someone was singing. I heard the voice. Sometimes it was several voices.

"Sing," I told them, "sing."

LUTHY

"I can't forget I'm shivering," I told Tanner from the wagon. "I'd like my black teapot with the cat head on the lid." My voice cracked thinking of my things in our cabin.

Tanner smiled. "You talk like yourself again." He put the boys on my lap with their red cheeks and chapped, runny noses.

"The log-cabin-pattern quilt I made, I liked it as well as any of your grandma's." Mark put his hands to his ears so he wouldn't hear me talk about what we lost.

"We have to think of the new territory," Tanner told me. "We can't give up."

The waves of snow scattered like ghosts. My family could scatter with them.

Sometimes people stopped in their wagons and carriages to watch us pass.

"If we were home, I would be poking the fire in the hearth, ЅWGRD!"

"Don't talk," Tanner's father said.

"How far did we go today?" Mark and Ephum asked, but I couldn't answer.

MARITOLE

The widow Teehee grew weaker every day. She groaned as the wagon jarred over the hard ground. If she lay down, the others protested. Only the death of someone would give her space. She clawed at my sleeves from the wagon when I walked near her. "Take care of the corn," she would say. At night I held her in my arms until she slept. Each day she went farther away. The cough deepened the rattle in her chest.

"I wish I could do something for you."

"Feed the chickens," she said.

"I will," I answered and slept awhile. When I woke it was dark and the old woman's breath rattled in her chest. I had been dreaming of the cannon sounds I used to hear, coming through the woods in North Carolina from town, shot when a meeting was called. But when I opened my eyes, I knew it was her.

"She needs a doctor," I told my father.

"There's nothing he can do." My father looked at her. "He told us that the last time he was here. It's pneumonia. He can only give her calomel and opium if she needs it."

The widow's breath got heavier. I thought she would wake

the camp. I heard the bear growl in her breathing. I felt her heaving chest. The claws of her hand reached for me, but I knew her eyes didn't see me. She looked somewhere else. Maybe she was back at the cabin. Her own quilts on the line. The wind high in the trees as she fed the chickens.

"The fire still burns in the woods when the sun goes down," I whispered to her. "Don't you see it? You're returning to the land. It will always be ours." Her breathing got slighter. Soon I thought I could not hear it at all, but once in a while her chest heaved.

My eyes filled with tears. I held the widow Teehee's hand as she went back to our cornfields like a hollow log floating in the creek. Her brittle fingers sticking up stiff as twigs I picked for tinder. I wanted to be with her, not on this trail to a new land. I wanted to get off, too. "Wait for me," I cried.

"It's the best thing that could happen to her," the soldier said.

"No, it's not!" I screamed. "Grave digger!" I jerked her away from him. "The best thing would be not to have left at all."

My father pulled me away from the body of the old woman. He pulled me away from the soldier.

I kicked and hit at him. He held my arms and pushed me against the wagon. "You can't cry like this. She's dead. There's nothing we can do."

I spit on the ground.

"Then walk with our enemies." My father looked at the soldier and let me go.

When my father left I got up and kicked the wheel of the wagon.

KNOBOWTEE

I knelt by the fire under a dark sky and remembered General John Wool's speech, over a year ago. "Why not abandon a country no longer yours? Don't you see white people daily coming into it, driving you away?"

It was Maritole's farm, but it seemed like mine. It had almost stopped breathing in the years her grandparents aged. I had made it strong again. ᏙᎥ ᏗᏏ (come together and act in unison).

"How can you stay in a country with a people whose customs are unlike yours?" John Wool had said. "It's a country better than the one you occupy, where you can grow more corn and game is abundant." Then why didn't Wool and the other generals move there themselves?

Wool had resigned even before the march began. He didn't have heart for this. General Winfield Scott had taken his place. General Scott and Chief John Ross, who was always making speeches, always making lists, getting everyone to think of what we left.

Maybe I should have gone earlier.

No, I never would have gone.

We had been cheated out of our land just as the Cherokee were who had volunteered to go earlier. Families had been lost. Children ran into the woods. Mothers were not permitted to get them.

One deaf and dumb Cherokee had been shot because he couldn't understand the orders.

I was so stiff I had to pull myself up with the help of my brother.

Cattle, horse, hogs, harness, implements, seed-corn, musket, farm. All had been lost.

MARITOLE

When I woke my father's blanket was on me.

"You can't give me your blanket again," I told him. His face was pale in the first morning light.

"It seems colder to me this morning," Luthy said.

"I think I dreamed of Thomas—" I rubbed my eyes.

"We're going north and it's winter," Tanner answered Luthy.

"Sometimes it feels like Thomas's with us."

A soldier approached on his horse, and when I looked it was Sergeant Williams.

"Knobowtee would tell you—" my father said.

"I know what Knobowtee would say," I interrupted.

"Daily rations," Williams told my father. "One pound of flour. Half pound of bacon. Make a fire," he said. "Soon we'll leave."

I remembered feeling warm in the night. Now I was cold again as my brother and father brought the wood and Luthy and I cooked bacon. The earth looked hard and ugly in the raw morning light. Patches of snow spread over the hills like lard. In North Carolina the pines kept their leaves. Here the trees were leafless. On parts of the trail, there were no trees, but only open fields. The earth seemed cleared away like the eyes of our people before they died. I thought the earth must be dying, too.

We marched again. What was it like to feel rested? My legs felt hollow. I was only bones with a blanket on them.

My father walked at first, holding on to the wagon as we started marching that morning. Tanner held Luthy's arm. The boys lay in the wagon making a loud humming sound. Letting the wagon rattle their voices.

MARITOLE'S FATHER

umgh. It waits for our hands to bring it life. It knows already we are coming. I say, *New land I'll see you.* I say, *Get ready.* You will be transformed by what we are when we get there.

MARITOLE

There was a lid of ice on the creek as we neared Nashville. The creek was nearly dry, but a thin sheet of ice covered it. As the wagons rolled through the creek, the wheels cracked the ice into a thousand pieces like kernels of corn without their cobs. Sergeant Williams rode beside us. I watched him for a moment then turned my head away.

The land flattened until I saw no hills.

"Still no trees," I said to him.

The pines squatted near the ground like children playing stones. The cold crept into my skin and stayed there. The soldier with the gray in his hair gave his horse to Mrs. Young Turkey, who had stumbled several times. He walked beside the horse with the reins in his hand. Another soldier passing said something to him, but he continued to let her ride. It was the private Knobowtee didn't like because he drank and tried to get the Cherokee drunk, especially the young men.

Sometimes the land rolled again with small hills, and the trees would come back and then disappear.

"In parts of Indian Territory there aren't any trees," the soldier said.

I looked at him. I must have had a strange look on my face because he laughed.

"The prairie is barren," he tried to tell me as I walked beside him. "But Fort Gibson, where we're going, has hills and trees."

"As many as North Carolina?" I asked. "Is it like the land we came from?"

"I don't think so," the soldier said.

Nothing would be like the land we came from. Nothing would be like the ceremonies we had there. I remembered the booger dance when the masked man ran through the town making fun of our enemies, and Knobowtee and I screamed with delight. Knobowtee. Where was he now?

How could someone change until I didn't know him at all? Other families walked together, but I was alone with my father and Tanner and his family. Ephum kept his head buried in my sleeve when the wind howled. There was always the great dark presence that hovered over us.

The men looked at a large farm we passed in Nashville called The Hermitage.

"Andrew Jackson's place," Fly Smith said.

"If I'd have foreseen this march," said Junaluska, who fought beside Jackson and saved his life in the 1813 war against the Creeks, "I would have killed him myself at Horseshoe Bend."

There was Knobowtee. He stood outside a circle of men who talked. Most of them were Tennessee Cherokee. They were Knobowtee's heroes. White Path, an old clan leader, Fly Smith, and Junaluska. Their faces hard with cold. In their ragged tunics. Coughing. Spitting up.

Sometimes I'd see Knobowtee walking in front of me or behind with other men. I felt as though he thought it were my fault we walked the trail. Knobowtee looked away if I saw him. Once I came face-to-face with his mother, but we didn't speak. I wanted to talk to him, but there was nothing to say. He walked the trail in his tunic and trousers with a blanket around his shoulders because I didn't get his coat when I went back to the cabin. It was in the attic wrapped in tobacco. I was too angry at the people in the cabin to think of Knobowtee's coat or baby's blanket. I started to cry as I walked. Sometimes without warning the tears ran down my face. Like Kee-un-e-ca, who always had tears in her eyes. I shivered with cold. The soldier walked beside me trying to say words of comfort. I made the sign of a baby for him.

He knew anyway.

I woke the next morning with the thought of the cabin. Mark was crying, trying to poop. The soldier lifted the tarp thrown against the wagon where we had slept that night. It was like lifting the lid of the night jar. My bones hurt and I groaned. I felt sick again, and the soldier gave me a biscuit. I looked away from him to let him know it didn't help. He pushed it to me. I took it in my hand and watched it for a moment. I put it to my mouth, chewed on it, but spit it out. He put the rest of the biscuit to my mouth again. "Chew!" he commanded. He held his hand over my mouth so I couldn't spit it out. Saliva ran over my tongue and moistened the hard lump in my mouth. I chewed and swallowed the dead lump. It seemed to stay in my throat, and I heaved as though it would come back up, but I felt nothing in my mouth. The soldier pulled me up straight and held my head back so that I looked at the sky. He held me there until the lump sank to my stomach. Luthy and the boys watched. He gave them a biscuit, too. Nausea filled my mouth but I didn't lose the bite I had swallowed. The soldier lifted me into the wagon, and I rode for a while that morning.

KNOBOWTEE

Somewhere in line, someone tried to ride a sick horse. It stumbled to the ground and convulsed. The man beat the horse to get up. I rushed him, pulled the stick from his hand, and raised it against the man but others held my arm. The man who beat the horse fled. The men let me go. I beat and beat the ground while my mother held my sister.

FROM THE *BAPTIST*

(a monthly periodical published in Nashville, Tennessee)

Four detachments of the emigrating Cherokees have, within a few days, passed through our city, and seven others are behind, and are expected to pass in a week or two. They average about a thousand each. Of the third party, our brother Evan Jones, who has been eighteen years a missionary in the nation, is conductor; and the fourth is under the direction of the celebrated Dta-ske-ge-de-hee, known among us as Bushyhead. In the two parties they direct, we learn there are upward of five hundred Baptists.

During two or three days, that their business detained them in the vicinity of our city, we have had the pleasure of some intercourse with these and others of our Cherokee brethren; and more lovely and excellent Christians we have never seen. On Monday evening last, several of them were with us, at the monthly concert of prayer for missions. It was expected that the meeting would be addressed by Ga-ne-tuh and the chief Sut-tu-a-gee, all in Cherokee, and interpreted by Dsagee. Some of these brethren, however, were sick, and others were detained by other causes, but their places were well supplied. We had a very crowded house. The services were commenced by singing a hymn in Cherokee, by brethren Jones, Dta-ske-ge-de-hee, Gha-nune-tdah-cla-gee, and Ahtzthee. After prayer and another hymn, we were addressed by Ga-wo-he-lo-ose-keh and Dta-ske-ge-de-hee, in English, and, in a very interesting manner, by Ahtzthee in Cherokee, interpreted by br. Bushyhead; and the services closed in the usual form. The effect was thrilling, and the people, though we did not ask a collection, spontaneously came up and contributed to the Baptist mission among the Cherokees.

Last night, br. Jones and br. Bushyhead were again with us. Two other Indian brethren, whose names we did not write down, and cannot remember, were expected, but the rain, which had been falling all day, in the evening poured down in torrents, and they did not come into the city. Our congregation was much larger than we expected. Br. Bushyhead addressed us in English, after prayer and a hymn in Cherokee, on the subject of missions. After pointing out our obligation to the holy work, he told us that he could very well remember when his nation knew nothing of Jesus Christ. He detailed to us some particulars of their past religious opinions, and method of spending their time, their habits, and domestic manners, and contrasted them with the present condition and character of his people, and thus illustrated the happy effect already produced among them by the gospel. He told us he recollected most distinctly the first time he ever heard the name of the Savior. He recounted to us some particulars of his conversion and that of his father and mother, and gave a short account of the effects of his own, and especially of the glorious revival that prevailed among them in their camps the past summer, during which himself and Ga-ne-tah and others had baptized over a hundred and seventy, upward of fifty of whom were baptized on one occasion. He adverted to the opposition to missions waged by some Tennessee Baptists, and presented himself and hundreds of his brethren as living instances of the blessing of God upon missionary labors. He closed by stating that it was now seen that Cherokees could be Christians; commending his nation particularly and the Indians generally to the prayers of the Lord's people, and beseeching them still to sustain the preaching of the gospel among them. He sat down in tears.

Br. Jones followed in a very eloquent address on the same subject, adding some interesting observations about the translation of the Bible in Cherokee, in the letters invented by Seequa-yah (George Guess) at present in progress by himself and br. Bushyhead. The effect produced will not soon be erased from our mind, and we trust the recollection of the numerous instances recited by God's goodness and mercy to our red brethren, will add fervor to many a prayer, and zeal to many an effort for the salvation of the noble-hearted Indian.

MARITOLE

Again, some people from a town we passed sat in their carriages along the road to watch us pass. I peered back at them from the wagon. What were they looking at? Didn't they have anything to do but stare at us? A ragged band of Indians. Half frozen. Hated. Sent from our land. They called us savages. Then it was all right to drive us from our land. Then it was all right to sit along the road and watch the spectacle of our march. Maybe that dark thing was in all of us. How could I go on without my baby? If I missed her, I soon thought how it was easier to walk without her. What was wrong with me? How could I talk to the soldier whose job it was to push us from our land?

"Jesus," I called when Reverend Bushyhead preached redemption to us on the trail. I would hold anything that would take away the pain in my body and the hurt I felt toward Knobowtee. Reverend Bushyhead said there was even healing for the anger we felt. There was forgiveness.

Sometimes I believed the spirits of my mother and baby were with the Great Spirit. They were waiting in the afterlife for us. Grandma was already thinking of the feast she would cook. Grandpa was probably already hunting. Or maybe their spirits were not there yet but stayed awhile longer on our farms, not seen by those who had moved in after us. The spirits collected Grandmother's cotton cards, her thimble, shell beads, butter ladle, so they seemed to disappear. The white people would think there were thieves among them. Or they'd look for our things and say they'd been misplaced. I was there on the farms with them, walking over the cornrows, listening to the birds. I could feel the earth under my fingers. I was climbing into the wagon to take the apples to the market. But it was Mark touching my hands when I opened my eyes, not the reins. Reverend Bushyhead was singing and Luthy was humming with him. I held Mark against me and listened to the hymn.

Bushyhead and the white minister who walked with us preached Christ as the corn god, the giver of life, along with Selu. I thought that if any of us made it to the new land, then it must be true. Both Christ and myth. It would take both.

I had no husband, no mother or baby. I shivered through the morning into the long and rainy afternoon when we rested on the trail.

The men said that General Winfield Scott had left the trail in Nashville. Something else was happening somewhere. Another skirmish or war.

"In Canada," Tanner told me.

"What do we matter to General Scott?" Luthy asked.

I could see far ahead into the sunset to the end of the flat earth. I sat against the wagon wheel looking off into space. Soon the soldier lifted me into the wagon again and threw a tarp over me. The doctor put camphor under my nose, and I tried to sleep by thinking I was chewing an apple.

I didn't have the strength it took to get across the trail. But our land in North Carolina was gone. We could never go back, any of us. We would never be the same. I would never see Thomas again. My father shunned me sometimes because I talked to the soldier. Soon Luthy would talk against the soldier again. There was nothing if it wasn't ahead. I had to walk. I shivered in my feelings like a scarecrow in the storm. If Knobowtee didn't have his horse and cornfield and hogs, he had nothing. I couldn't tell him I was relieved the baby died. I couldn't carry her anymore. I couldn't bear to hear her fuss against me. What was he? What was I? Did my mother have her things with her again or didn't she care? Was life just a peeling away of ourselves down to our core? The shiny pointed seeds within us? Was there anything to plant in the new land? What would come of us? Somehow I felt soil within myself. The seeds cracking. The root coming forth. It hurt in my spirit the way the baby hurt when she came from me.

I wanted out of the wagon, but I found I couldn't walk in the mornings. I slept in the wagon with my head against Luthy as we tossed and jolted over the moving earth. Maybe the whole world had gone wild and whirled somewhere out across the sky. Was it always cold and harsh there? Yes, at night it was. I looked up at Luthy's plain face and her dull black hair. Her shawl was ripped and dirty. I felt a lump in my throat for all the times I had resented her.

"Do I look as pale as you, Luthy?" I asked, but she didn't answer.

I lay in the wagon and felt the hard sting of my toes and fingers. My runny nose made sores above my mouth. I watched the ashes fly from the small fire when we stopped for rest. They were our ancestors with black wings flying up there in the air, flapping their wings away from the snow. Or were they the Raven Mockers carrying off the spirits of the dying? The earth grew old before my eyes.

"Hush, Maritole," Luthy said.

"The bear's at my feet," I told Luthy. "My toes feel like the bear's eating them!" I could feel the bear's teeth tearing the skin from my feet. "Luthy!" I jerked my legs, but they were weighted to the wagon. I couldn't move. I felt the bear's claws holding me down. "He's eating my legs!" I screamed to Luthy. I kicked in the wagon, but the bear didn't stop. I tried to sit up, but Luthy held me as I jerked under the blanket. I pitched with the wagon over the hard ground. The bear kept eating my body. He ate my stomach. My chest. There was nothing anyone could do. The bear kept eating until I was inside him. There was nothing left of me in the wagon. I could feel the bear's warmth. My whole body was stinging. I saw nothing but the dark.

What was that spasm? It was the shaman over me. Sucking me out of the bear. I had been warm. Now I felt cold again. I heard the shaman talking to the bear. He looked at the sky above the wagon. He chanted. I tried to kick him away with my feet but someone held my legs.

When I woke, Mark and Ephum were leaning over me, looking in my face.

I stayed in the wagon for several more days, until my legs felt stronger and I wanted to walk again. I wasn't going to ride to the new territory with the old ones. I wasn't dead. I would get out of the wagon and walk if that's the way it had to be.

WAR CLUB

Found a pouch from a pack dog and tied it around my neck. Nothing was in it. Maybe the dog had run off with the goods. At night, when it was cold, I tied it on my head because I'd lost the pelt. Why's Quaty Lewis frowning at me? *"Yawp,"* I bark at her.

MARITOLE

Sometimes the soldier talked to me as I walked beside the wagon. I looked into his face. The strange blue eyes. He reached his hand to me, held it a moment, leaning from his horse. Sometimes he dismounted and took my arm to help me walk. He smiled and said some words I didn't understand. The English words the soldiers spoke had the sound of trees and streams and the hiss of wind. My father pushed me away from the soldier. He told the soldier to leave. Who was I to talk to the enemy? The ones who drove us along the trail. The ones with ears and eyes closed to the Great Spirit. The ones who hated us.

But the Williams soldier talked to me in the evening shadows. He thought he knew Cherokee, but he didn't know the North Carolina dialect. I understood some English now, though Quaty said I didn't. Often, she told me what the soldier said. She knew English because her father had worked for a trader in New Echota. She knew English because her husband who stayed behind in North Carolina was white.

"You're not much more than a child," Williams said.

"Yes, I am. I'm older than I look," I told him quickly. Then we sat together a moment without speaking. "Don't you have children?" I asked, remembering the care he took to bury my baby.

"Yes, I do."

"And a wife?"

"No, not now. I had a wife and we had two children, but . . ." He paused.

"But what?"

"She left me for another man and took the children with her."

"Didn't you try to get her back?"

"No," he answered.

"Why?"

"Because I decided she was right in what she did."

"How can that be?"

"I left her alone so much. The army. I was gone sometimes for months. I guess she got tired of waiting. She wanted a husband and a father for the children."

"Why were you gone so much?"

"I studied Indian languages for the army—I had a knack—"

"For Cherokee?"

"Yes. How else could we speak?"

"You don't speak it very well."

Williams looked at me.

"I can understand what you say—sometimes. But you make a wall of your words. You don't speak like my father—or like Tanner," I told him. "Our language is one with itself. It makes a song—" I didn't know how to tell him these things. "Do you see your wife and children anymore?" I asked.

"No."

I thought of the shame that belongs to a man who has lost his family, but didn't say anything about it to him. "Do you miss them?"

"Sometimes I wonder what they must be like now." He paused. "You remind me of her, Maritole. I noticed you from the first."

"Your wife?"

"No," he said. "My daughter."

"She was Indian?"

"No, but there's something about you that reminds me of her."

I felt the soldier near me even when I didn't see him. If I turned sometimes, I saw him behind me watching. If he was ahead, I could follow and it made the journey easier. I felt him wherever he was. I watched him dig graves along the road. If the ground was too hard, I saw him lift the bodies into the wagon to bury later. I saw him wrap the sick ones in blankets. When they died, the digging sometimes lasted after dark. Always, always we moved pushing ahead against the animal that pushed back at us.

One afternoon another blizzard came across the open field. It raged through the night. I pulled the blanket over my head. The next day no one could see to walk. The soldiers halted the march as soon as it began, and we sat under wagons or hovered under tarps thrown over the low branches of thickets. We didn't even have a fire. Out across the howling dark that night I could hear the thin prayers of the DᏏᎠᎪ, the holy men, and the low chants of my people.

Someone was in the shelter under the wagon in the dark. A hand covered my mouth. It was the soldier.

"What do you want?" Tanner asked.

He had clothes for us, he said, because we wrapped the boys in our blankets. I wouldn't take them. No! I fought against him in the dark. He had to hold me down. He tried to tell me something, but I wouldn't listen. He said sharp words to me. Luthy told me he brought us clothes. I knew I was supposed to hold still. My father had told me it was wrong to bury the dead without their clothes. But the soldier took my foot to pull up some trousers. I jerked my foot up and down so he couldn't get ahold of it. He was over me. I felt his weight holding me down. The way Knobowtee came over me when he loved me. When the soldier buttoned the trousers around my waist he pulled my skirt down. He put another shirt on me. Then a man's short coat. He wrapped me in a blanket. He held me in the dark. He rubbed my feet with his hands, held them against his chest inside his jacket. He buried my face against him. For once, the shivering stopped and I lay quietly against him.

All the time I knew they were clothes from the dead. Probably the trousers and shirt from some boy. The blanket from some old woman who had given up her life. The coat likewise from some man, maybe some white man in a town we passed. I felt my arms against my chest. Deep inside the blanket I felt warmth.

The next day I walked in the cold. The ground was hard and the wagons would have moved easy but for the snow. It was a white cover on the road without threads to hold it together. I picked it up and ate some, remembering my thirst in the stockade. The snow parted with my feet. The trousers stayed up on my legs. The socks. The coat held my arms. Birds spoke to us with their chirps. See, they were telling us, it is possible to live in the cold. The bitter cold steamed from our mouths. The boys laughed at it. They jumped up and down with Tanner, who tried to warm them.

"There's a fire inside us. See the smoke?" Tanner breathed into the air. "How can we be cold?" he asked, and jumped until they laughed, wiping their watery eyes, their noses matted with mucus.

The birds moved quick and impatient on the low branches. I listened to their sounds among the coughs and sniffling noses of the people. I watched the sun lead us west across the sky. If I could see it in my head, I could follow with my feet.

Kentucky

NOVEMBER, 1838

MARITOLE

It rained and turned to snow the day we passed into Kentucky. A fence along one side of the road hung with 0ᵖ∫lᐤᏏᏔW, icicles. The soldier told me the name. I heard a word that had sparks from campfires burning in it. I couldn't make him understand that each word told its own story when it wasn't with others.

My legs walked in the trousers under my skirt. My arms were covered with the shirts and jacket, which felt like the soldier's arms still around me. I watched my moccasins in the snow. Sometimes I saw blood in the footprints of others.

At times I still waited for the Great Spirit to take me to the afterlife. I felt the white man's presence in the land we crossed. It was a new world that had come over ours. We didn't fit. Sometimes we just looked at the ground and walked.

In Hopkinsville, Kentucky, the townspeople gave us blankets and boots. They gave us coffins. They cooked for us, and at night there was shelter. Some of us slept in a schoolhouse and some in the town buildings. The soldier wanted me to go in, but the old people and the mothers with their small children needed it more.

"You can take Ephum's hand," Tanner said.

"No, let Luthy go with the boys."

Tanner looked at me. "Stay away from that soldier," he said.

"He gave us clothes. You're the one who said he could."

White Path, an old clan leader, and Fly Smith, a member of the old council, had been sick since we left Nashville. I heard the men talk. They said both men were dying. White Path had walked leaning on a stick. Sometimes Fly Smith rode in the wagon. They had resisted the white man's ways, especially the treaties, which they called "talking papers."

I only wanted to stare at the South Fork of the Little River where we camped. I had cramps and was sick to my stomach. My hands and nose stung. I thought I had hurt my toes and rubbed them in the cold night air. I coughed with the others. Anna Sco-so-tah, Quaty Lewis, and the other old women slept together for warmth.

In the morning, Ephum tripped over me. My lips and fingers were split from the cold. I tried to talk, but only moans came from my throat. I listened to my moans. It was how I knew I was alive.

When I stood, I had to catch a branch to keep from falling on the slippery bank. There was something warm like cornmeal mush they gave us to eat. If we could stand in line.

Luthy ate with tears running from her eyes. Behind her, some men were digging graves for Fly Smith and White Path. We would leave them behind.

We waved to the people when we left Hopkinsville. Their kindness had been like salt on an open wound. There was something about it that stung.

A WHITE TRAVELER
FROM MAINE

. . . detachment of poor Cherokee Indians . . . about eleven hundred Indians—sixty waggons—six hundred horses, and perhaps forty pairs of oxen. We found them in the forest camped for the night by the roadside under a severe fall of rain accompanied by heavy wind. With their canvas for a shield from the inclemency of the weather, and the cold wet ground for a resting place, after the fatigue of the day, they spent the night. . . . Many of the aged Indians were suffering extremely from the fatigue of the journey and the ill health consequent upon it. . . . Several were then quite ill, and an aged man we were informed was there in the last struggles of death.

We met several detachments in the southern part of Kentucky on the 4th, 5th, and 6th of November. . . . The last detachment which we passed on the 7th had about two thousand Indians with horses and mules in proportion. The forward part of the train we found just pitching their tents for the night, and notwithstanding some thirty or forty waggons were already stationed, we found the road literally filled with the procession for about three miles in length. The sick and feeble were carried in waggons—about as comfortable for traveling as a New England oxcart with a covering over it—a great many ride on horseback and multitudes go on foot— even aged females, apparently nearly ready to drop into the grave, were traveling with heavy burdens attached to the back—on the sometimes frozen ground, and sometimes muddy roads, with no covering for the feet except what nature had given them. . . . We learned from the inhabitants on the road where the Indians passed, that they buried fourteen or fifteen at every stopping place, and they made a journey of ten miles per day only on an average

KNOBOWTEE

The cold is here as a helper
The snow is here as a helper.

I could hear my dead father's voice. Or my great-grandfather's.

The snow is a spirit being.
Speak to the snow.
Ask it for help.

QUATY LEWIS

"Crunch. Crunch," I said as we stepped through the snow. "Sounds like a horse eating corn. Sounds like War Club belching." I heard the men chuckle to themselves. *"Crunch,"* I said again to make them smile. *"Crunch,"* I said to our feet reaching the snow

TANNER

Still we walked. The detachments of wagons. Thirteen of them, if I counted right. With their conductors. Hair Conrad. Elija Hicks. Jesse Bushyhead. John Benge. Evan Jones. Captain Old Fields. Moses Daniel. Choowalooka. James Brown. George

Hicks. Richard Taylor. Peter Hildebrand. No, there were twelve detachments. John Drew, the thirteenth, went by boat.

Then the horses. Mules. Oxen. Dogs.

The Light Horse Guard. The government teamsters.

The long line of people in their seven clans.

My father. Luthy. Mark and Ephum mimicking a soldier they'd seen shaving that morning. Maritole and that damned soldier riding beside her.

Somewhere I heard a prayer in Cherokee. Somewhere I heard a negro's dialect.

Despite the trips to Washington. The hearings. Harangues. Murmurings. Pleadings. Councils. Votes. Petitions. Acclamations. Resolutions. Sermons. Divining stones. Until the land got tired of listening. No wonder it drove us away.

We walked sometimes in silence. Except for the groan of wagons. We camped in silence also. Driven inward, we hovered over the small campfires of our hearts.

MARITOLE

"I remember trying to get you on my horse that first afternoon." Sergeant Williams's laugh broke the silence that morning. "I remember you in your cabin when I let you go back—your strength—" He shook his head.

"I wasn't going to leave my farm," I told him, "and it wasn't funny."

He squatted on the ground next to me. He tried to speak Cherokee and I tried to speak English. Sometimes Quaty Lewis told us what we said.

"The openness still scares our people," I told Williams. "In North Carolina we're always surrounded by the hills and trees. There's a Cherokee legend about a magic lake, DWଽꝊ, and it's here in this land," I said.

"Kentucky?"

"No, Tennessee. West from the headwaters of the Oconaluftee River in the great Smoky Mountains."

"We're west of the Smokies now, in Kentucky."

"I know, but it's still the same land. Your boundaries don't mean anything to us."

"Don't tell a soldier that boundaries don't count."

"No one has seen this magic lake," I continued, wondering if Williams was still listening.

"Then how do you know it's there?"

"If a hunter comes near the place, he would know it by the whirring sound of thousands of wild ducks flying over the lake." I spoke in Cherokee whether he understood or not.

Williams pretended to shoot at ducks.

"No," I protested. "Sometimes you let things live."

"Not if you're a soldier."

"Do you want to hear the legend?"

"Yes, ma'am."

"But on reaching the spot the hunter would find only a dry flat without birds or animals unless—"

"Unless?"

"Unless he first sharpened his spiritual vision by prayer and fasting."

"There's always a catch."

"Because it's not seen, some people think the lake has dried up, but this is not true. To anyone who kept watch and fasted through the night, it would appear at daybreak. In the water all kinds of fish swim upon the surface, and overhead there are flocks of ducks and birds, while around the shore, bear tracks cross in the four directions."

"That's quite a place," Williams said.

"It's the Medicine Lake of the birds and animals. Whenever a bear is wounded by hunters, he makes his way through the woods to the magic lake and plunges into the water. When he comes out on the other shore, his wounds are healed."

"Do you really believe that?"

"The legend? Yes."

"No one has ever seen it."

"The animals keep it invisible because the hunters would take advantage of it."

"Do the men have a place to go to when they're hurt?" he asked looking at me.

"Yes, everyone has a place."

"I would like to think so. But I see a lot of Indians suffering without any magic lake to go to," he said.

That night I dreamed of my grandmother. I was still a girl. I could see her standing with her old hoe made from an ox shoulder, saying ᏔᏬᏙᎩ when the pollen dropped into the cornsilk and fertilized the ear. I could see back to when I was my mother's baby playing at her feet as she mashed grain in the hollowed tree stump. I heard her grinding cornmeal. I thought the Great Spirit was taking me because I wanted to be with the soldier. I woke before dawn and could not sleep again for fear I would die. The old ones always talked about long ago before they died.

But still, I thought, I was alive.

REVEREND BUSHYHEAD

"Woe to those who rely on horses, and trust in wagons—Isaiah 31:1," I preached. "Our strength is not in horses, but in God." I looked over the little group of people around me.

War Club burped.

"I hear the spirits with us. We are not abandoned. At night I hear the angels groaning under the weight of their wings. We can't see them—no—" I shook my head. "They're rolling our wagons on the long path to the new territory. We're wheezing and jerking and spilling our way." Suddenly I felt distracted. My widowed sister, Nancy, stood beside me. My pregnant wife sat at my side. "Does not our blood stain the snow?" My voice cracked. Not since the smallpox epidemics had so many died. Even the animals dragging the wagons collapsed.

"And how do we make it? How?" The words were in my head, but I said them aloud. "The babies cry and then are silent. The old men fall. The women weep. Our young men look at the snow. If that's all that's ahead of us without our fields to plow."

"Why doesn't he mention the soldiers who sleep with our girls?" someone asked.

"Why doesn't he talk about the soldiers who give our men whiskey?" War Club belched.

"What do we do when our feet don't walk?" I paused. "We leave our blood leaking on the ground." The words were heavy. My sister, Nancy, held my arm. My wife held her stained shawl to her mouth. My small flock watched to see if the Lord God who sent angels to pull the wagons could get me through my sermon.

"We look at our sorrow and know it's not all," I reminded. "Somewhere people are warm and singing in their churches. We will again. Our children. Some will survive. We are the land. We'll have a remnant—We'll—" I coughed back my grief and began at another place. "Our journey—the one ahead—the one after this walking—will begin again from nothing. This is how we go. Always back to nothing." I stumbled as if my words were a bundle I carried. As if I were top-heavy with my sermon. "These tears don't hurt my face. I'm not crying for myself. I feel—"

The people became alarmed. My wife cried out. My sister couldn't decide which one of us to comfort. "There's nothing to be afraid of—" I stammered, and fell to the ground

MARITOLE

Doctor Powell came, but Bushyhead would not leave the meeting. A holy man, a ᏗᏓᏁᎮᏉᏴ, spoke then for him.

I watched Bushyhead shiver in the miserable wind. Nothing held up the sky. The land was flat, the hills shaved off.

Bushyhead's sister coughed beside him. I held two fingers to my nostrils under the thin blanket and felt the warm stream of my breath.

"I hear the string of angels above us," the holy man said, "and the spirit beings. They fly with us. *Hold us up, spirits,* I say. *Our legs are weak and sometimes we can't walk.*"

"I hear the angels," someone said. "Hold on to your hope. The spirits rub our legs while we rest. That feeling we can't explain is an angel."

A HOLY MAN

After the meeting, I prayed for Bushyhead. The reverend sat quietly against a tree, wrapped in a blanket. He was the leader of our regiment and had to be able to walk. He had tried to make sense of everything, but the trail we marched didn't make sense. It didn't fit into an understanding of the Christian God. "Slip between both worlds," I told him, "like our feet slip over the snow."

This (Is) to Cure (Them) with
Whenever They Have Forgotten Their Voice

These (five barks) cure them with: Cherry, small acorn
oak, flowering dogwood, bitter apple, big (white) willow.
The medicine against hoarseness drink from the bark of
trees and he will vomit phlegm which clogs his throat. Some
(of it) rub on neck. The bark from east side of tree.

I sang as if I had the five barks. But some said, "What if those trees don't grow outside Cherokee land?" Or they said, "What if the words only work on land where we were born?"

KNOBOWTEE

I heard the singing as I walked beneath the dripping trees. Sometimes I wondered if it was the people or if the song was only in my ears. The trail could do things like that. Maybe it was the little people. Making me see what wasn't there. Making me hear. Sometimes I looked at my brother to see if he was singing. Sometimes I thought I heard my father. Calling a bird.

Sometimes I could hear the singing in the night with the wind. Sometimes I could hear it in the day when I walked, my arm bent as if I carried my musket. I looked around me. Yes, I saw the mouths moving. Sometimes when the people sang, I smiled because of Quaty Lewis. If only she could sing like she thought she could. But if I tried to sing, the words caught in my throat.

I walked silently beside O-ga-na-ya. Sometimes when she

seemed to gain strength for a while, our mother walked between us. My sister walked behind us holding the corner of the blanket over her nose and mouth like Maritole.

At first the soldiers tried to stop the singing, but it kept on. *Sing*—I gave the sign when the soldiers passed—*sing*.

SONG WE SANG ON
ᏘᎠᏏᎾᎠᎷᎢ (THE TRAIL OF BLOOD)

ᏚᏙ ᏓᏣᎤ

ᏚᏂᎵ ᎯᏍ

ᏍᏒᏙᎵ ᏣᎬᎾᏠᎬᎠ

ᏍᏚᎵᏚᎵ

ᏠᎤᏙᏍᎤᏴᏃ

ᏁᎩᎷᎾᎪᏓᏂᏗᏍ

ᏍᏚᏙᎵᏚ

ᏣᎬᎾᏠᎬᎠ

ᏟᏙᎵᏚᏃ

ᏣᎬᎾᏠᎬᎠ

ᏍᏚᏙᎵᏚ

ᏣᎬᎾᏠᎬᎠ

ᏟᏙᏒᎵᏚ

ᏣᎬᎾᏠᎬᎠ

KNOBOWTEE

"We could protest to the Tennessee Cherokee," I said to my brother one afternoon. We had stopped to build a fire for warmth and to dry our blankets and coats. "We need representation in council."

O-ga-na-ya looked at me. "Yap," he said.

"We could form a petition. Not all of us signed the treaty."

I knew the women listened. Often they made their minds known. I looked at Lacey Woodard. Mrs. Young Turkey. Anna Sco-so-tah. The other old women.

There was silence.

"They can't have meetings without us," I continued. "We're walking the trail, too—"

"We could tell the soldiers we're not going," I heard the men's voices. They were listening, too.

"We could tell the sky to shut its mouth."

"Yop. This snow's worse than white flour."

"It's got teeth."

"We could ask the Great Spirit if he knows what he's doing."

"Yar. Whar's my toes?" War Club asked. "They feel like rocks in my socks."

The Tennessee Cherokee could hold all the meetings without them. What did I care? They could decide who had wagon detail, who sat on guard at night against the wolves and renegade whites, who had burial duty.

I felt my stomach churn. I cared more than I wanted to know.

"We could form a council of our own." I worked with the wagon hitch as several men watched. My hands were cold and my fingers moved stiffly pulling the wrench.

"I think we ought to take the knife to them," one of the men said.

"The Tennessee Cherokee?" I was surprised.

"Maybe them, too." The man coughed. "I meant the soldiers, Knobowtee. They're getting tired of the trail."

"We can't be making more than five miles a day now." The man who spoke had a large cold sore under his nose. It turned my stomach to look at him.

"Not even that."

"We could call a meeting right now. Decide how to speak to the Tennessee leaders. Maybe they would listen." I blew on my fingers to warm them.

"No, they wouldn't."

"We could speak to Bushyhead." I turned the wrench.

"And Mackenzie."

"Leave them gentlemen out."

"We don't need no holy noses," War Club muttered.

"I think we need anyone who could help." The wrench

jumped from the wagon hitch. I cursed. "This wagon's going to wobble all over the road. Nothing I can do."

"Let me try," O-ga-na-ya said.

I wiped the grease from my sore hands. If there was ever any water to wash in—ever anything warm to feel . . .

O-ga-na-ya couldn't fix the wagon, either. He gave one last jerk with his hand and the wrench flew, jamming his hand against the wagon, scraping the knuckles. Blood oozed over his dirty hands. He cursed and kicked the wagon wheel until I stopped him.

QUATY LEWIS

Aaahhchh. Sometimes Kee-un-e-ca says she smells wood smoke. She thinks of her cabin burning in the North Carolina woods. Waves of grief sweep over her. Kee-un-e-ca turns her head almost backward. She flaps her arms like wings. *"WHHHOOOOOO"* is what she says. You can see her cabin burning in her eyes. Sometimes she cannot be consoled.

KAKOWIH

Womens cry and make sad wails. Childrens cry and men, all look sad when peoples die but they say nothing. Just put heads down and keep going toward west. Many days and peoples die very much. Sleep under thin blanket. Wind howls. Make me weep to see them. Each day look like maybe all be dead before we get to new Indian country. Maritole growl like a bear when she sleep. She got eat by bear. She have bear strength. Always keep marching. No one never smiles. Just walks. Stumbles. Gets up. Walks

TANNER

"We hardly move." I put my head between Luthy's knees in the dark. I'd always tried to protect her, but I felt my weakness now. I needed to bury myself in her.

Each day the disheartedness and anger increased. A blacksmith from New Echota walked with us. He'd been moved from his place in the back of the line and shackled. The men said he'd tried to stab a soldier with a metal file as he fixed a wagon wheel. It was only a matter of time until it happened again. A wrench flying through the air would hit a soldier or a Georgia Cherokee.

I leaned into Luthy as we camped that night. My father nodded by the tree. Maritole was probably under some wagon talking to the soldier. When the boys were asleep, I pulled up Luthy's skirt and got between her legs, in the soft part I missed. Quietly and hardly moving, I tried to enter her, without a leg cramp causing me to cry out in pain, without a sudden release causing me to sob with the resignation that was either hurt or love.

VOICES IN THE DARK

There's a world that moves of itself. It doesn't care about us. Well it cares, yes, maybe some of it wishes it wasn't the way it was.

It's a world that doesn't see.

It never will.

But look at Reverend Mackenzie. Remember Reverend Worcester? There's also a soldier who has eyes-that-see.

Well, some of the people of that world, then.

Yes. Some.

Listen to the day wheeze.

Listen to the shovels digging graves.

Listen to the little hive of women buzzing. Anna Sco-so-tah. Lacey Woodard. Luthy and Maritole. Quaty Lewis. Kee-un-e-ca. Mrs. Young Turkey. With their little bee wings you can see right through.

KNOBOWTEE

I sat in the woods calling a bird. *"Come here, bird,"* I sang, and whistled the way I remembered my father did. But the birds just sat on the branches of the trees and looked at me. Soon they flew away. *"I'm hungry for you,"* I called. *"Anything but this salt pork and white flour."*

Maritole's father watched me. He wanted to say something, but didn't.

I turned to him. "Could I borrow your musket?"

"There aren't any musket balls."

"But you go into the woods."

"I act as if I have them."

"I wondered why we didn't have bird meat."

"Here. Maybe you can shoot without musket balls. Bring it back."

"Don't I always return what's yours?"

"Not always."

"Maybe a few tools. But what difference do they make now?"

"I remember you didn't return them," Maritole's father told me. "That's the difference."

I took the musket, but a soldier yelled at me. The younger men weren't allowed to carry muskets. The soldiers didn't trust us. Before I could hand back the musket to Maritole's father, the soldier knocked me on the ground with his bayonet.

I raised my arm to let the soldier know I wasn't going to do anything.

"It's rusted, too," Maritole's father said when I got up out of the mud. "I don't have any way to clean it."

"I thought I heard musket shots when you went in the woods."

"I act like I shoot. It makes me think I still can. Maybe it makes you think I can."

"No wonder the birds sit and watch. They know we don't have anything to shoot with."

"Bird, my relative, come into my hand." I wished for my blowgun. Maybe I could turn myself into a bird. Or if I thought I was a bird, maybe I could become a bird spirit. It was the way my father had hunted. Fished. It was the way he became another. If

only I could remember how my father did it. *"I'm hungry,"* I told the bird. *"Give yourself. I honor you with song."* Still the bird flew away.

REVEREND BUSHYHEAD

I read the Bible as I walked the trail that morning, my wife holding on to my arm. I tripped over uneven places, bumped into whatever was ahead of me. But it kept me warm. Maybe the whole nine-mile line of Cherokee through Kentucky should read the Bible as we walk.

I remembered something about the year of Jubilee in Israel when everything returned to its owner. Every fifty years. I looked through the pages of Leviticus. A drop of snow or cold rain from the trees spotted the pages. There it was, in the twenty-fifth chapter, twenty-third verse. "The land shall not be sold forever: for the land is mine; for ye are strangers and sojourners with me." Even the Lord God was a sojourner! What ideas the white God had! He didn't stay on his land like the farmer. But what did it mean? I had trouble thinking at times. The land was returning to the white man? No, it wasn't his to begin with. The land would return to the Cherokee? No, this wasn't Israel. It meant nobody owned anything permanently.

"It means the Redbird saved a piece of ice for the Mockingbird when he returned in the spring," Nancy said, smiling as she helped my wife and me walk.

Yes, it was that, I nodded to her. But it also was something more, I thought. I could say the Cherokee were going through a year of Jubilee. Giving our land, that wasn't really ours, back to God. Then we could travel. Maybe that was the idea. If it would help the people walk, then I would tell them.

KNOBOWTEE

Again I spoke to the birds. I was so cold, my voice jerked. But they recognized my voice. I knew it. One would have given itself, but I had nothing to kill it with. A stone. Maybe a pebble. If I hit it just right. Where was a rock in this snow and mud?

Where was anything? I hit himself in frustration and the bird flew away. Everything was gone. Even the voice to catch birds.

REVEREND BUSHYHEAD

I remembered the little table in the church in New Echota. The bottles of wine and anointing oil sitting on it. How I needed the oil, I thought, as I listened to my young daughter cough. Behind the table there had been a white wall. A staff and candle snuffer crossed on the wall above the table. Why did I remember that wall? It was white and barren as the fields of snow in Kentucky where we walked. And as pure. How could that be? But everything came from the spirit. There was nothing without spirit. My wife couldn't keep up with the walking line as she grew heavier with our second child. She couldn't bear the bouncing of the wagon. "Stay in there," she said to the baby. "You're warmer than you'll be out here." Someone put my wife on a horse for a while. Then I had time to think about the detachment I led. I had time to think about the next sermon. I would say we were blessed with a year of Jubilee. We had to give back what wasn't ours.

TANNER

I saw two conjurers working their magic over a family. The woman quivered with either cold or fear. "Why do you scare her?" I confronted them.

The conjurers hissed at me. I pulled back. A haze seemed to come between us. Luthy held the boys. She stood behind me. Maritole, who had been walking with the soldier, froze in her tracks.

"You live the white man's way." The conjurers spit words that burned the snow. Smoke rose from it. The men around them hopped back.

"I'm not afraid of your magic," I said. "You couldn't do anything when smallpox came—"

"Traitor," the conjurers said. "The new ways have caused this trouble."

"What can you do? Call down the sky to hide us?"

"What can *you* do?" The conjurers spat again.

"I walk by faith in the Great Spirit." I stood my ground.

The conjurers waved their arms and the people screamed. Sergeant Williams shot in the air as the soldiers always did when there was trouble. The conjurers raised their arms at Williams and spat. There was a terrible smoke. Williams fell back. Maritole and Luthy begged me to keep still. The conjurers left the sergeant on the ground.

KNOBOWTEE

I called a meeting. Few men came, other than my brother. I was discouraged and my throat was sore, but I talked as though we had council.

I reminded the men of Wilson Lumpkin's speech. *"The earth was formed for cultivation and none but civilized men could cultivate it."* Lumpkin was Commissioner to the Cherokee, and he said the savages the white men found on the land were not fit to subdue it.

But the civilized race should treat the heathens with magnanimity. *Magnanimity.* That had been the word. Therefore, the Cherokee should be removed to the West.

I felt my anger. Nothing else mattered. How could we deal with men who thought like that? How could we do anything? No one came to the meeting, but they stood on the outskirts or walked past, looking. I cursed them. My fist pounded something—the side of a wagon. The sick ones cried out. I pounded the ox who tried to pull the wagon.

TANNER

I listened to the men grumble in Knobowtee's meeting. I listened to Knobowtee stumble over the English word *magnanimity* when he tried to say it. I heard him curse. O-ga-na-ya pulled Knobowtee to the ground when he beat the ox with his fists. I knew how Knobowtee felt as he sobbed against his brother.

I wanted to kill, yet I wanted to heal at the same time. Where did these two opposing forces come from? Not from the white soldiers. It wasn't their fault. Hadn't they loosened their hold as they grew weary of the trail? No, those feelings came from within.

Not everyone thought like Lumpkin. I remember a Cherokee trying to describe a horse he couldn't find. He had trouble talking, and the white men concluded that the Cherokee language wasn't fit to be spoken. The sooner we forgot about it, the better off we'd be.

But Reverend Worcester had argued for the Cherokee keeping our language. He said our speech had meanings and sounds not found in English. We said things in our own way in Cherokee. We had our own ideas and feelings and relationships between our words.

Sequoyah had written our spoken language with his syllabary. His "talking leaves" made the Cherokee literate. In 1828, some of the New Testament had been translated into Cherokee "so they could bear the weight of the divine in their own way," Worcester explained. For all that, Worcester had gone to jail while Wilson Lumpkin would probably be elected senator or governor in Georgia.

"They wanted our voices silenced so we couldn't complain about the loss of our property, the murdering and plundering," the men complained. "They don't want us to be able to talk. They know our language gives us power."

"Who are we to enter the Divine Providence of language and replace it?" Worcester argued. That was God's place alone. "We have forced the Indians along the dark trail. And worse yet, we would render the trail wordless?"

"Let us be without words like my sister," O-ga-na-ya spat. He held Knobowtee, who slumped beside the wagon.

"No," I argued. "We push our words on the trail with us to see what's in them. We shake them in a sifter, burn them with fire. We are made for words." I felt the old power as my words came from my mouth.

"We're sacks of words, like Tanner says," Knobowtee agreed with me in his raspy voice. I saw him stand by the wagon. He trembled with shame at his anger, but he knew the men listened. "We're whole cornfields carrying the kernels of our words."

"*ypmph,*" War Club said.

O-ga-na-ya stood to his feet beside Knobowtee, who nuzzled the ox with his hand.

LUTHY

The men buried a young woman without a name I had held that Sunday morning. I didn't even know her clan. The digging started as soon as Reverend Bushyhead's sermon was over. The young woman had died while he spoke, but I didn't cry out. Bushyhead had talked about giving back the land because the Great Spirit didn't stay in one place either. What was Bushyhead talking about? Who farmed the land then?

"The white man," O-ga-na-ya said.

That was sure.

HEALING SONG

The holy men struck our heads for every song we could remember. Even in sleep we searched.

This Is for the Purpose of (Curing) Children
When They Cry Constantly.

The people are scaring them, they say, when the children are constantly crying, the people living in the mountain (that is). Old tobacco should be blown on them, all over their bodies. Their heads should be blown first. It should be repeated four (times), each time at night. While they are being cured (that is) four nights, they should not walk about. And this (you ought to be careful about): If there are any feathers (inside the house), put them all outside (just) like when they are being treated for the (disease that is called) "they are eating them." And any skin (that might be inside the house) all has to come (outside). The medicine is just old tobacco.

(When the children cry constantly there are spirit clans playing ball in the stomach, and he calls on the Thunder to swoop down like a hawk on its prey and drive them out into the Night Land.)

KNOBOWTEE

I sang my spirit song. *"Here bird, here bird,"* and the bird came. The bird's wings moved in my dream in time to the shovel digging the hard ground. Was the sky as hard? Maybe the bird would bump his head against it and fall dead into my hand.

MARITOLE

We came to the edge of Kentucky at the Ohio River. Ice and snow had frozen the river, and the ferry was not able to take us across. Neither was the ice thick enough that we could walk to the other side. The weather worsened as we camped by the river waiting to cross. Other detachments joined us as they caught up. Our old ones lay on the ground with the edges of their blankets fluttering. Sometimes the blankets blew away in the wind and people ran after them. At night the conjurers hummed with stories of the water spirits who waited to drag us into the river with them, or stories of the Raven Mockers stealing the dying. We heard the old stories of Uk'ten' again.

"Who's Uk'ten'?" Sergeant Williams asked.

"I don't know. A large snake."

"Where does he live?"

"He lives somewhere."

"By rivers," Luthy told him.

"Oᵒ$i," Mark said, trying to scare his brother.

"What does he do?"

"Kills people."

"He was someone who turned himself into a snake."

"You mean he wasn't really a snake."

"Yes, he was," Anna Sco-so-tah said.

"But he could be other things," Luthy said.

"Nothing's ever clear with you people."

"Yes, it is," I told Williams.

"He had horns, too," Mark reminded Ephum.

"And he smelled."

"Because he was fierce," Mark finished

———

Still we sat on the edge of the river in the whipping cold. I covered my head with my blanket. I got up and hopped. I cried at the wind to go away.

Behind us, people held their blankets around someone who was trying to start a fire.

"Ho," War Club joked. "Even the fingers of the fire freeze."

I saw the line of people sit in a stupor. The cold was changing us into itself.

"Don't sleep," said someone walking along the line. "You won't get up, Maritole." Someone jarred my shoulders.

I felt the cold sting my eyes.

We moved as if in slow motion, the way a bird would glide over a cornfield.

My father had ice under his nose. Knobowtee's mother had it in her eyebrows.

Some days later, we heard that one of the leaders feared his family would not survive and decided to take them back to the last town we had passed. We watched them depart on horseback from camp one morning, the man's wife so weak she held the neck of the horse.

A few days later, Lewis Ross decided he would go to St. Louis for supplies. He was supposed to help us, but we didn't always know where he was.

KNOBOWTEE

We had nothing but a blanket against the cold. I looked at the old ones on the shore. Should I give my blanket to one of them? Would it help? I could see snow when I closed my eyes. My sister shivered so violently her mouth made noise. I held her next to me, inside my blanket. Had we come to the end of the earth? Were my sins before me? That's what Bushyhead called his wrongdoings. The Cherokee held slaves. My father had told me stories of the wars against the Creeks. I knew the cruelties, the beatings. I remembered running with my friends at the festival. I remembered the girls that smiled at me. Now the frozen earth rubbed my shoulders. I remembered once throwing a cat into the creek, again and again, fifteen, maybe sixteen times, until it had spasms and died before I could throw it back. Was it the spirit of the cat who scratched me now? I tossed under my blanket. The hard ground, the endless cold. I thought of Maritole. How I hated her at times. Her spite. Her power to talk to the soldier in front of my brother and friends.

I had to walk now with my mother, helping O-ga-na-ya to hold her up. Why couldn't Maritole be like my sister, who never said anything?

How often my feet walked, but they didn't seem to move. The long procession had slowed to under five miles a day. Sometimes we made only two.

Now we had stopped at a wide river. The Ohio. I had never seen such a river. Not only was it wide, it was turbulent and full of ice. At night my mother slept between O-ga-na-ya and me for warmth. My sister seemed buried under her torn blanket. What would I do without Maritole? I'd lost my horse and the few belongings I had. Would we be stranded forever on the bank of the Ohio? I heard the old ones cry and moan. They asked the Raven Mocker or Great Spirit or the Christian God to take us, whoever we could believe in, in this cold, white, brittle life.

MARITOLE

A few days later, maybe a week, Lewis Ross returned with brogans and mackinaws and blankets and other supplies for the five thousand or so of us camped by the river.

There had been questions about the money the government had given John Ross for the removal. Knobowtee said Lewis Ross had used his own money for the supplies he passed out. But the men didn't seem to listen.

That night, Tanner and my father covered Alotohee, who chewed the air and said he was not hungry. He said the trees were in his stomach.

Still the conjurers chanted. Nothing the Cherokee leaders or ministers could do would stop them. Sometimes we heard the thunder in their chants, and some of the leaders said it was a good omen.

Still the stories of Uk'ten' were told at night.

Long ago Uk'ten' and Thunder had a fight. Thunder was underneath and Uk'ten' was winning because, you remember, he was fierce. A boy saw them fighting. Thunder called out to him, saying, "Help me, nephew. Uk'ten' will kill me and then he will kill you."

"That's not so," Uk'ten' said. "When Thunder thunders, he will kill you."

They both kept saying these things.

But because Thunder was losing, the boy decided to shoot Uk'ten' with an arrow. Uk'ten' was weakened and Thunder was able to thunder until he killed Uk'ten' with his noise.

Thunder won and the boy had helped him win. That is the reason Thunder is around us. He is not fierce. He remembers it was a boy who saved him.

This is how it was when they were telling stories long ago.

One day Evan Jones, who followed with another detachment, rode forward in the line. He said we would all die unless we began crossing the river. He had prayed and his prayers would hold us up.

He persuaded some of us that the wagons could cross on the ice. He started three wagons loaded with old ones and sick ones across a frozen place in the Ohio. One wagon almost made it before the ice gave way and the three wagons overturned, dumping their passengers into the river. We heard their screams and watched them flail in the water before they sank. We cried out to them. One of the men from the shore jumped across the ice and into the cold water to save them, but they were gone.

More people died in the cold waiting to cross. Even the pack dogs died of hunger.

Several days later, when the ice chunks seemed smaller, the rest of us began crossing slowly on the ferry, the rafts, and small boats. The water lapped at our feet. We didn't have enough to hold on to on the platforms that shifted above the water. We swayed awkwardly, bumping one another. Everyone was frantic. The conjurers said the spirits that walked with us couldn't see across the water. We believed the water spirits would pull us into the river. But Reverend Bushyhead said that God was with us. I saw the boat ahead of us shift and turn over. The people looked like scarecrows jumping up and down in the water until they drowned. I heard the wailing voices of the women. I heard the thunder again. In the long nights afterward I saw them dance in the river, the cold water making them rigid, soaking their lungs until they sank like sacks of white man's flour.

KNOBOWTEE

The soldiers and government teamsters buy soap and coffee and sugar for their men, but we don't get nothing, I thought. "They cheat us and rob us." I must have spoken out loud as I crossed the river, because I heard my own voice. "They rob us."

"Even our own people cheat us," someone answered as I pitched with the raft midriver. "Some say Ross got two hundred and fifty thousand dollars for our removal."

"Some say he got five million."

Another man losing his balance on the raft cried out and knocked others off balance. We tried to hold ourselves upright so the others could keep their footing. The raft shifted so severely once that cold water from the river washed over our feet. Yet we held on until we were across.

My words were still in my ears as I struggled to get my legs back after the river crossing. The ordeal had left me dazed and weak.

If I weren't so weak, I'd jump the soldiers who rode past and pound them into the ground. I'd jump my own people. No, I had to keep my head in balance to survive. My anger at the soldiers gave me strength. My weakness tempered my ability to take revenge. My knees buckled as I walked, thinking of beating the soldiers. My brother grabbed my arm as I fell but I jerked away.

Yes, I could walk because of Uk'ten'. The snake that could kill with his breath. I thought Uk'ten' was like the Christians' devil, but once Uk'ten' was defeated, the reverse was true. Then his scales were healing. Protection. The stories fueled my walk. Yes.

illinois

DECEMBER, 1838

KNOBOWTEE

At a camp near a cemetery on the other side of the Ohio River, past Golconda, Illinois, my sister, Aneh, dreamed she was bitten by a snake. She made sucking sounds, clamping her fingers to her arm. Her mother held her and told the conjurer what happened.

"It's too cold for snakes," I told Aneh. But my sister held herself while the others ate that morning. She held herself while the others passed. Maybe it was the stories of Uk'ten' she'd heard. Maybe it was the river crossing.

The land, which had been flat, now rolled with steep hills and frozen cypress swamps. We kept thinking the trail would get easier, but it only got harder.

"It's the same as if she were bitten," the conjurer said, the skin of a fox squirrel on his belt. I knew it was true.

The cure was different for an imagined bite, but if it wasn't treated, Aneh still would be poisoned. Already her arm reddened.

If Snake Have Bitten Them, This Is the Medicine, the conjurer sang in Cherokee.

> *Ya! Ha! now, Black Snake, they have caused you to come down, it seems. The snake that has bitten is only a ghost, it seems. They have caused you to come down, it seems.*

> *The ever-living bones, the ever-living teeth it has advanced toward her, it seems. It was only a black snake that laid itself about the trail, it seems. But right now, it seemed to bite her.*

I felt my mind wandering. I could take Maritole's father's musket and club the soldiers to death. Yes, I could. The anger shook me as much as the cold. I thought of the musket splitting the soldiers' heads when I heard the conjurer again.

But at this moment you Two Little Men, you Two Powerful Wizards, have caused you two to come down. It was a black snake, it seems, but the snake is merely a ghost and it has feigned to put the disease under him, it seems; it thought its track would never be found.

But now you two have come to take it away. Where the black boxes are, you two have gone to store it up. As soon as you two have turned around, relief would have been caused at the same time.

I watched the conjurer with my sister. Maybe she'd offended a snake or fish and one of them had returned to take vengeance, causing her to dream of snakes crawling over her, breathing their breath into her face, spoiling her saliva until she was bitten with a dream and lost her appetite. The medicine would cause vomiting. She would spit up the spoiled saliva and recover.

Aneh coughed and spit up. The conjurer chanted. Two Little Men were taking his sister's disease to the Night Land in the West to put in a black box or coffin. Then she'd be healed. I heard her gag. I saw her throw up the venom.

Why would Aneh dream of a snake? Didn't we have enough trouble on the trail? Did we need to think up something else that wasn't there?

Illinois was hilly and rugged. Sometimes we made only a few miles a day. Wasn't it also true that you could be bitten and think you weren't? Couldn't you speak to the wound as if it wasn't, and it would dry up, and the poison along with it? How much was in the thinking? Like those who denied the trail. It wasn't really happening. Sometimes I passed them talking in their own world. Maybe for them there wasn't a walk. It could be dissolved in thought.

I wanted to ask the conjurer to make us warm. I held my eyes together. I pictured a fire. Now I saw my field in North Carolina. How I plowed behind the horse, sweat running off my face. Maritole coming through the field with a gourd full of cool springwater.

MARITOLE

"There's a split in our ways of thinking," I said to Sergeant Williams as we helped push a wagon up a hill. "The Cherokee lived in agreement with the earth. But the white man told us God's curse separated us from the earth."

What was wrong with our relationship to the land? I thought. Why hadn't we known of the curse? Some of it the white men had right. Before light there was sound. Bushyhead once preached from the beginning of Genesis that there had been a world that dissolved and then became earth again. The Cherokee believed that after this earth, there would be another. One without the white man. The conjurers only wanted to get back the agreement of man and earth. They hissed and their faces transformed as if they wore masks.

The men put a rock behind the wagon wheel so it wouldn't slip back while they waited for another horse to help pull it up the hill.

The white man told us we had been left out of God's world. There was a way to get back with God—Christ. But there was no way to be reconciled with the white man.

I rested on the ground while the men hitched another horse to the wagon. I stood and pushed against the wagon again while a drunk teamster whipped the horse. The wagon jerked forward, but the horses slipped and the wagon rolled back, hitting my knee. A man yelled on the other side of the wagon. The wheel was on his foot.

The men couldn't back the wagon off his foot. It was loaded with the sick. My father got a branch, and the men levered the wagon back. The man's foot hung from his leg. He yelled with pain. My father called for a doctor again. The sick moaned in the wagon. I picked a splinter from my finger and sucked the blood and thought of the creek near Du'stayalun'yi so I wouldn't have to listen.

KNOBOWTEE

The soldier kept talking to Maritole. I would kill him if I could. She was my wife. I was supposed to protect her. Now I wanted to push her into the snow because she looked at the soldier. But I had to keep my mind on the trail through Illinois. The hills wore on us. Dixon Springs near Vincent. Anna. Ware. Then at Clear Creek, we tried to camp on James Morgan's farm. But Morgan told us to move so we packed up, walked on for nearly a mile, and camped again. The farmer there wouldn't let us cut or burn wood on his land.

"The snow is a spirit being," I repeated to myself in the cold. *The snow is a helper*, I thought in the dark.

THE SOLDIERS

"Gawd, they're quiet sometimes."

"When they're not yelling with pain."

"I would like to be home tonight."

"All of us would, sir. Especially them."

"I'm afraid sometimes to close my eyes."

MARITOLE

Somewhere close to dawn, a bird called out and I thought I heard my baby's voice. Maybe it was Quaty who squeaked in her sleep. Or Mrs. Young Turkey when the air whistled in her nose.

KNOBOWTEE

In the bright dawn, I remembered my mother's cabin my brother helped me build. We cut the logs with our axes, filled the open places with mud. We had gone to a white settlement to see how it was done. I had pulled up grass, knocked dirt from the roots, stirred gravel and water with it. My sister had mixed the mud with her feet.

The cabin would have gone to Aneh. The women owned the possessions. That's why I had lived with Maritole and my other wives before her. I only had a horse and two pigs. I wanted

an ox and some sheep but hadn't had time to buy them as yet.
Now I would never have them. I knew it. What good did Maritole's talking do? Everything would be all right, she said. We
could not be wiped off the earth

> *In the mountains (East). In the new territory (West). There*
> *would be a ΘβЉ, a remnant. The land was their power. They*
> *were of the earth. The turtle island. They were the ҶiЛT (the*
> *everlasting people).*

How I had danced with my wife who died. Stamping one foot at
a time in the long line. I had been afraid the first time I danced
with her. I remembered her near the fire later. She had stripped
the corn, pounded it into meal, and mixed it with mashed
beans. She formed the dough into loaves and wrapped it in corn
husks and baked it in the hot ashes of the fire I built. How I
longed for her bean bread. Maritole didn't have patience yet
with her cooking. She'd make something just to get it done. But
the baby had taken her time. I walked with my brother and
thought of my first wife. I felt the tears come into my eyes and
wiped them away quickly with the sleeve of my worn tunic. I
didn't want my family to see. But O-ga-na-ya was making funny
motions with his hand as he walked. Sometimes his mouth
moved. Maybe he was remembering, too.

"*Haaa-ya-hoop-hoop,*" I yelped, as if at the end of the round
dance. O-ga-na-ya was startled from his reverie but caught on.
He made the mince step of the eagle dance. How handsome we
had been when we danced half naked in the town square. Our
painted bodies sending the missionaries and Christian preachers
back to their church to pray.

MARITOLE

The road made the same raw, jagged cut to the west as we
crossed Illinois.

I heard Luthy hum to her boys. How could she hum?

"Nothing keeps you down, Luthy," I said. "You always had
everything."

"My parents are gone. I watched your mother do everything

for you," she snapped. "When you had a girl, I wanted her."

"You can still have other children." My words spit at her in the bitter cold.

"So can you." She paused. "If you wouldn't shame Knobow-tee."

"He shames me! Is there anyone who doesn't know he left me? You don't know how that feels." I hated Luthy again. "You took the clothes, too, when the soldier brought them. You didn't lose your children," I choked. "You have Tanner to sleep against at night!"

"I'm sorry, Maritole," she pleaded. "I never liked to argue."

I walked out of the shelter and stood behind a tree. I felt a sudden warmth in the rush of anger and felt I could march even through the dark.

THE BASKET MAKER

John Benge's detachment caught up with Bushyhead's group sometimes, then fell back. I talked to Maritole and Luthy as if I marched with them.

"I can feel my hands weaving in the night," I said. "I can feel the river cane between my fingers. That's how I stay warm. See, my hands are not raw."

"ᏍᎪᏈ," Maritole said when I held out my hands. Other hands were bleeding and covered with sores.

"Haven't you felt your religion in something other than the Christian ministers who send our wagons into the rivers to drown us? The conjurers do it, too. I don't always understand what they're talking about. But my religion's in my hands."

LUTHY

"It's thievery." The men talked beside our group of women. The boys, who were sitting in my lap, turned to listen to them.

"They stole our land. It was as if they cut open my chest. Took my breath."

"Let's get up. Keep walking."

"Use your anger. Use whatever you have. Keep walking." Knobowtee always was agitated.

I pulled the boys' attention back to the basket maker. Why did Tanner listen to the men?

"As for the removal, it wasn't legal." That's all Anna Sco-so-tah could say.

"I walk," Quaty added.

"Walk."

"God is a just God who demands justice. What does he do with injustice? You, white man? It may take a while. But you'll feel the cold against your back."

"What did we do to deserve this?" I asked.

"We were in their way, Luthy," Maritole answered.

"It must be more than that."

Somewhere behind the group of men, another man sobbed.

Ephum chewed his fist as he sat in my lap.

Maritole and Quaty stood painfully and limped a few steps. Quaty's legs would hardly move. She said they felt like logs. "Why do we rest? It just gives our legs a chance to stiffen." Maritole was young, but she limped, too.

THE BASKET MAKER

"Now this is the story of my baskets."

ᏍᎵ.

"Some think the idea for weaving baskets came from the earth, which is the holder of our cornfields. Which is the holder of our lives. Yes, the baskets just copy the land.

"But others think the idea for weaving baskets came from the sky. An upside-down holder of the rain. So it falls back to us.

"But I say, the idea for baskets came from our stories. The baskets hold fish and corn and beans. Just like our stories hold meaning. Yes, I say the baskets copy our stories."

"You're making that up."

"What's wrong with that?"

"I don't like it."

"We need new ways."

"You can't make stories on your own."

"Why not? The trail needs stories."

"No. Leave it unspoken."

"How do you think stories got made in the first place?" I asked.

"The ancestors had permission from the spirits to talk."

"And we don't?"

"No, the spirits gave us the stories. When they still talked to us. I think they're mad at us now. Why else would we walk the trail?"

I said, "Sometimes in the night I dream the patterns of my baskets. I think of gathering the river cane and walking to my cabin with the bundle on my back. I think of driving a wedge into the cane and dividing it into four splints. After splitting, I peel the splints. I trim them so they're even. Then scrape the inner surface so it will be shiny as the outer."

"You just can't wait to get to the new territory to make more baskets," a woman said.

"And what do you weave with the fingers of your tongue?" I asked. "No wonder you don't have anything to say."

The woman jumped on me, pounding me like corn in a stone mortar.

"Hey," Maritole said. "Don't fight."

Knobowtee separated us before the soldiers could arrive. His brother and the other men held us apart. Another woman screamed until one of the men held his hand over her mouth.

But the fight didn't stop me. I talked all that day as we walked.

"You know the rim around the top of the baskets—the hickory withe. That's the edge of hills that used to surround us. I'll still rim my baskets with the hills in the new territory."

"What if there are no hills there?" Maritole asked.

"Then the rims will be clouds so my baskets will have new stories to tell."

KNOBOWTEE

What was I thinking? No, I was remembering. My father once burned out a log, chopping at it, to make a canoe. His head shaved. One braid in back with wampum and feathers, beads and stained deer hairs tied to it. On this cold night we shivered in the frigid air. I remembered my father rowing. I remembered our words. Our voices and the meaning of our stories. The feeling of wholeness that held back the cold. To heat me. To be my fire. To be my means to survive the night. Voices interacting. The sound with the thought behind them, just like Maritole's father said. Connecting with others. That was the spark that made the fire.

It wasn't the words, just the words. But rather the heart that went into the words in the warmth of the head, then passed through the mouth, which the Great Spirit had made pliable enough to talk.

QUATY LEWIS

"How can we still be in Illinois?" I chewed the edge of my blanket as we walked. "Ain't nothing more than a finger width across," I said, looking at the trail on the soldiers' map.

"Tell me more about the baskets," Luthy said when we camped again that night. Sometimes Mark sucked on Ephum's fist as they listened. I told Luthy the wetness would chap his hands worse.

Even Maritole looked like she wanted to hear more from the woman who had been irritating when she talked. As the sun went down, I looked back and saw the hills we'd started from that morning. The people were suspended above the earth. I'd always suspicioned it. We would never get to the new territory but were stuck forever with our legs walking below us. Not one comfort carried with us.

THE BASKET MAKER

The woman who'd been in the fight with me picked at the dried blood on her collar. Drawing back her mouth to see below her chin.

"It was all a process," I said, "staining the river cane splints with bloodroot, pokeberry, boiled black walnut root. Weaving patterns I copied from ripples in a river. Or deer hooves in the field. Or hatchet marks on a log canoe."

"Maybe stories got started by watching the late afternoon sun on the river—" Quaty interrupted.

"The baskets speak like the river," Luthy agreed.

I frowned at their interruptions.

"Cherokee baskets don't mean nothing," Anna Sco-so-tah said.

yompa. Maritole chewed a piece of dried meat and looked at Anna.

"You women have to have some way of carrying things other than your hands," one man said and the others laughed. "You have to have something to sell to the traders for that calico to make your dresses."

"Not much of our calico dresses left."

"You women have to have talk," another man said, "so you make a story. You have to have something to carry yourself in. What are we without something to say?"

I saw they'd lost their interest in my story. I sat with them under the tarps and handmade tents with the wind riffling them. It was so cold we could hardly talk. We blew on our hands, sat on them. We were so cold we couldn't be still. I heard the coughing. I heard the wheezing lungs, which fought the frigid air we had to let in.

KNOBOWTEE

My father had paddled the log canoe. I remembered the sun and shade passing across my face. It was something like the flickering fire I could imagine to keep me warm. What had my father said? What story had he told? My father was dead. The Cherokee land gone. But I had memories of my father. Could Maritole say that about me? Women could feel hurt, too. I saw that. If I died that night, what had I given Maritole? I reached out to my father in the night.

A man's basket was his log canoe.

The thought of it held the times I remembered.

THE BASKET MAKER

"We worked with the baskets we traded to the white men for calico and the goods we wanted. We worked to get what the white man wanted," I continued my story. "Lids and handles.

Design and shape. It was a long process. I remember eating acorn butter on corn bread as we talked."

"Chestnut bread was better," Quaty Lewis said.

"The traders said the *cheerakes* didn't have good baskets," Anna Sco-so-tah told us.

"Yes, they liked our baskets," Quaty disagreed. "They just couldn't say our Cherokee name."

KNOBOWTEE

I listened to the women and covered my face with a matted pile of dead weeds I'd pulled from the underbrush. It seemed warmer if my face was covered. It seemed warmer if I remembered instead of thought.

During the fish-kill, the women had pounded chestnuts and scattered them in the still place in the river. This made the fish dizzy, and they floated to the surface. The women gathered them up in their fish baskets. I remembered holding a basket beside my mother as she called the fish between her hands.

I heard Reverend Bushyhead talking to someone. "Yes," I heard him say. "Even the angels need blankets tonight."

THE BASKET MAKER

"Even the angels need baskets tonight," I thought Reverend Bushyhead said.

"Trade baskets.

"Market baskets.

"Pumpkin baskets.

"Potato baskets.

"Hominy baskets.

"Peas-and-beans baskets.

"Corn baskets.

"Game baskets."

"ß," Quaty interrupted. *"Shut up!"*

"—Trinket baskets," I kept on.

"Trunk baskets.

"Hulling baskets.

"Winnowing baskets.

"Fanning baskets.
"Sifting baskets.
"Storage baskets.
"Carrying baskets.
"Shallow baskets.
"Flaring-mouth baskets.
"Sunday collection baskets."

MARITOLE'S FATHER

Even the spirit beings Bushyhead called angels needed to understand stories. If they'd never had their feet in the earth, they needed to know that men were woven from the land. Hollow as a basket, with a hollowness that pulled things into it. Because its purpose was to hold things, like the stomach, I thought, feeling my hunger. But how much more like a basket were our stories? They held our fear and hurt and resentment and anger. They gave us a place to order our disorder, a direction for our directionlessness.

They gave us a place to argue with ourselves. Men felt a need to fight sometimes. Even women. Not because soldiers took our land, but because they took the order that couldn't be seen. They opened us up to the old disorder, and we would have to build the world again—and that took so much time and energy. They were unweaving the weaving that we had taken generations to complete.

And what was wrong with that?

What if we were hollow like our baskets? Like our stories? Nothing remained empty. There were too many things running around with nowhere to rest.

Maybe that was the Great Spirit's rule. Didn't he allow things to happen, though he didn't always cause them? We could weave for only so long and then had to suffer unweaving. To know that was to know an old truth: Our hollowness drew hollowness to itself, so the shift to creation would begin again.

That was the horror of the trail—we saw beyond our cornfields and cabins and villages into the west, where the sun disappeared. And worse, we knew the black space inside our heads was only a copy of the nothingness itself. And because of the hollowness, we were meant to hold things, and would always hold things, as long as there was something to hold.

MARITOLE

I wondered what Knobowtee was thinking as he listened to my father and the basket maker. Quaty Lewis took her elbows out of her mouth, and Luthy came down from her post. Even some of the soldiers listened. Yes, maybe the Great Spirit had created us out of his own hollowness. We could understand the emptiness that caused him to create us, more than the spirit beings or angels. They did not belong to the earth, which the Great Spirit must sorrow over as he watched us march. We knew his loneliness and despair. We had a place the angels and spirit beings could not fill. It was our job to be companions to the Great Spirit. They could only help us. That was their job. Though they probably muttered to themselves, wondering why the Great Spirit would want anything like us.

Yes, we had to grace the nothingness, and in that we would know the Great Spirit and the nature of our own being.

All our weaving brought the unweaving. We walked as if falling into the black space we moved toward while living, though now, on the trail, at a slower pace.

REVEREND BUSHYHEAD

Somewhere in the dark, I held a small Christmas service. I offered prayer to the four directions. The red of the east, the blue of the north, the black of the west, and the white of the south. I thought of their meanings. Strength, defeat, death, and peace.

For some reason, I wanted to burn four candles in the open, but the wind would blow them out. There were no candles, anyway. But in the end, it wasn't the powers of the four directions, or the winds, but the strength of our utterances.

"Our hope is in words." I sat in the dark with my wife, who was near herself to giving birth. "We are in this predicament now, but there's a place we won't be. We're on our way to it now."

KNOBOWTEE

Somewhere in the line, the fire carriers kept the embers going from camp to camp each night. Not only the fire that warmed the corn mush, but the spirit fire—the Keetoowah fire.

It was the smoke as well as the fire.

They kept it going through their ceremony. They said they were the Cheerakes, the possessors of the holy fire.

"I see the fire spirits like ashes flying around us," Maritole said. "When I close my eyes I still see them."

"That's how I see them, too," Luthy answered her. "That's where they are."

MARITOLE

Suddenly one day we came to a huge river. The people cried, remembering the Ohio. The soldier told me it was the Mississippi. We would cross it into Missouri. We camped under the cover of brush and watched the ice chunks float by Green's Ferry landing. The earth and sky were ghost white in the frozen air. Sometimes there was a wailing.

"Look at the terrible outcropping of rock upriver."

"A bluff," the soldier called it.

The hills were higher than they had been when we crossed the Ohio, and the trees shorter, allowing the heavy sky to push down on us.

Many more of us died waiting for the ice to pass. Knobowtee and the men sat spitting into the fire.

"That bluff is where the earth steps up to the sky world," Anna Sco-so-tah said.

I felt my fear of the river grow.

"How can we cross that water?" I cried in panic to Tanner one evening. "We'll die! We'll drown like the others." Mark and Ephum heard me and they cried, too.

My father didn't say anything. His hair had grayed, and his eyes were dull and hollow in his head.

Luthy held her boys. "We'll make it the rest of the way."

"Look at it," Quaty Lewis said. "It's a spirit river."

I watched the ice pass for a few more days. Then one morning I woke with the taste of peaches in my mouth. I heard the soldiers preparing to cross the river. We had always been toward the front of the line. We would be among the first ones to cross. My heart pounded wildly. I held something in my hands, but always, always, I found they were empty.

The bear camped before me as usual. I tried to push him away, but he did not move. I felt the stirring of his breath in the cold morning. "Old bear," I cried to him, "today we cross the river." I patted his hide. "Move over. I go, even if it's to the afterlife with Mother and the baby."

The boys fretted as we waited for the raft that would take us across the river. They cried frantically when the soldiers herded us toward the landing. I felt a tightness in my chest. My arms hurt. Surely the land and the trail we walked would fold under the earth with the sun. I heard the trees mourning for us. "We go," I told the boys. They would not hold still. "Don't run," I told them again. Above us the clouds wore my grandmother's bone-carved hairpin. "Grandmother," I called. She smiled. Her face was now gray and lovely above the wind that snarled up river. I saw the spirits eating from my feather-edged dishes. I heard them in the wind. They put down their knives and forks. They came and held the sides of the tossing raft as we stepped onto it, some of us falling, others crying out. The spirits wore bright tunics and turbans, and I couldn't see beyond them as we crossed the river. They held the raft steady as it jerked between large pieces of ice. I spooned more corn bread to them, more squirrel meat and peach cobbler. I had cooked it just this morning in my dream. "Hold on. Hold on," I heard them say as we crossed the river, their ghost voices laughing to the freezing wind.

Missouri

JANUARY, 1839

MARITOLE

ᏍᎩ.

Just north of Cape Girardeau, Missouri, we sat near the fire as though it could thaw out our bones. Quaty Lewis. Anna Scoso-tah. Mrs. Young Turkey. Kee-un-e-ca. Since Hopkinsville, Kentucky, some of us had shoes, which made blisters on our feet. I decided to wear the shoes anyway because the rocks hurt worse than the shoes. One man's hands bled between his fingers. Someone couldn't stop coughing.

Again on Sunday Reverend Bushyhead preached. Would we come to the edge of the earth? No, I thought. I felt I kept walking, but there was no end. I felt I walked because I hadn't died when the others had.

ᏍᎩ.

We listened to the soldiers get drunk at night. They celebrated their new year with cold and discord. One soldier, Private Raburt, who had joined the march somewhere in Tennessee, drank and gambled with the Cherokee men and won whatever they had. Even their blankets. Then he'd sell them to someone else. Sometimes we heard the other soldiers argue with him about it.

We celebrated our new year with the Keetoowah fire in the fall. We lit our small campfires from a larger fire. One of our leaders spoke of our legend of the phoenix, who rose from the ashes like we would in the new land. I remembered the new soil spread over the square ground. The sound of the large fire. Then we burned cedar, and a ᏗᏓᏅᎥᎩ prayed.

REVEREND BUSHYHEAD

Soon after my sermon, I was called to my sister's side in a makeshift tent stained with soot. She was dying as my wife went into labor. Some women sat with Mrs. Bushyhead in a small copse of trees beside the tent. Other women sat with me as Nancy called for her dead husband, John Walker. *Murdered.* I could see the word on her lips. My brother-in-law had been killed by James Foreman, one of John Ross's men. Nancy had never spoken of it, but now in her delirium, she called it out. If you crossed Ross, you feared for your life.

I could hear the turmoil of the Cherokee people in Nancy's mumblings. The dark nights when men had been killed for signing agreements with the government to move west. But that was years before the present turbulence of the final removal. Still, there were nights when boundaries ceased between what was known and unknown, when the nightgoers walked among us. There were nights I felt nothing before me. I wanted to put an arrowhead under Nancy's head to cut her delirium to pieces, but I belonged to faith. I had to hold on to certainty as though it was there.

I held my sister. "ᎤᏩᏯ," I whispered her secret name under my breath. I listened to the moans of both her and my wife. As Nancy died, my second daughter, Elizah Missouri Bushyhead, was born January 3, 1839, in a clump of trees.

LUTHY

Look at Maritole sitting with the widow Teehee and the older women. All Teehee talks about is Selu, the woman who gave us corn. She doesn't care that Maritole walks with the soldier. Maritole doesn't sit with anyone her age. She wants to be with women like her mother, who would ignore what she does. Let Maritole talk to the younger women. Let her sit with us.

MARITOLE

On the trail again I felt the soldier's arm hold me up when my legs folded under me. I had been strong. I could run almost as fast as Knobowtee.

I told the soldier more of our language as we walked. "ᏣᎷᎬ, the screech owl. ᎫᏍᎩ, the black snake. ᎣᎲᏟᏁᏯ ᎠᏘᏘᎿ, the water spider."

"The smallest thing has the largest name?" Williams asked.

I felt him beside me on the trail as I walked. I felt his chest against me in the dark. His blanket over me. A white soldier. I held to his collar with my fist. I held my hand to his cheek and felt the scratch of his whiskers with my hand. I felt his hands rubbing the ache in my legs. Even Knobowtee hadn't been life to me as this soldier was. I nearly slept, but he moved and I woke. He put his hand to my face. I cried for the cold I felt. I cried for the people who had no comfort on the trail to the new territory west of the Mississippi. I cried for my baby wandering somewhere in the next world. No, my mother had her. She wasn't alone, whatever world she was in. I wondered what her voice would sound like in the afterworld. Maybe I had heard it already.

I cried for the blood from the split feet I saw in the snow. I cried for each suffering body that walked through the cold. The soldier felt the tears running across my face with his hands. In the dark he kissed them with his mouth. He lifted my head to him in the dark. He kissed my mouth. I was hollow as the log where my grandmother had ground her cornmeal. Yet his love was comforting. He touched my skin inside my shirt. He felt my legs. His ankles were over my feet. One of his hands held my braids tight. I felt stretched like a rabbit ready to be skinned. He pushed away the pain inside my head. I let him touch me. Let him enter. I gave him my life in the dark. I let him feel my hurt. My wounds inside. I would always be cut in two. Part of me in North Carolina. Part of me in the new land. I held open my wounds for him to soothe.

The next day as I watched Sergeant Williams fixing the broken axle of a wagon, Quaty Lewis walked up behind me. "Is he your husband?" she asked bitterly.

"I lost my husband on the trail."

"ᏎᎤᎦᏇ," she spit. "You agree with the Georgia Cherokee who gave away our land. You deserve the trail."

Was Knobowtee a husband to me? Could I talk to him? Did I hear his voice in my ear? Did I feel his strength in my body?

ᎡᏏᏍᏬᎢ, I heard Quaty try to be a holy man saying ᎱᏓᏓᎩᎩ, but she was only copying.

"You're one of us, Quaty," I snapped. "Your father may have come from Tennessee, but he was a trader in Georgia."

"That's what's wrong with doing something wrong." My father startled me as we stood by the fire. "—even something little at first. It makes way for other wrongs, bigger ones, later on. What if the wrongs kept coming and couldn't be stopped? Nothing we do is done alone. Everything is connected."

"I know," I answered turning from the fire, my face burning from the heat, my back cold in the wind. The smoke stinging my eyes until I put my hands to my face. "But you're not saying how not to do something wrong."

We crossed a stream and stopped to build a fire to warm our hands and dry our feet. It was the Whitewater River. Or Castor River or Cape Creek. I looked at the map. We'd been on the trail nearly four months. Since we left North Carolina our trail had been northwest through Tennessee and Kentucky and Illinois. Now in the southern part of Missouri, we still walked northwest. Some of the men questioned the way we walked. In places the trail narrowed to horse paths and crude wagon ruts between settlements.

"The trail's longer than it should be." Tanner looked at the map. "Look how far north we've come."

"Maybe there's a swamp. Maybe the hills are steep."

"We'll stay north with the trail marked on the map," my father said. "Somewhere we'll turn south to Arkansas into Indian Territory."

"Jackson, Missouri." Knobowtee read a sign on a stage stop and shook his head.

"Andrew's been here, too," O-ga-na-ya spat. "The Chicken Snake."

The men slaughtered a horse when rations were low. They divided it for the women to cook over several fires. The saliva in my jaw made a sharp pain. The pack dogs snarled for bones. Behind me I saw the long trail of cooking fires of my people. How many would one thin horse feed? Were there other animals to eat?

Each day we agonized along a few miles to the land we didn't know. There we would start over with nothing. Would we plow the fields with our fingers? Plant corn with our toes? Cut down trees for cabins with our hands? Would Jesus rain seedcorn on us?

WAR CLUB

Yop. Our strength is in horses. I chewed.

MARITOLE

"I would put you on this horse with me, but it would make your people hate you," Sergeant Williams told me.

"More than they already do?" I asked.

Someone threw a rock and hit my head as I talked to the soldier. I fell on the trail and passed into blackness. When I came to, Williams sat beside me.

"I would do anything for you."

"Take me back to my land," I said. "Get that white man and woman out of my cabin. Get my mother and baby back for me. My animals."

He wiped the dried blood from my head with his kerchief.

"Go back and get our corn out of the storage house so we'll have something to plant. Give us back what is ours. Open your white heart and become Indian. Walk as one of us along the trail like Reverend Mackenzie. Or like Reverend Worcester, who crossed on an earlier trail. The Cherokee have been moving west for years."

"Why do you always ask what I can't give?" He looked away again, and Quaty said something to me.

"What'd she say?" he asked.

"You don't want to know," I answered Williams.

In the dark we sang our hymns. Somewhere a cry went up. I saw a shooting star fall over us, and Williams disappeared into the dark.

Sometimes I woke thinking the baby sucked at my nipples. Sometimes I ached to feel the cabin around me, the dark walls chinked with clay. I wanted to hear the cords of my bed creak. I wanted to hear the wind in the corn tassels. But we were left out of this country. We'd been pushed to the margin. Now we would find out how to build nothing. Plow nothing. But always, always in my bitterness, I thought of the Great Spirit, who stood above me. He knew the steps we took.

"You shame me," Knobowtee interrupted.

I opened my eyes. It was my husband. Just as I thought. In the Great Spirit's voice, I heard my husband's. And rightly so. But anger flashed across me. "What have you been to me?" I asked, without thought for his feelings. "Haven't you ignored me since we started on this trail? Haven't you been the one who hurt me? I try to understand. But you have left me alone! Don't tell me anything!"

Knobowtee tried to rip the man's coat from me.

"You're still wearing the clothes of our dead." He jerked the coat, and my body jumped toward him.

"Better than dying." I pulled back and screamed at him. "You have someone's musket. How can you be angry about my clothes?"

"You aren't fit to wear them." He shoved me down to rip the coat from me, but saw the trousers on my legs. He was trying to grab them off me, too, when Williams took Knobowtee with his hands and ordered him away from me. Knobowtee pounded Williams. Williams hit back. I screamed at them to stop fighting, and a principal soldier shot his gun in the air. Luthy begged Tanner not to fight. Knobowtee had Williams around the neck. The Cherokee men, who often spoke in whispers, roared. Other soldiers and government teamsters arrived and pulled Knobowtee and Williams apart. A woman spit at me. Knobowtee spit at me. I saw hatred in his face as I crawled to the shelter of the tarp.

Everyone moved away from me except Mrs. Young Turkey.

The next day my father told me to get behind him. I didn't even look for Knobowtee or Williams. I walked on the road, stumbling as I went. My legs were always weak now. I followed my father on the road as if it were a field that had been furrowed. The wagons hopped like frogs. I hardly knew I was walking. I saw only my father's back and followed him as though he were the whole world.

Williams rode up and handed the coat back to me. Luthy gasped. "Put it on," he said.

My father didn't say anything.

The soldier who rode beside Williams led him away from me.

MARITOLE'S FATHER

I knew Sergeant Williams faced a hearing. He probably would be leaving the trail.

"I've watched you walk when it was all you could do." Sergeant Williams knelt beside me. "I've seen you Cherokee lift your feet even when it was your last step. What's happening is not lawful. It was shoved through government. I wish there was something I could do."

Williams turned to Knobowtee. "Take care of your wife."

"You take care of her."

"I can't."

"You already took her. Now you tell me I can have her back?"

"Knobowtee," I warned.

"I'm tired of losing," Knobowtee snapped.

Williams tried to stand, but Knobowtee pushed him down. Tanner and another Cherokee held Knobowtee while Williams walked away.

MARITOLE

Later that day, Sergeant Williams was relieved of his duties as easily as if he were an Indian removed from the land. I couldn't watch him leave so I buried my face in Tanner's blanket. Tanner told me Williams looked back as he was taken away. Maybe they were sending him to another place in the army. Maybe he was going to jail.

"Why?" I argued with Tanner. "Why was it wrong?"

"You ought to know why, Maritole," he said.

I walked in shame in front of the others. In the shame of my people, I brought more shame. The leaves had ripped away from the trees. The trunks and branches were bare. The birds had nowhere to nest.

KNOBOWTEE'S MOTHER

Longer than long ago, a Cherokee man and woman left their cabin for a trip to town. For four days and four nights they traveled until they came to the town. They bought what they needed at the general store, then the woman became angry when she saw the man skip away to gamble. She picked up the man's stone ax and hit him on the head. Then she dragged him back to their cabin in the woods. They didn't go to town again.

TANNER

The soldiers argued with a teamster hired to watch the march. I held Luthy and the boys against me in the dark. Now several men from the two groups argued. Once I thought I heard Knobowtee's name. Like the Cherokee, not all white men agreed with one another.

MARITOLE

The land sounded different here, but the trees still spoke. There was one leaf hitting the sapling, clicking. I listened. It sounded like a soldier's bayonet hitting his saddle as we walked. It sounded like the women weaving their river cane baskets. I closed my eyes with the memory. My eyes swollen nearly shut from crying. The white traders had bought as many baskets sometimes as they did deerskins.

The leaf kept clicking in the cold wind. I watched it again. It was telling the story of our march. I would have the tongue of a leaf. I would tell our story, I thought.

KNOBOWTEE

"They're even here," I grumbled. I saw the farms across Missouri. "Cape Girardeau, Jackson, Fredricktown, Farmington, Caldonia, Massey's Iron Works, Waynesville, Springfield." I followed O-ga-na-ya's finger on the government map. "Look there—after Waynesville we'll be dropping south. The direction of warmth."

"How far do we have to move to be safe from them?" O-ga-na-ya asked.

The white men had seeped into the land like water. Everywhere the Cherokee walked, it was soggy with them.

I could see the trails of their smoke through the woods. Up there into the air. Where the trail of the Cherokee was going. Their cabins and fields. This far west.

A baby was given away to a passing farmer at one camp. In another place, I passed two children hiding in the bushes. Maybe they'd been put there by their parents who couldn't care for them. Or relatives after their parents died. Let some farmer pick them up. The Cherokee would be scattered everywhere.

Soon the white man would spread everywhere. Probably already had. I could feel the power of the country. The United States government had called itself mighty. It had a Declaration of Independence. A Bill of Rights. A Constitution. A president. A Congress. A creed of Manifest Destiny. The God of their Fathers had heard their words. He had set spiritual boundaries over their country that couldn't be seen. A nation had been established. Hadn't the Cherokee felt it? Wasn't that why they were quick to farm, to form new government?

"This damned country is going to work." I could feel the weakness in my knees when we talked.

"They don't understand what they're doing, Knobowtee," Maritole's father said to me, "how they set principles into being when they act."

"Their injustice to us will come back to haunt them," O-ga-na-ya said.

"They'll have to answer for their deeds."

"Maybe they'll realize," Tanner said.

"Maybe the time will come when we get our farms back."

"Never," Maritole said. She had fallen behind the wagon where she walked and I hadn't noticed. She looked pale as she spoke to me. Like she was disappearing.

WAH-KE-CHA

Yop. The damned farmers take our moneys. But one named Wilson in Missouri where we camp now opened his log barn. Let us sleep in the hayloft and stalls. He brought his dog that sang *yaa yaahhhh yahhh*. Dog said *wooooo woooooo woooah* he said. We laugh at dog who talk. Except Anna Sco-so-tah cry.

"My neighbor," she say. "My old neighbor, Kinchow, dead."

Maybe she wanted to forget him, but he pushed back into her head. Yop. That's what we do to walk.

MARITOLE

Fredricktown, Missouri. Fodder for the horses, mules, and oxen. Flour and salt pork for us. No more horse meat. I carried a weight on my chest like the anvil in the blacksmith's shop in North Carolina, where I had watched the fierce flames and felt the heat. Now I knew that cold burned like heat. I held my tiredness against my chest and rode in the wagon across the St. Francis River.

Luthy was holding the boys and crying when I woke. "You don't look like yourself," she said.

The doctor tended the sick when we made camp. He gave me something to chew. Quaty interpreted for me. She called me lovesick.

ᎿᏆᎨᏏ ᎠᏆᏤ ᏬᏆᎵ
ᏇᏋ ᏇᏋ

She sang facing east, the holy direction. She sang four times and blew her breath upon a comb she held.

"Stop it," I cried, but she kept singing.

DCSⱭꝶꙆ	to comb one
AꝚꙆꝞꙆ	to make one
ꙄZУꙙꙆ	to sing one

(I am combing my hair and singing to become more than I am as I sing.)

I turned my face from the doctor. Quaty made fun of me being in love with a soldier. The song was to make me better looking so another white soldier would love me. I put my hands to my face. Luthy tried to quiet Quaty, but she kept hounding me.

"You had a white husband who stayed on your farm when the soldiers took you," I blurted. "Everyone knows it."

Luthy put her hand to her mouth. Quaty looked stunned.

Tanner lifted me and carried me to the sick wagon. I sat next to a man who looked yellow. His body was stiff, his eyes crusted. He wanted to breathe, but the breath couldn't go into him. I saw splinters in his fingers where he tried to hold the side of the wagon to keep from bumping. He was scared of the death that waited for him. I held his arm and tried to remember one of my father's songs for him. "You'll be in a land where you forget the trail," I told him.

The soldiers rode away for supplies. Later that day they handed out the rations. Someone cooked our supper. It was Luthy or Tanner. Or Mrs. Young Turkey. Or the birds. Or rabbits. Or the spirits.

Someone cooked breakfast and a meal to take with us the next day. We moved on. I cried for the soldier as I bumped in the wagon. Everything was like a fog in the North Carolina hills, gone by the time the sun climbed to its attic.

WAR CLUB

"Hey, soldiers. Think of this. The debit of stolen land in your ledger book."

MARITOLE

I shivered in the night. The heaviness on my chest worsened. The bear, I thought. I heard him thunder in the night. The whole sky flushed with lightness. There was a cloud formation I hadn't seen. The land swelled up to it. We had walked across a huge land. It had entered us. Along with the cornfields we left. I was full of trees. Full of corn. Full of walking. My feet churned inside me at night as if they entered my body when I slept. I thought of Alotohee. I felt the blacksmith pounding. The bear licking my face. I couldn't live without the soldier. I was going to sink into the rolling fields of Missouri. My ears heard the ancestors singing their song. Maybe it was just the creak of the wagon wheels and the voices around me. I felt the wagon jarring under me. It was rolling over trees. The trees in Alotohee took root in me.

THE STORY OF THE BEAR

A long time ago the Cherokee forgot we were a tribe. We thought only of ourselves apart from the others. Without any connections. Our hair grew long on our bodies. We crawled on our hands and knees. We forgot we had a language. We forgot how to speak. That's how the bear was formed. From a part of ourselves when we were in trouble. All we had was fur and meat to give.

KNOBOWTEE

Tanner called me again to be with Maritole. She was out of her head. I thought she would die as I walked beside the wagon. Sometimes I wanted a new wife anyway. She hadn't been faithful. I felt her body shiver when we stopped for a rest. She was a scarecrow in the wind as I held her head in my lap in the wagon. Her teeth chattered like dried cornstalks on an autumn day. The conjurers chanted. The holy men.

Maritole's father cried as the walking started again. Tanner put his arm around him and led him like a child.

That night, I sat for hours with Maritole's head in my lap. Then I had to get up and stretch my legs. My mother was dying. Aneh spoke to me without speaking.

Luthy said she'd stay with Maritole while I was gone. The boys curled beside her like two leaves on a cornstalk.

There was nothing I could do for my mother. I stroked my sister's head. The men's voices talked quietly by their makeshift tent.

"That soldier—Private Raburt's drunk. We could stab him. Get 'em back for the ones of us they cut."

"No," I said. "We don't have strength. We can't bring the whole army down on us."

"Wha'd they do to us then? Humiliate us in front of the women."

"Let's just sit here," O-ga-na-ya said.

"Be like the women then."

"Let the soldiers lick us—"

I was on O-ga-na-ya in an instant. Pounding him into the ground. The sound of the fighting brought the drunk soldier to his knees. Sensing he needed to stop something, he struck with his bayonet. I felt the cut across my face. I lifted my arm against the private, knocked his head against a tree. The Cherokee men rallied with me. With hardly a noise we beat Private Raburt until he was unconscious. He died in the night.

A conjurer stopped the bleeding on my face. "Where were the other soldiers?" I asked. "How had the Cherokee gotten away with it?"

My eye was nearly swollen shut in the morning. I heard the Light Horse Guard riding toward the detachment. I crawled under the wagons back to Maritole. She moaned when I touched her face. She rattled like the corn. She was still out of her head. A sob came from my chest. I held her as if she were the farm.

The soldiers made quick work of finding the private. Some old man quivering with fear pointed into the woods where a tarp had been thrown. The dead soldier was under it.

The soldiers asked who beat the private. No one answered.

They searched the men for those who had bruises on our hands. They dragged me from beneath the wagon. They beat me and the others, shot one of the men who tried to run. Then they shackled us and started the march that morning, the stronger ones helping the weaker, pulling them along.

MARITOLE

When I could sit up in the wagon, I looked back and saw our trail through the Missouri hills. Walking. Walking. The line shorter than the ten miles it had been in the beginning. Maybe eight miles now. Maybe less. I saw some stumble and large flying-beings rush to swoop on us. They carried us over the sky. The living ones couldn't see them. There was a war over the walking ones. An animal with little tight clouds on it seemed to lead. Some of the flying-beings didn't want us to go to the animal. They hit us away with large clubs. They flapped their wings at one another. *Hey. What's going on?* I hit back. But they didn't see. Their hands flew like wings of insects. Hit Indians. Half-breeds. Negroes. Say *walk. Hey you, walk!*

There are places the earth draws us away from ourselves. Each of us in our own way. Quaty baking corn bread over a fire. Anna Sco-so-tah conjuring the black-winged flyers. The basket maker weaving her hands as she sleeps. It must be night again. The soldiers sleep against the tree.

Hey, speak louder here.

Luthy. There's a tree above me. I reach for the branches. My baby—Mother—I could reach them if I wanted.

But my father hasn't come through yet. He might need me. I go back—There's time—

The earth is a brittle husk that can be broken away. Easy—I could step out—If I want—Or go back and walk.

ANNA SCO-SO-TAH

Sometimes I could hear the silence. What happened? I wondered. Where were the voices of the others? Why were they quiet? Leaving me alone to wonder where to go.

I wanted them to talk. I wanted to listen. I felt a grief so deep it was nearly silent. We were the land. The red clay people with mouths that would talk. Sometimes I even thought I could hear the hens cackle on my farm. I looked over my shoulder. If only I could listen hard enough.

LUTHY

Between Fredricktown and Farmington, I thought we were in North Carolina. The hills were steep and the valleys wider. I walked beside the wagon where Maritole rode. My sister-in-law had always done what she wanted. She hadn't been afraid to displease anyone. I always thought first of what others thought. Now Maritole rode without her mother and baby. I watched my boys on a mule, their heads bundled with turbans I'd cut from a blanket. Ephum didn't want his turban to come down so far on his head, but he and Mark had cried too often with earaches.

Each day the men pushed the wagons uphill. Then they walked with ropes behind the wagons trying to hold them back as they went downhill. The roads were rough and wagons broke down. I was afraid we'd come to another river like the Mississippi and the Ohio. I knew there was a Missouri, but we wouldn't have to cross it, Tanner assured me. At rest stops, we stood looking over the cliffs and rock outcroppings into the valleys far below. Sometimes I told Maritole to look, but she only cried. Some of the people also wept, remembering our farms in the hills of North Carolina.

THE WIDOW TEEHEE

Well, get up. We're moving on. You think you walk alone? Let me tell you there are spirit-makers and dead ones walking with you. I died in Tennessee but I still walk. Yop. They didn't leave me there. You can't see the dead, but they come to talk to you. They say the spirits and angels walk. The animals. Get up now. Move on.

KNOBOWTEE

I had the ability to lead, but not the opportunity. That's what they took from me. But I could still lead. I felt it in me. Maybe not in government, but among the men.

I walked in chains with my brother and a few other men. The holy men walked with us, praying. One man fell, and we could no longer carry him between us. We were too weary and the pain of the ankle chains cut into our strength.

The holy men told the soldiers they'd have to remove our chains. We couldn't walk. We had to help the old and sick ones walk. The trail was too steep and uneven. There were caverns where the soldiers were afraid the Indians would hide. At the stops by the spring to drink, they watched us nervously. Everyone was needed.

The private had struck first in the dark anyway.

"The Cherokee are responsible for our own removal," Maritole's father reminded the soldiers of the Light Horse Guard. The Cherokee would make sure our men didn't attack anyone else.

A lieutenant rode away for a while. When he came back, he leaned down and unlocked the ankle chains. The metal ring pulling off my bleeding ankle made me cry out with pain. I sat on the ground quivering.

When I was able to walk I limped to the wagon where Maritole rode. I had heard from Tanner that she was dying. I wanted to tell her to live. She had the desire to walk that I needed. When I found her, her eyes were open to the sky. I touched her face. Her eyes looked at me. She was still living.

THE SOLDIERS

"Wha'd they let 'em go for?"

"It's what the lieutenant said to do."

"Who'd he talk to?"

"I dunno—the captain."

"Them Indians get away with killing one of us—who's safe then?"

"Them damned conjurers'll change into muskets and shoot us in the night."

"Raburt caused a lot of trouble—he came from some other company who couldn't handle him. Maybe someone wanted Raburt dead."

"We need all of us we can get. Them Indians haven't figured out how outnumbered we are."

"Maybe they did it themselves."

"Who?"

"The lieutenant—or someone else. And it just looked like the Indians did it."

"Naw. It was the Indians."

"They didn't have strength to walk in chains."

"We should have tried 'em on the trail— Shot 'em at dawn. It ain't right. This's the army."

"But this is their march. The government contracted with their chief so they could oversee their own removal. Let it go."

"Maybe we'll get 'em later."

"Maybe the captain was afraid it'd bring more trouble."

"I'm watching my tail from now on."

TANNER

Didn't the grandfathers say a shadow would come into our land? Didn't we remember the stories, then push them away?

"But we didn't know we were naked until the white man showed us," Reverend Bushyhead said. "We didn't know we were nothing without our farms. Our council fires." Bushyhead had come to see about Maritole, but she turned away from him as he spoke.

"But their nakedness showed, too," I said. They just couldn't see it yet. Not until their stolen farms were taken.

The grandfathers didn't tell us that the shadow was as hard as field rocks when our plows stumped them. It was not a darkness we could pass through like the night.

It came with the white man dragging their ships across the ocean. *"Mine,"* they say. They wanted to find new because the old was dark. They wanted to leave their dark. They came and took our new. Soon they had it dark again. But some of the men and Bushyhead say the darkness was here before they came.

Yes, the Great Spirit allowed the white man to show us what we were. We didn't have in us what the Great Spirit was. We had to know. His world was over ours. A world of better-than-we-were, and we couldn't get there without the Great Spirit making the road for us.

Maybe there were other choices for the afterlife. Some Cherokee didn't believe Christianity. No. They believed the white man was bad and the Indian was good. But that didn't make sense either. We were all full of the darkness we felt. It penetrated every being. Just give it a chance.

The darkness hard as a field rock. If we thought of ourselves more than the Great Spirit and others. If we built our own hard place in our thinking, if we didn't allow the light and the darkness to show us what they were like, the darkness would be a growing rock until it filled the head. "Then a man could die while he still walked on his feet," Luthy said as we talked. "He could die before the breath stopped in him."

We walked now to another place far from North Carolina. The blood of Selu, who gave us corn, also gave us strength to walk. *But, inside it was another blood,* Reverend Bushyhead insisted. And it gave us the likeness of a light we could have in our lives. The story of Jesus that could hardly be understood—That didn't seem to make sense. We had to face the darkness and know a Savior had been made darkness on the cross so he could take the darkness with him into death. He built a fence on the edge of the field so darkness couldn't get in and fill us again.

We only had to believe.

KNOBOWTEE

Caldonia, Missouri. The Meramec River. Then down a steep hill. Across the Little Piney Creek. Then up again through the heavy woods.

MARITOLE

In the cold I heard someone snore like a bear's growl. Maybe Kee-un-e-ca killed a field mouse, eating it with her beak. Or maybe it was someone dying in the wagon. Sometimes death-breathing and snoring sounded the same.

I could see the bear through the snow. Sometimes I could see my dreams before I was asleep. Often I saw a booger mask in the dark of my head, or spirits I hadn't seen before. *Go on, bear,* I said and clapped my hands.

How could anyone sleep? It was so cold. My hand twitched and pain leapt through my fingers now and then. It was the bear gnawing my bones again.

Go on, I said. Not with words. But deep inside myself where the bear walked. I felt my legs jump with exhaustion. I made a thought-song. It was more than words. It was feeling woven with a command. It was the spark of firelight in the dark.

The bear had once been a person. But he was not conscious of the consciousness he was given. His darkness was greed and self-centeredness. It was part of myself, too. It was in all of us. It was part of the human being. Why else did we march? No one was free of the bear.

O-ga-na-ya came by and threw some twigs on the fire. It blazed for a moment. I could feel its heat inside my head. But then it went out and the smoke made me cough.

I sang my thought-song, like I'd heard my father sing, where no one could hear. It was more than words. It was the intent behind the words that counted. That's where the power was. I wanted to stay with that power. I wanted my own life, away from Knobowtee. I wanted the soldier, but I knew I wouldn't see him again.

I tried to make myself sleep. I wanted to leave the trail and disappear. But my thoughts tossed like the sick ones moaning in the wagon. I bumped against some old man or woman and pulled away. I didn't want to touch whoever it was wrapped in the blanket. A head poked out. It was Kee-un-e-ca. That crazy old woman who thought she was an owl.

I wasn't going to go crazy to forget the trail. No, I thought. I would get up in the morning and walk. For one more day. Walk. I remembered my mother, my grandmother and baby. I laughed inside myself. I saw one of the spirits dancing beside the trail. I didn't care if I sank into the land. Even if I became like one of the dead ones in the wagon with my eyes frozen to the stars. The Great Spirit was just. He was to be honored. I had heard the stories. I thought of Nancy Ward. I would not ignore them and fall into darkness. I didn't care how much it looked like I would, how much it looked like the stories didn't matter. I trusted in those stories. They would hold when I couldn't.

"I'm sorry for what I said about your husband taking your farm," I told Quaty. She poked Kee-un-e-ca in the wagon to see if she was still alive.

"I saw him decide," Quaty answered quickly. "Before he knew what he was going to do, I knew. He'd turn in the night and I'd feel the bed wet from his sweat."

"It was hot, Quaty. We all sweated."

"His sweat was cold."

I felt weak from talking and started back to the wagon.

"He couldn't help it," she said as I walked away.

"Yes, he could," I said to myself, and O-ga-na-ya looked at me.

I thought of the white people married to Cherokee who stayed behind on their land. I wondered what Quaty's husband felt when he slept at night. Maybe nothing. Maybe sometimes he remembered he had abandoned her. He had taken her land and let her go alone on the trail. Maybe he sweated sometimes until the bed froze.

KNOBOWTEE

Roubidoux Creek. Up a hill. Down a hill. From the next ridge I looked into the valley. Waynesville was a stage stop on the side of a hill in a valley surrounded by hills. It would make an advantageous fort for the soldiers. How far their outposts had come.

TANNER

Knobowtee was right. The white men were everywhere. How much farther did the country go? We crossed the Gasconade River. I helped the boys while Luthy held on to the ragged edge of my tunic. How much was there I didn't know?

REVEREND BUSHYHEAD

"But as for me, my feet were almost gone—Psalm 73:2." I looked up from the Bible and smiled. How often my life joined up with the scriptures.

When I thought of the burdens of the people in my regiment, or when I thought of Nancy, my sister who had died, I watched the land as the Cherokee crossed southern Missouri. After the hills and valleys we passed through earlier, the land seemed to be without definition. A gently rolling place that had no substance. Yet each step I took was something solid in the nothingness I felt. If I counted it solid.

I saw a wire fence.

I saw a rock outcropping along a creek.

An opossum.

A row of short trees, maybe an orchard.

A church. Yes, there it was.

A road off somewhere.

The land was quiet. Maybe shy or asleep. Look at the scrub trees and stalks that would be alive in the spring.

I saw a stone shed or springhouse.

A farmer's large pile of wood.

"He must have been gone for the winter," I heard someone say.

"Or when the farmer used one log, the little people replaced it with two," Quaty Lewis grunted.

There were big gray-and-white clouds like rocks in the sky. Why did they look so ugly?

I saw Knobowtee's sister. Her silence seemed to multiply like the loaves and fishes in the Bible. Like the deer, rabbit, quail, fish, and honey story of Anna's old neighbor. Yes, I nodded to myself. I would not be one of those ministers who tried to rid the Cherokee of their stories. It would take everything we could muster to start again.

KNOBOWTEE

There was a voice somewhere. With all the voices on the trail. Ancestors. Conjurers. People. Even the voices of the animals and the land. I was almost sure I heard a voice. *You brought us through fire and through the water*—Maybe it was Bushyhead preaching in his sleep. It sounded like one of the Psalms. Maybe it was a voice beyond hope. A certainty I could hear in the ministers' voices. It woke me in the night. There was something that made sense. I just couldn't see it. But look at the churches in the towns we passed. It was their God. Those people who made the Cherokee walk. It was men like Schermerhorn. Chief Justice Marshall. Though Marshall tried to be just. Andrew Jackson himself probably sat in church Sunday morning near the comfort of a woodstove. A hearth fire and supper waiting in his house. How could I understand? It churned in my head like Maritole's dasher stick in the milk. How could God allow men to walk a trail? Should I just swallow my pride and say their God was my God? How my brother would laugh.

My mother said we should have joined Tecumseh when he wanted the tribes to fight the U.S. government.

O-ga-na-ya agreed.

No, I thought.

"Your father wanted to fight, Knobowtee."

"No," I told her. It was no use. I know it now.

LACEY WOODARD

I unbraided my hair and covered a small girl with it to keep her from shivering. "You are a small animal," I said. "Feel your fur." I took the child's hand and rubbed it over my hair. "You are warm under your fur, little rabbit."

MARITOLE

I sat under the blanket near Lacey during the rest stop and looked through a hole at my feet. I felt the bruise on my ankle. I saw my swollen legs. I rocked my arms as if I held the baby.

O-GA-NA-YA

"Even in the shadows of the new country there is light. Not the light it could have shined with, no, but a remnant that will carry it awhile." Knobowtee talked with me, but his eyes were on Maritole as she rocked under her blanket. Knobowtee had as much hurt as she did, I thought. Maybe more.

"Remember when all we had to do was shoo the flies on the step of our cabin?" Knobowtee got up and limped away on his stiff legs.

I saw Maritole watching her husband, and I must have frowned at her.

"I want to feel the anger you make me feel," she said to me. "It makes me get up and walk." She held out her arm to me.

I pulled her up.

REVEREND BUSHYHEAD

"*Hyaaa!*" the Light Horse Guard yelled at the horses and oxen.

"*Hyaaa!*" They beat a mule that stumbled.

The women cried.

The men tensed but what could they do?

"What the shit?" the soldiers said looking into a wagon.

"A bell? Some boards?"

"They're roof beams and the bell from our church," I told the soldiers with authority. "We bring something of our past."

The soldiers rode carelessly around me, sometimes coming close enough that I stepped backward, off balance. Involuntarily.

"Leave the boards alone," I repeated. "The ox will move. Give it time." Some of the Cherokee men took the ox by his bridle and walked him.

"Who told them they could bring that shit?" a soldier repeated.

I stood my ground. "The bell and roof beams go with us."

WAR CLUB

"What'll we do now?" I asked.

"Why don't we walk?" I answered myself.

"Yes, that's what we'll do," I joined.

"Walk," I said.

"Walk," I repeated our conversation.

"Walk," I repeated once more.

"Walk," I said to myself again.

VOICES AS THEY WALKED

The Light Horse Guards were always trying to list us. They were always counting us. Don't tell them our names, we say. Hide under the tarp. Under the wagon. Move back, there behind them.

A LIGHT HORSE GUARD

U SI TA NEE. 15 fullbloods. 5 farmers. 3 farms. 6 readers of
Cherokee. 1 weaver. 3 spinners.

ROBIN LOWER JOY. 6 fullbloods. 2 farmers. 2 readers of
Cherokee. 1 weaver. 2 spinners.

ARCH SKIT. Two families. 18 fullbloods. 1 quarterblood. 5
farmers. 2 farms. 4 children.

Here the dark lead in my pencil smeared as I recounted and marked over the number of children.

JOHN SATTERFIELD. 1 halfbreed farmer. Intermarried with
the white race.

DANIEL DAVIS. One halfbreed. 9 quarterbloods. 23 slaves.
1 marriage into the white race. 8 readers of English.
0 readers of Cherokee. Owned 2 mills. 5 farms. 6 farmers.

1 mechanic. 2 weavers. 2 spinners. 1 reservee. 10 descendants of reservees.

LEWIS RALSTON. 5 quarterblood Indians. 1 white marriage. Owned 1 ferryboat. 1 farmer. 2 readers of English. 1 weaver. 1 spinner. 6 descendants.

Here my blunt pencil skipped a grease spot on the page.

VOICES AS THEY WALKED

Why didn't they make a roll of our way of life? Sometimes a man reminded us to remember our ways. Sometimes someone encouraged us to walk.

We plant our outer fields when the wild fruit is ripe because the birds are busy eating it. Which is the beginning of May, about the time the traders leave for their English settlements. The people work together. A holy man warns the people to be ready to plant. On a certain day, men whoop at dawn. The new year is moving away, and those who want to eat must work. If someone won't work, he has to pay a fine or leave town. The chiefs work in common with the people. About an hour after sunrise, the men enter the fields. Sometimes the orators cheer us with jests and old stories. They sing wild tunes beating an earthen pot covered with a wet deerskin. All of us move from field to field until the seed is sown.

The corn is planted in straight rows. Five grains are put into one hole and covered with clay like a small hill. In the vacant ground the women plant pumpkin, watermelon, potatoes, mallows, sunflowers, beans, and peas. Everyone works together in our individually owned fields.

Late October is our new fire. Debts are canceled. Grudges forgiven. Offenders pardoned. The unity of the town is restored. Our goods are shared. Distributed among us.

The women make dippers and birds' nests out of gourds. They sell their gourd wares when traders come again.

We still carry water in gourds through the cornfields. Until we left them. *Umph.*

LACEY WOODARD

I walked as if on a white field of clouds, my feet not touching the ground. I was so cold I felt warm. Still I walked beyond anything I could have endured.

Oh ᏢᎾᏣ. Oh mystery. Oh unexplainable God.

MARK

I came running to my father to tell him. Ephum's screaming behind the wagon. The people looked. My father sprang back to him. Ephum jumped up and down. Mamma screamed, hollering at Tanner. "What's wrong, what happened?" The people looked. Ephum jumped his hand to his nose. My father held him down to look. Something up his nose? "There's no blood." Aunt Maritole stood over him, too.

A button. It was a button he had up his nose.

"Ephum, wha'd you do?"

My father held Ephum down, Mamma helping. Ephum screaming. My father trying to get at it. Wouldn't come. A doctor came with pinchers and got it out. A soldier's button up Ephum's nose. Off whose uniform? Where'd you get that, Ephum?

Harmmff. The people laughed. The soldiers looked at their uniforms while I say, "Look," but no one saw the man walk away through the woods.

WAR CLUB

But whar he go whan he run? Off to the white man's farm? Move in wif 'em? They say, ho, have a piece of our land?

QUATY LEWIS

"Whooooooooooooooo." She hooted all day.

That night Kee-un-e-ca disappeared.

"The soldiers took her into the gully and killed her," Anna Sco-so-tah said.

"She thought she was an owl," Mrs. Young Turkey added.

"Who got the feathers?" War Club asked.

MARITOLE

I dreamed of hominy soup, cornmeal, and squirrel. DӨᏚᎱᏽᏮᎱ. Mark and Ephum laughed at me when I woke. They said my mouth chewed when I slept. I got out of the sick wagon and walked again for a while using Luthy's cane.

ᏮᏐᎾ.

Once we made brush arbors around an open field. We hung fish on a pole for a game. We had small stones we hit with sticks. We always played games. Was I dreaming again? Was I in the sick wagon? I couldn't tell if it was afternoon or morning. I thought sometimes I was eating apples and peaches from our orchard. I would wake, but there was nothing in my mouth.

In the nights my spirit walked a slick road. I dreamed all the land was white as the inside of an apple. It would never be anything but white.

The spirits seemed to say, "ᎯᎱᏃ Ꮅ Ꮒ Ꮒ, Maritole the bird girl is flying."

"David sent the bear running," I heard someone talking to me. I tried to open my eyes. It was the white minister, Mackenzie, who walked with us. He was praying for me. Telling me about David who killed the lion and the bear. I tried to lift my arm toward him but felt it shaking like a sapling in the wind. It was fatigue I shook away. At times my own body was the bear I pushed on the trail.

A GOVERNMENT
TEAMSTER'S JOURNAL

The various contingents followed one route west, though some took alternate roads and trails because of the harsh winter of 1838–39. From the Mississippi River crossing to Jackson and north to Farmington, the Cherokee traveled well-defined roads. Beyond these eastern Missouri towns the route followed Indian trails, horse tracks, and poorly maintained postal roads connecting scattered settlements.

At Farmington, the route turned west through the Bellview Valley to Caldonia, then northwest to Steelville. The trail crossed the Meramec River at the Iron Works, then joined a road west from St. Louis. For the Cherokee, the trail west passed through or near Little Piney, Waynesville, and Onyx before reaching Springfield, Missouri.

the 17th Halted at Whitewater Creek, 4:00 P.M. Issued corn and fodder, cornmeal and beef. 13 miles today.

the 19th Marched at 8:00 A.M. Halted and encamped at Wolf Creek. 14 miles today.

the 21st A refusal by several to march today. Allegedly they would wait for sick families to catch up at that place. Marched at 8:00 A.M. in defiance of threats and attempts to intimidate. None remained behind. Passed through Caldonia. Halted at Mr. Jackson's. 14 miles today.

the 22nd Marched at 8:30 A.M. Passed through Lead Mines (Courtois Diggings). Halted at Scott's 4:00 P.M. Issued corn and fodder and cornmeal. 13 miles today.

the 24th Considerable sickness prevailing. Halted at Huzza Creek. 12 miles today.

the 25th Dr. Townsend Official advised a suspension of our march in consequence of the severe indisposition of several families for a time sufficient for the employment of such remedial agents as their respective cases might require. Sickness continuing to increase. Moved detachment 2 miles further to a spring and schoolhouse. Obtained permission for as many of the sick to occupy the school as could do so. A much better situation for encampment than on the creek. Sickness increasing.

the 29th Buried Corn Tassel's child today.

the 4th Marched at 9:00 A.M. Buried George Killian and left Mr. Wells to bury a Wagoner (Black Boy) who died this morning. Scarcely room in the wagons for the sick.

the 8th Buried Nancy Big Bear's grandchild. Marched at 9:00 A.M. Halted at Piney, a small river. Rained all day. Encamped and issued corn only, no fodder to be had. 11 miles today.

the 9th Marched 9:00 A.M. Mayfield's wagon broke down at about a mile. Left him to get it mended and catch up later. Halted at Waynesville, Mo. 4:00 P.M. Encamped and issued corn, fodder, beef, and cornmeal.

the 14th Halted at James Fork of White River near the road, but which does not cross the road. 3:00 P.M. Mr. Wells taken sick. Issued cornmeal, corn, and fodder. 15 and miles today.

the 15th Joseph Starr's wife had a child last night.

the 16th Passed through Springfield, Mo. Halted at Mr. Click's 4:00 P.M. Encamped and left Mr. Wells.

the 17th Snowed last night. Buried Ellidge's wife and Charles Timberlake's son, Smoker. Extremely cold weather. Sickness prevailing, all very much fatigued. 10 miles today.

TANNER

In the dark I heard the breathing. The anger. The determination to survive. I heard the counting.

It was the blacksmith saying,

Anvil.
Vise.
Screw plate.
Hammer.
Rasp.
File.

It was William Griffith saying,

1 double hewed log house 20 × 20, 18 × 16, plank floor, planed and nailed down in each, above and below stairs, a pair of stairs and closet in a room and a double chimney between and connecting the two houses.

KNOBOWTEE

When the roads thawed, I worked with the men bedding mud holes in the road with brush so the wagons could pass.

I ached for my cornfield as I worked. In North Carolina I would soon be plowing. My thoughts turned like soil over my single-blade plow.

I needed to feel the cornfield. The trail had left me with a hollowness, and I had nothing to fill it.

Maybe that's what Maritole could be to me. But she had slept with a soldier in front of me. Cut off her nose. I'd heard that's what other tribes did. Let her be shamed in front of everyone. Wasn't that the way I felt?

For now she was a reminder that I was always dissatisfied with my life. I had to look to other measures. Other than horse, hogs, plow, field, wife.

LUTHY

I sat by Mark and Ephum while Quaty told them the story of the Trickster Turtle. She spoke first in Cherokee, then English, word for word through the story. "So you won't forget," she said.

WYb	box turtle
Z♂	and
DӨ	deer
SᏮᏞᏁ ᏋᏁT	challenged
ᎤᏧᏸᎩ ᏁT	seventh
ᎦdDᎱ	mountain
ᎧhMᎯᏬᎫ	to reach
WYb	box turtle
ᏆWᏁᏁᏋᏁT	challenged
ᎫWYᏬ ᏬᎫᎯ	that he would leave
	behind and win
DᏬRZ	but
ᏆWMᎱ	before
ᏆWOᏣ♂	the race
ᏆWOᏣ♂	schemed
WYb	box turtle
ᏕᏟᏬᎩᏁ	seventh
ᎦdDᎱ	mountain
ᎫӨ♂hᏬE	beginning
ᏂSOᏬWᏁ	he placed along
WYb	box turtle
ᏂSOᏬWᏁ	as he placed them
SᏁᏤ♂T	he told them
hᏕMEӨᏬ	before he got there

ᎠᏫ	deer
ᎠᏙᎯᏍᏗᎥ	to holler
ᎰᏎᎢ	
ᎠᏫ	deer
ᎱᏨᏍᏔ	as he ran past
ᏔᎩᏏ	box turtle
ᎾᎾ	right there
ᎤᏁᎢᏙᎶᎩ	in the leaves
ᏥᏊᏄᏰᏍ	it crawled into
ᏬᏓᏍᏗᏬ	as he ran
Ꮍ ᎣᏓᎠᏄ	other mountain
ᏏᏫᏂᏕᎹᏣᎾ	before he got there
ᏧᎠᏙᎰᏍᎰ	hollered
ᏄᏔᏍ	another
ᏔᎩᏏ	box turtle
ᎢᎬᎣ	first
ᎤᏝᏁᏄᏔᏁᎡ	the challenger
ᎤᏁᎢᏙᎶᎩ	in the leaves
ᏊᏄᏰᏄ	had crawled
ᎰᏒᎥ	
ᏔᏥᎩᏲᎢ	was defeated
ᎠᏫ	deer
ᏕᎶᏄᏢᏬ	cheating
ᏕᏧ	with

ANNA SCO-SO-TAH

"That's what we'll do. We'll take away the power of our stories out of the earth. That will get 'em."

"But they don't know the power anyway," Luthy said, falling over a tree root in the path where the ground had eroded.

"Our stories're here whether they know it or not. Yop. They'll feel it when they're gone."

KNOBOWTEE

Maybe I could be in the council in the new territory. But now things were broken. The Tennessee Cherokee hated the Georgia

Cherokee. I listened to the remnant of them on the trail. What did I care? I was a North Carolina Cherokee, but the anger wouldn't go away. Sometimes I couldn't think of what was ahead in the new territory. It made the trail harder. Not just planting corn. But the politics. There, that was the word. It kept me warm at night. In my head. Deep inside where the soldiers couldn't come. Nor Maritole. Nor any girl. Nor even O-ga-na-ya. But what was there for me to do? The men had taken the power from the women to emulate the white man, to show we could also dominate the women, but the women would assign farmland in the new territory. I knew it. They would enforce the laws in their behind-the-scenes way. But there would be something I could do. I knew it. Weren't all things possible according to the Christians? Forget Anna Sco-so-tah and the others filled with bitterness. Listen to Lacey Woodard. Listen to Bushyhead. Even Maritole thought it was true.

REVEREND BUSHYHEAD

For some reason, I carried an old list of things needed at the mission. I found it one morning when I looked through my bag. The smoke from the campfire burned my nose, and I needed a rag to cover it. The list was in the bottom of my bag. I sat reading it.

15 reams Royal Demi Paper
1 ″ ″ paper suitable for covers, say Retre Cartridge paper
1 ″ ″ Letter Paper
1 cheap Sand Box
1 doz. Monroe's Pencils
2 Penknives
2 oz. wafers
1 gill red ink or 1 paper powder
½ doz. Reference Testaments, if on hand
A small assortment of simple Sabbath School Books. Among
    them Hymns for infant minds
½ doz. 24 to Walls & Select Hymns
1 Hone
1 Pocket Comb
½ doz. Cakes Windsor Soap

1 lb. Chalk

2 oz. Indigo

2 oz. Gum Arabic

2 phials each 1 oz. E. Tansey

2 bottles Opodeldoc

1 lb. Salt Petre

1 lb. Cream Tartar

1 bottle Tartaric Acid

2 oz. Paregoric

2 lb. Redwood

3 bed cords (be so kind as to take special pains to have them good; for if we receive such as were sent last year we shall have to send annually.)

1 Oxford Grey Cloth Coat. (My coat last year was too small, yet so that I wear it, but much too fine.)

1 Oxford Grey Cloth Vest

1 pr. " " " " " " Vest Cloth or Cassimere Pantaloons

1 pr. Lasting Pantaloons

3 pr. men's calfskin shoes, no. 9

1 pr. woman's Morocco walking shoes, No. 8 one-half or 9

1 pr. shoes calfskin (Mrs. Worcester's feet are such that she cannot comfortably wear horsehide shoes.)

2 prs. calfskin shoes No. 4 one-half

10 yds. brown Tow Cloth

1 piece fine American Gingham

2 yds. English Pink Gingham

2 Handkerchiefs

9 yds. Calico suitable for little girls

2 large Hair Combs

2 Side Combs

3 steel-topp'd brass Thimbles

6 fine Darning Needles

6 common mixed Needles

2 Tape Needles

1 paper needles No. 5 sharps

1 " " " " No. 4 betweens

1 " " " " No. 6 sharps

1 " " " " No. 7 sharps

1 piece unbleached Cotton Shirting about no. 20

6 yds. red Flannel

2 prs. large woolen Socks

10 lb. Black tea

2 lb. Green Tea

1 oz. Nutmeg

1 oz. Cloves

1 Lantern

1 Sausage Filler

12 sheets Tin Plate

10 cents U.S. copper coin

2 6-qt. Milk pans—tin

½ doz. Cups & Saucers with Teapot and Sugar Bowl

2 small Oval Dishes

2 large Chamber with covers

1 pair Iron Candlesticks, to admit a good-sized candle

1 pair snuffers

1 oz. Beet Seed

½ oz. early Cabbage Seed

½ oz. Late ″   ″   ″ ″

½ oz. Lettuce Seed

½ oz. Early Cucumber ″ ″

½ oz. Late   ″   ″   ″ ″

1 oz. radish   ″ ″

1½ oz. Onion Seed (Be so kind as to get from two or three different places, so as to secure seeds that will grow.)

1½ oz. Parsnip Seed

1½ oz. Carrot ″   ″

1 Roll Paper Hangings

1 bottle Spirits Turpentine

1 lb. Peruvian Bark

Mr. Boudinot wishes:

50 reams Super Royal Printing Paper

4   ″ ″ retre cartridge Paper

2 Cannisters Printing Ink

4 lb. Twine

2 lb. Full-faced Brevier Capt. Type

2 lb. ″ ″ ″ ″ Long

Primer Type

2 lb. Brevier Antique Type

½ lb. small pica letter

16 Bevil Column Rules (such as are apparently used in printing in the N.Y. *Observer*)

1 ream Letter Paper

1 Sand Box

1 Paper Sand

½ doz. Pencils

2 oz. Wafers

2 Papers Ink Powder

½ doz. cakes Windsor Soap

½ lb. Chalk

2 oz. Ep. Tansey

1 bottle Opodeldoc

1 box Lee's Pills

1 lb. Cream Tartar

2 oz. Paregoric

4 good Bed Cords

1 blue cloth Frock Coat

1 pr. " " " " Pantaloons

1   " " " " Vest

1 pr. lasting Pantaloons

1 silk Vest. (Mr. Boudinot is 5 ft. 7 in. in height, and 2 ft. 8 in. around the waist. He would like loose pantaloons.)

2 Handkerchiefs

2 prs. woolen Socks

2 prs. cotton   " "

2 prs. dark cotton Stockings

2 pieces dark. Am. Gingham

9 yds. Calico for little girls

7 yds. English Buff Gingham, double width

1 pr. Brogs calfskin no. 5 and one-half

1 pr. Morocco pumps No. 5

2 pr. Women's Shoes calf good thick No. 5

½ lb. cotton thread

½ lb. assortment thread

½ lb. Sewing Silk

7 yds. British Shirting

15 yds. unbleached Cotton Shirting No. 16

1 large Hair Comb

2 Side Combs

1 ivory Comb

4 sheets Tin Plate

2 long flat Tins

2 10-qt. tin Milk Pans

Garden Seeds (the same as for the mission)
1 flute & directions for playing (cost not to exceed $6)

Mr. Wheeler will be thankful to have the following purchased for him:

1 4 pail Brass Kettle—bailed
2 rose blankets
1 piece good Am. Gingham dark
7 yds Calico—good
1 pair iron Candlesticks
1 pair Steel Snuffers
1 Pea Pot
2 lb. black Tea
Garden Seeds (same as for the mission)
1 pair Cassimere Pantaloons. Same size as for Mr. Boudinot
15 yds. bleached Am. Shirting
1 piece common Table Linen
1 teakettle (I cannot tell the name of the kind he wants. It is
     malleable iron cast and tinned within.)

Also, if it's not too late, a neighbor wishes very much to have me procure for him, through you, the following medicines:

Jewett's improved Vegetable Pills or, German Specific
     Dr. Rolfe's Vegetable Pacifick, and Antibilious Pills
     Of each of the above enough for one case of dyspepsia
Vegetable Lithontriptic and Specific Solvent Powders—
     enough for one case of the Gravel
A little Corn Plaster

Mr. Weir, a young man who has been at work for me several months, wishes for the following:

1 most approved school arithmetic. Not Colburn's
1 Goodrich's *History of the United States*
1 Worcester's *Epitome of Geography & Atlas*—latest edition
1 pair high quartered Calfskin Shoes, no. 9
1 best Razor and Razor strap
1 silk handkerchief
1 waterproof hat. Circumference at the band 23½ in.

Mr. Boudinot wishes added:

1 lb Redwood
1 pair mantuamaker's Shears
1 doz. good common knives and forks
Mr. Wheeler's teakettle, already mentioned to contain 6
    quarts

I shall be enabled to oblige some of my neighbors if you send
me 1 doz. *Webster's Spelling Book.*

WAH-KE-CHA

Hey what that noise? Two pack dogs snarling over scraps. I
reach over grab a stick. Hit one he yelp limp away.

MARITOLE

As we neared the edge of Missouri, I woke one morning with
the thought of my younger brother, Thomas. How long had it
been since I'd remembered him? Was he all right? Had his spirit
come to tell me something had happened?

No, I thought, rubbing my eyes. I put my blanket over my
head. I sat by myself awhile. I knew what had happened. I felt
separate. On my own. Individual. I'd heard that word. Now I
knew what it meant.

At one time we were one. I was one of everyone. I could
feel my parents on their farm. I could feel Knobowtee in the
field. Tanner hunting. Thomas running in the woods. I knew
the boys Luthy carried before they were born.

Now everyone had gone away from inside my head. Though
Tanner and Luthy slept beside me. And Mark and Ephum curled
at my side.

That's what woke me. Ephum kicked in his sleep. His foot
had pushed me into waking. Into knowing the blackness of being alone. I held the blanket to my face. I looked out through
one small narrow hole.

Arkansas

FEBRUARY, 1839

A GOVERNMENT
TEAMSTER'S JOURNAL

From Springfield, several contingents followed an ancient Indian path that led south past Monet and Washburn. This trail passed into Arkansas close to Elkhorn Tavern and continued to Pea Ridge, Arkansas. After reaching Arkansas, several contingents took various routes west toward Indian Territory—

MARITOLE

The stars twisted above me at night. I felt the soldier cup his hands under my chin. I felt him bite into my hurt like an apple. I sat up in the wagon wanting to put my arms around him, but he wasn't there.

"Williams knows where we're going," I whispered. "He could find me if he wanted."

"We'll be spread out in Indian Territory," Luthy answered. "He wouldn't come and ask—The men wouldn't tell him." I heard her sigh.

Soon I walked on the hickory cane again with Mark and Ephum coaxing.

When I closed my eyes, I heard the conjurers long ago. Sometimes in the boys' voices I could hear the stickball games or the old council fires at Red Clay, Tennessee. Sometimes I could even hear the land ahead. We must be getting near. Park Hill. Fort Gibson, Indian Territory, was just beyond Arkansas.

The wagons bumped up and down over the rough trail. The soil was rocky, and there were old stumps along the trail. The trees were thick with vines and heavy underbrush.

Somewhere, down one of the hills, we passed a trading post.

There were razors and straps. Staples of flour and lard. Molasses and sorghum. Calico. Needles. Pie wheels and spurs. Fleem and hocking knives. We looked in the windows until a white man told us to move.

What were they burning in the stove? It didn't smell like our fires. I remembered the small grass fires in North Carolina. The trading post smelled something like the underbrush we burned off the fields near our farm so the deer would come and eat in the corn and we could harvest their meat. ᏚᎣᏉ ᏃᏒᏍᏉ. The thought of the farm swept over me again.

Suddenly there was a holler from within the store. A Cherokee ran from the store holding his hand in the air. Tanner rushed to him, yelled for someone to pump water. The white men laughed. The Indian had put his hand on the pot-bellied stove and burned it to the bone. "Or someone had done it for him," Quaty spat.

The doctor held the hand in the bucket of water. Then he took bear grease and spread it on the man's hand. Soldiers brought him whiskey to numb his pain. Where was the snow when he needed to put his hand in it? My father called him Him-who-we-see-the-bones-of-his-hand.

The Indians gathered to watch the man with his new name. The doctor bandaged the burned hand. He howled until he no longer sounded like a man. Tanner and Knobowtee held him on the ground. I remembered the little burns on my hands when I pulled the cooking pot out of the fire in the cabin. I wanted my father to cry against. But he stood over the man

TANNOS-WECH

"We got burned. Yop." I sat with Maritole's father and Tanner as they sat with the hurt man that night. "How many times our corn and barns and sheds been fire? Yop." Every time I closed my eyes, the hurt man groaned and wakened me. I wished he would be quiet. I wished the man were out of his pain. "Like the phoenix we fly on again," I said. "Get up. Wave your hands. Go on."

KNOBOWTEE

The reflection of the trees in the creek let me see another view of the trees. How it changed the way I saw. While my father and I had fished, I looked into the water but not for the fish. I was watching the mud that trailed my father's footsteps. I watched the image of the trees rippled by the water, distorted by the mud. I heard the trees tell their story. The other voice was there for a reason. I had to let it in. I had lost my land and there was a just God. Just try and reconcile that. A man got his hands burned to the bone, yet there was a Great Spirit who protected. To think of all that put a chunk-of-fish-meat-full-of-bones in my mouth that had to be chewed. Once when I was a boy, I had nearly choked on a fish bone. My father and I had been fishing and hadn't eaten in a while. I bit into the fish as soon as it was out of the fire. I ate too much too quickly, burning my mouth, trying to cool it by taking quick breaths, and I had choked. My father had beaten me on the back to get me to breathe. Hunger could do that. Maybe the white man had a hunger that made him take more than he needed. Maybe it would choke him.

"Maybe I would have been better off if I'd choked to death on the bone," I told O-ga-na-ya. But I had felt the long fingers of a spirit pull it out of my throat.

Maybe that was the Great Spirit's lesson. Nothing was mine. I could receive and lose in the same breath. The burden the white man carried was that he didn't know the lesson yet.

"Maybe the Cherokee are like ripples in the creek," I said to O-ga-na-ya. "No." I changed my mind. "The Cherokee are the trees on the shore—Yes, that works."

"Then our walking is only a reflection," he said.

"Or maybe the soldiers are only the reflection in the water," I thought further. "Yes, the soldiers who carried out the orders to march with the Cherokee are the ripples."

"But the others"—O-ga-na-ya paused—"the ones in Washington who told them to do it, then they are the trees on the shore."

"But the trees on the shore are the Cherokee," I said to O-ga-na-ya. "How could they be the men in Washington?"

"Well—Isn't there more than one kind of tree on the shore?" he asked.

"Yes, there had to be room for different kinds of trees, different kinds of reflections, and different kinds of thoughts."

"Which will confuse and frustrate you more."

The image of the man's charred hands lodged in my head. How would I get the sobs out? I thought about my baby daughter. I felt like I was choking again. I'd keep thinking. It gave me a place to be when the sobs wanted to choke me.

My wife had slept with a soldier, and my mother couldn't stop coughing. When I closed my eyes, I couldn't see my mother in the new territory. In fact I couldn't hear the new territory at all or the cabin I would build there.

I thought of the old log cabin in North Carolina chinked with clay and roofed with bark. I remembered the moss on the bark roof. The cabin was a part of the land. I remembered the leaves. The sun in the clearing. I could almost hear the sound of the leaves over the cabin. I was trying to find a way to go on, I told my thoughts. I was trying not to hear the howling man in the night. I wanted to remember the gourds and skins hanging on the wall of the cabin. The rows of corn. The trellis of beans. The pumpkin vines and columbine by the cabin. The peach and apple trees. The greenness of the woods that was always something apart from the trees.

I wanted to forget my cabin in the clearing as we camped near Little Sugar Creek. Across a grassy field I saw a shed that looked like a corncrib. I saw a cow eating in the grass almost as tall as its head.

Only a few trees gathered, like the men who came when I called a meeting.

What's there to understand? Sometimes there was nothing. That's what the Raven Mocker taught. Just accept it.

Why was it hard to face?

It was the reason the ministers were always trying to make sense of the horror that happened.

It's the trees where they stand on the bank of the river. My thoughts were only the ripples—Unless, of course, the creek dries up. Unless, of course, the creek freezes over.

Yes. The trees showed me a part of myself. The easy part that could be divided between trees and ripples.

HIM-WHO-WE-SEE-THE-BONES-OF-HIS-HAND

All winter we was driven into blowing cold and snow. I hear a Cherokee beat an ox whose legs fall. I hear sick ones' coughs. The white mens talks as if the land's theirs. Don't they know we been here long?

I saw over them. Yop. There into the sky.

The old frog looks over. He can bite the sun. He can bite earth. He bite soldiers if he can.

They better watch.

Sometimes I hear old corn cry.

I hear the sumac burning in the trading post. The *das' das' das'* of its tongue. I hear it talk.

The white man says you want to see fire?

He puts my hand to the stove.

I yell.

I send him ᏰᎾᏛᎧᏬᎫ, the little people, to fix his cabin good.

Yo stone-clad man.

Yo snake-with-horns.

Go get him. I send all.

I part of old earth. All walking ones. The falling and stumbling ones.

I see over the trading post. The black sky we walk, our hands held up to the sun.

MARITOLE

"Your soldier husband is gone now—" Knobowtee said coming up bitterly behind me. "—your government man."

I looked off into the distance and didn't answer. The red sun sat low on the horizon.

"And there's your apple orchard," he said. "As far from us now as the horizon will always be."

My father argued again with Knobowtee.

"Don't try to make him walk with me," I said. "He's not my husband. I feel it in my heart."

"You can't give up like that, Maritole," my father said. "Knobowtee's your husband. The trail doesn't change that."

I don't remember signing any treaty. I don't remember anything but the soldiers who came and ripped us from our farm.

ᎬᏓᎢᎢ. The screech owl woke me soon after I slept. Even in sleep I felt my anger.

My feet felt like they were walking. My legs tingled. I always dreamed they were moving. My knees felt hollow and my legs jerked. I put my hands on them, tried to quiet them like the animals I tamed. I spoke softly to them, told them to be quiet and quit their walking, but they did not hear. Like some animals, they would never be gentled. My feet walked to a new land. Sometimes in sleep I felt the bear still gnawing my toes. But I couldn't find the teeth marks. It was only the cold that bit my feet making them sting. I flaked some skin off my legs. Some people's feet turned blue and then white, but mine stayed red and swollen.

Always now in the dark I heard the voices of our ancestors. They said to keep walking. The spirits who had held the raft across the huge Mississippi River told me the road would come to an end and I would see the new land. They did not promise I would be happy.

Sometimes stories didn't seem to make any difference, but now I wanted to ask my father for a story again. I didn't think he would want to remember how I'd curled up in his lap as a girl. Suddenly I felt the magic of the stories again. They could keep life with me when I would let it go. On the outside we had only the cold that bit us, but inside the Keetoowah fire burned and some of our legends lived. The thought of the magic lake, ᎠᏯᏍᏗ, would always heal.

When I got up the following morning, I tied a rope around the waist of my skirt and trousers to keep them up. I marched on holding my father's hand or Luthy's, telling the boys it was a little farther each time they asked.

Then we saw a trading post covered with antlers. Every part of the logs covered. Antlers from herds and herds of deer and elk. How could they kill like that? Some of the women wailed. The men turned away. We passed in mourning. The weight of our sorrow pushed our feet farther into the ground. The antlers were like stiff gray flames. The white man's trading posts had always been trouble. Often they cheated us when we traded there. But sometimes we cheated also.

"AAAHHHHHHthggggt." My father's grief suddenly came upon him. He wept, bent over to the ground. Luthy and I wailed with him. Even the boys. Tanner sat on a stump with his back to us until my father quit his grieving.

"The clouds over us are like blossoms of apple trees in the orchard," I told my father as I walked beside the wagon. I wanted to hear one of our legends. If he couldn't tell me, then I would tell him. "At one time all things were in the sky," I blundered on. "All living things spoke the same language, so they understood each other. But we misused this privilege and were stricken deaf to the talk of animals and birds."

I heard my father groan on the floor of the wagon as the wheels jolted up a slight embankment.

"Do you want me to keep talking?" I asked him, but his eyes searched the sky and he didn't answer.

"I want to hear, Maritole," Luthy said.

"As the birds and animals grew in numbers, the sky became crowded until there was danger of being pushed off." I saw my father clutch his chest with his hands. I called for Tanner as my father gasped. "No. *NO!*" I screamed. "I can't bear your death, too." I saw how old he was. His hair was white and his eyes stared like nutting stones. I could not bear to see Tanner leaning over him. I looked away and continued my story for him. "So a council was called to decide what should be done. Finally the water beetle was sent to see if he could find a place where the animals could live." Luthy tried to talk to me. "He dived down under a large body of water and found mud." I continued as though she wasn't there. "He brought the piece of mud to the surface."

"Maritole," Luthy said.

I had my fingers in my ears. "The mud began to grow until after a long time it covered much of the surface of the water," I screamed at the sky.

"He's dead, Maritole," Luthy sobbed against my shoulder.

"No." I tried to push her away, but she held on to me. "My father, my mother, my baby—Thomas." We held each other and cried, our shoulders jumping together like wagons that crossed a rough field.

Finally I closed his eyes with my hands. "We're like the animals in the sky pushed off to find a new place," I told him.

REVEREND MACKENZIE

"Do you know how many've been converted?" I asked Bushyhead as they stopped at a spring to drink.

"No, not many."

"Some?"

"Yes, some."

"Then maybe the trail was worth it."

I saw the spring was beside a stage line. There in the trees was a rest stop. Then there would be another trading post. It was always the beginning of their towns.

MARITOLE

Sergeant Williams was not here to bury my father, but someone else would. Tanner, I suppose. I put my head into his sleeve and closed my eyes. Everything I had was gone. I looked into the dark pit of myself where nothing moved. I hated life. I hated the God who made it. I would die here and be buried with my father. I would go with him to the afterlife to be with my mother and baby again. I would go see who was there. What God was behind this? I wanted to see him. I held my eyes closed so tight the stars popped behind them. Maybe we were in the heavens already. My head felt dizzy.

I stayed in the wagon beside my dead father, waiting for the God who loved us to lift us off this earth. My eyes were open to the sky to see him. That's where our trail ended. I felt my father's arm already growing stiff as I lay beside him. I could not even cry any longer. My own fingers dug into myself. Let me see the God who dared to make us.

I held to my father's rigid arm and cried. Knobowtee pulled at me, but I wouldn't go. He wasn't going to take the only thing I had left.

"I'm going to bury him, Maritole. Let go of his arm." Tanner lifted me from the wagon, and Knobowtee and another man took his body. Even the boys helped.

Reverend Bushyhead said something as the men dug my father's grave. Knobowtee handed me my father's leather coin pouch. I felt between my fingers that there was one coin left.

I saw my father wrapped in a torn flannel blanket. The men lowered his body into the shallow hole. I was going to touch my father one more time but tripped over the mound of dirt beside the grave, knocking my father's body from the men's hands.

"Maritole!" Knobowtee tried to pull me up, but my arm slipped from his hand. For a moment I felt like I was in the sunken DᎧT, the old sweat house where we'd slept when I was a girl and the winter was cold. For a moment I felt like I was back farther than when I was a girl: I saw the daub-and-wattle dwellings we had before cabins, woven with river cane and covered with red clay mixed with grass. I saw my grandfather or great-grandfather returning with fish to eat. I heard my grandmother dancing with turtle-shell rattles on her legs.

I heard the whole voice of the earth calling him back.

Tanner stepped to the grave and held me while I sobbed. "I'm glad Thomas can't see us," he said.

ELLA ROGERS

I was a spider now. Didn't I walk even when I couldn't feel my feet? Not the two feet I started walking with anyway. Out of North Carolina into Tennessee and Kentucky. Across Illinois into Missouri. I walked through the fall and into winter I walked. I walked nearly into spring. I walked through Arkansas. I walked toward Indian Territory. More than with two feet I walked. Ha. I walked on many feet. Ho. I had spider legs. As many feet as I needed. I walked to a new land to weave a cabin from my web.

LUTHY

I am part of the earth as I walk. I am the harvested crops. I should not mind the trail any more than the corn minds the harvest.

When I hear the voice of the corn, I know I'm a part of the earth.

Not the stalks nor leaves nor kernels, but the process. The sheen which is the voice of things.

A living essence which walks of its own accord, whether crop or animal or man.

It doesn't matter if I walk or cause the walking.

Voice speaks for all who come and go. It travels through time. It's a woman with bloody feet. A child crying for its mother. Voice reaches into the animals and insects. Voice is in the trees of the woods.

It's in the corn. It's in the boys. All the same. It doesn't matter.

TANNER

"Why do we survive when others die?" Maritole asked at the campfire.

"Our grandmothers and grandfathers prayed for us," I answered her. "They directed us on the long path when we were born. They spoke us with their words."

"They didn't speak us here," Anna Sco-so-tah said. "No, they wouldn't do that."

"Your family's always talking about words," Quaty told me.

"They don't make nothin'," Anna said as Quaty slapped her batter onto a piece of bark.

LUTHY

A stray dog from somewhere attacked one of our pack dogs. All along the trail there had been the sound of dogs barking at our passing. Sometimes they fought with the pack dogs. Sometimes the pack dogs had run off. There were not many left.

The stray dog bit the pack dog, clamping his teeth on her neck. There was growling and fierce yelping as the pack dog tried to run.

"Stop them!" I yelled, but no one could.

The men didn't want to get bit. They tried to separate them with sticks.

I hid the boys' faces, but they broke loose to watch.

"Stop them, Tanner," Maritole cried, but the dogs fought. I covered my ears from the noise.

They continued to fight until one of the men hit the stray dog hard enough he ran away.

Tanner took a knife and cut the throat of the wounded pack dog, whose sides heaved with the pain and tumult.

The boys cried, remembering the dogs we had in North Carolina. How suddenly things come back.

That night, the boys tossed in their sleep.

KNOBOWTEE

I called Maritole into my family's camp. My mother was dying. My brother and sister sat around the fire. The memory of my father was in our voices. Maritole sat behind me as we prayed.

MARITOLE

I heard the conjurers. I heard the Christians. I believed them both. I heard the humming of the ancestors and the words of the living as I sat behind the tent where Knobowtee's mother was dying. Bushyhead said that Jesus made a way for light to penetrate the darkness so that darkness couldn't be all dark again. Didn't he hold up his infant daughter as the light that was ahead for us. It was in us. Our new birth was in how we thought and what we did. The light was a knowledge beyond feeling.

I had hurt since I left North Carolina. I guess I had even hurt before that. Maybe I'd married Knobowtee because I wanted a husband. Not necessarily him. But I saw other girls want him. The soldier had been closer to me than Knobowtee. Knobowtee had too many eyes always on others. But I was Knobowtee's wife. That was legal. I heard Knobowtee's mother in her death song. She cried about the trail, her hatred of the white soldiers, her hatred of the white people who had watched us pass on the trail from their carriages under the warmth of their lap robes. She cursed the people in her cabin in North Carolina. She called her husband's name. Maybe now he'd be there, when she entered the afterlife. She'd see him again. "If Jesus was his Savior," Bushyhead said. O-ga-na-ya spit. He didn't want any god the white man preached. Knobowtee shut Bushyhead up.

I saw Knobowtee's sister watching O-ga-na-ya and Knobowtee preparing their mother for her journey. Maybe she would catch up with my father and they could walk together for a ways. Or maybe they could stay and help us. We were all going to a new place. None of us was sure of the trail ahead. How much more it would hurt. How much else we could lose.

"We have ourselves," Reverend Bushyhead harped. "We have a place the white man can't touch."

Knobowtee and O-ga-na-ya looked away.

Their mother's breathing was shallow and raspy. Her breath was her song now. Death was usually fast on the trail. In the cabins, a sick one could hold on. But here the cold took them quickly.

I leaned back against the tree. It seemed like Knobowtee's mother would live forever. I felt the weariness in my body like a rock. I went to sleep crying for my father.

When I woke there was a faint light in the sky. Knobowtee's mother's body was wrapped in a blanket. Knobowtee, sobbing, was digging her grave with his brother.

Reverend Bushyhead started to speak but the conjurers pushed him back. The Christians with Bushyhead told the conjurers to stand aside. A conjurer struck the ground with a stick he carried. A puff of smoke rose to his knees. One of the Christian women screamed. Bushyhead raised his Bible. The Christian men rebuked the conjurers in the name of Jesus. The conjurers pushed them back and struck the ground again. I heard Luthy praying beside me. One conjurer chanted with a wild voice. He fell on the ground. A soldier stepped toward him, but the Cherokee warned him to stay away. The conjurer looked like he was dead or asleep, but his spirit had moved into something else—a deer or smaller animal. The soldiers would be killed by that animal if they touched the conjurer. The other conjurers hissed at the Christians.

"ZZZZZZZZZZZZZZZ."

They danced and spread their arms like wings. But the Christians stood still and prayed. I stood with them.

Our words pulled like wagons without horses, flew without wings. Our power was the Great Spirit, the *being one*, full of eyes and ears, and around him, animals and spirit beings. And men who believed his voice.

Our prayers were our actions. They carried on forever, waves of movement spreading north, east, south, west.

I saw the horses and oxen and the few dogs left with packs on their backs walking with the people. Even the corn walked. The spirits walked. Even the Great Spirit walked. That's what we all did in this world-that-walks.

Another conjurer hissed and went into a trance. He trembled and waved his arms. He turned into a bird in front of us and flew away.

KNOBOWTEE

"Everything's broken," I said to O-ga-na-ya as we sat back from the fire. "Even my wife loved a soldier— She's broken for me, too." I smoothed my sister's hair as she sat between us.

"We're all torn and hurt," O-ga-na-ya said. "But we're nearing a place where we have to start over. Maybe what Maritole did doesn't matter."

MARITOLE

We pushed south toward the edge of Arkansas in the early spring thaw. Now it was mud that slowed us. Wagons stuck in it. We pried the wheels with boards. The ragged oxen were beat so harshly the women cried. Even Knobowtee protested. The men worked all afternoon on a broken axle. It was the orphan wagon. Luthy and I and other women watched the children. I held two girls on my lap and combed their matted hair with my fingers. Knobowtee brought us some jerky to eat, but it was so tough the children could not swallow it. Saliva ran from their mouths as they tried. I chewed some pieces for them and put it in their mouths. Knobowtee came back with a pail of milk. Someone had found a farmer's goat by the road.

"We'll get in trouble for that," I said. "The old farmer will come after us with his shotgun."

"The soldiers watched us milk it," Knobowtee said. "The farmer won't know."

"He must be gone," Tanner said. "How could he not know we're passing?"

Sometimes the farmers sat along their fields with their guns. As though we would steal their mud. As though we could settle on their land as they did on ours. Maybe they thought we'd take their stock. Sometimes I think we did. I remembered a night we had fresh meat. No one asked where it came from.

"Look at Maritole with those girls on her lap," Tanner said.

Mark and Ephum brought the girls twigs to play with. The girls were thin, their noses raw from running. I felt the bones of their hips against my leg. I moved one because she was hurting me.

"What's your name?" Ephum asked one, but she didn't answer.

"Maybe they don't know," Luthy said.

"Is your name Beulah?" Mark guessed.

"Don't name them," Knobowtee said. "They'll be yours."

I looked at him to see what he meant. Why was he not bitter as he always was? Why was he not with O-ga-na-ya? Luthy had a girl on her lap, too. She cooed over her like she did everything. Knobowtee picked at a callus on his hand and looked at me now and then.

"The Bone-girls," I said, seeing what he would do. "The Running-noses or Where-is-my-mother? girls," I said, looking at their faces. They struggled to eat the jerky. The white milk ran down their chins when they tried to drink and breathe through their noses at the same time.

"Their eyes wild as new cornstalks in the wind," Knobowtee said.

I asked Mark to bring my blanket from the wagon. I wrapped them in it on the ground beside me. I took an edge of the blanket in my hand. It was the one the soldier had thrown from the cabin into the cooking pot.

The orphan wagon couldn't be fixed, so we moved on that afternoon carrying the children among us.

The trees had come back. Arkansas had almost as many as North Carolina. Finally there was something to catch the beings that fell from the sky. I thought I could even see the buds. Someday there would be leaves. But the soil was not rich. It was too rocky to farm. I wondered if the new territory was the same way. I knew we were getting close to it.

KNOBOWTEE

I shouted at the people who seemed to be giving up so near the end of the trail. Some of them I knew just disappeared. Others walked not caring where they walked. They kept their heads bowed in the sprouts of rain and didn't talk. *"We walk together and we're strong,"* I told them. *"Husband and wife. Brother and sister. Friend and friend. We walk. Ugh. Why? We're driven into ourselves like dogs howling. We walk all day. At night our feet still walk. Our feet move in sleep. Our legs jump. Our rib bones cry. Say to one another, we move like wind in the cornstalks. Something happens when we walk."*

WAR CLUB

"I split their heads. Yep. Them white mens. In my dream, my fist pound 'em. Wha'd this? Hey! Look up. Spring? Warm?" I put out my hand to the air. "Spring sits on it. It early yet. But them trees buddin' out. Uumph."

KNOBOWTEE

I saw Maritole take off the trousers the soldier put on her. That night I sang a song for Maritole.

I am called poor and ugly, but I am not this. I am going to take this woman home with me, as I did not know that there was such a good shell-shaker, none like her. I'll take her home to my settlement. We are going to touch each other.

I thought of the rest of the song in the dark. In the morning I would take Maritole's hand. She would know what I had been singing.

ᎤᏍᏗ ᎤᏣᎦ	pretty woman
ᏒᎦ Ꭿ ᎯᏂ Ꮟ	I am going to take home with me
ᏗᏴᏍᎢ	where is my town?

LACEY WOODARD

"Jesus knew all his life he would push the bear because of us," I told Maritole as we walked. "The claws piercing his head like thorns. His feet and hands nailed with claws. The darkness licked his fur up and down when he was on the cross. Yet he was the man ᎭᎥ ᎦᎦᏂᎠ° who pushed the bear."

MARITOLE

I remembered following Knobowtee through the woods in North Carolina. The trees laughing. The creek. Our words came out of the land. Would our words leave their place? Did they walk, too? Would we have language when we got to Fort Gibson in Indian Territory? Would we find our words hadn't migrated?

If the language didn't cross on the trail, it would sink back inside the trees and rocks. It would be buried in the land. It would go back to where it came.

Let Knobowtee catch some words. Let him talk to me. That will be the bird he catches.

LUTHY

Tanner walked with his father's musket. I saw him stumble, but he caught the side of the wagon. His toe had been broken. He couldn't remember when. I'd seen it crooked when he took off his moccasin. I loved him. I burned with hope, not bitterness. I beat it away as if I had my broom. I could almost feel the broom in my hand.

MARITOLE

I heard a woman's moan again, then sharper cries, somewhere back in another wagon.

"What's happening?" I sat up.

"What do you think?" Luthy answered.

I heard the woman again. They were childbirth pains. She was screaming in labor. Who else besides Mrs. Bushyhead had been pregnant in our detachment? There had been another woman somewhere—but I hadn't seen anyone near us like that.

The woman continued her screaming. There were no intervals now. I felt a sob in the pit of my stomach. The sky grew almost white. I felt the pushing out of new life. I heard the baby's squawl.

KNOBOWTEE

"You hear our orators, our story keepers, talk of our way of life, Maritole?" I asked, startling her from behind. "October is our new year. You got till then to forgive me, Maritole," I said as we walked. "You got till October to hold your grudge."

"It's just turned February," Maritole told me.

I didn't know what would happen in the new territory. There was a bear larger than the one Maritole pushed. It was greed. *I'm going to have it all. I'm going to push them out of the way.* It stretched over the land. I knew it now because of all the farms I saw along the trail. They would even come into Indian Territory. Push the Cherokee over there, too. It would only be a matter of time. It was in the heart of men.

Maritole's father spoke to me in a dream. At first, I thought it was my own father, but soon I realized it was Maritole's. He asked me to help his daughter. I was on earth as she was, as he was with my daughter in the afterlife.

Maritole's father told me life was more than the trail. More was happening than a bitter walk through the cold. They still cried where he was. Yes, some. They were angry their farms were taken. How long, Lord, how long? They cried for justice in the afterlife. Still, the walk meant almost nothing when it was over. It was fading into a morning fog for Maritole's father. But I still had to walk. *Do it right*, Maritole's father told me, *so later you'll have no regrets.*

MARITOLE

"You're still my wife," Knobowtee said.

"You said I wasn't."

"I was angry." Knobowtee looked at me. "I had a dream about your father. He told me to take care of you."

"You look at all the girls."

"You're the one I see."

"Should that make me forget?"

"What will you do when we reach the new territory?"

"Start over."

"By yourself?"

"I can live with Tanner."

"How long do you think you'd get along with Luthy?"

"I could stay with Quaty."

"Or you could listen to Anna cluck," Knobowtee said. "There's no one you could stay with, Maritole. But you could come with my brother and me."

"How long do you think I'd get along with you?"

"We had a farm together. We had a baby."

"That was in another land."

"We could keep the two girls."

"Why aren't you walking with O-ga-na-ya?"

"I got strength from him on the trail. I looked at you and all I thought about was how I could do nothing for you. It was easier to stay away."

"You could have done everything for me! You could have been my friend. Instead you ignored me and left me by myself. Maybe I'll be like Nancy Ward, our beloved woman, our ᎩᎦᎤᏅ, who fought in the place of her husband."

"She married a white man after her husband died."

"The soldier's gone. There'll be no marriage."

"Nancy Ward told the British about the Cherokee warriors," Knobowtee reminded me.

"She worked for peace, not war."

"She could be called a traitor by the Cherokee."

"You could be called a deserter by your wife."

"You don't forget anything?"

"Nancy Ward preserved peace. If it meant protecting American settlers and informing British soldiers about the plans of hostile Cherokee, well, that's what it took to be a woman of peace."

Knobowtee walked beside me without saying anything more.

LUTHY

I reached down to an old pack dog holding up his back leg as he hobbled. I wanted to untie the pack that hanged sideways. There was nothing in it anyway.

Tanner had to cut it loose with the knife he took from a man he had buried. He talked with some of the men in front of us. There would be hard times, they agreed. The Georgia leaders who signed away the land and fled to Indian Territory would have to face what they did. The Tennessee Cherokees would vent their anger against them no matter what the leaders and ministers and ᏠᏓᎣᎲᎠᎩ said. Even Reverend Bushyhead preached forgiveness every Sunday along the trail.

Mark wanted to play with the dog, but it growled, and Ephum pulled him away from the dog, who only wanted to limp out of the way.

TANNER

The men still grumbled.

Would there be the fiercer plains Indians to contend with again? What kind of animals would there be to hunt?

I listened to the men as we walked. We had not sided with the Shawnee chief Tecumseh in 1811 when he wanted the southeastern tribes to join and fight against the U.S. government.

We had been for nationalism.

"Even when the traders thought they could get us in debt so we would have to sell our farms to them."

"That didn't work."

"Even when our crops and cabins burned."

"Then we made land concessions until we had only a portion left."

"Sixteen eighty-four. The first treaty?" Knobowtee couldn't remember. He knew for sure that 1785 was the Treaty of Hopewell. Seventeen ninety-one the Treaty of Holston. All had been signed to settle boundaries once and for all. No more land would be ceded. But our territory had shrunk to a handful of land and disappeared. Now we owned the-land-we-haven't-seen.

"We've been doomed since 1540 when DeSoto came," I said, "and a scribe recorded the first sight of the Cherokee."

"Yes, writing was the beginning of our end, Tanner," Knobowtee agreed.

"But Sequoyah made a beginning for us in writing."

"What do we need it for?"

"To sign treaties."

The men laughed.

We had changed from the old ways. Even our prayer. We used to dance on the square grounds. That was our prayer. Now we used words. They had changed everything.

The white man had a way with words. The men remembered the laws that came into being with words. The Cherokee couldn't mine gold on his own land. He couldn't testify against a white man in court about the continual raids on Cherokee farms. The white man even got us to agree to our removal.

We could do anything with written words. We had to be careful we didn't use them that way. Our words would turn on us. Like summer into winter.

Indian Territory

FEBRUARY 27, 1839

KNOBOWTEE

Along the trail through the woods, there was a small marker beside the road. Some of the Cherokee who passed didn't even see it. It was a territorial marker for the end of Arkansas and the beginning of Indian country. We were the last and largest group of Cherokee to be removed from the southeast into the new land. We'd make a way into it with our voices. We'd call the orators to open our fields. And what were those dark things off to the side of my vision? A war in Indian Territory? Over the whole land? Maybe it was later. No, I didn't want to see. But the black thoughts came back. Large wagons on wheels. Maybe they were someplace else. Yes, that was it.

TANNER

"Did you see that marker beside the road?" I asked Knobowtee.

"Yes, I saw it," he answered.

KNOBOWTEE

"*Hey-eeey.*" I called the horses to hold back. The trail was steep and the wagons slid over the rocks. We traveled down a hill all morning, then crossed the Illinois River midday. The Light Horse Guard had found a shallows. The Illinois was not the Ohio or Mississippi. It wasn't even the Gasconade or Meramec or Whitewater in Missouri. It was more of a creek, like the Hiwassee that began the trail.

"*HEEEEEYYYY!*" O-ga-na-ya called.

I remembered the trees along the creek bank in North Carolina as I helped the people cross. I remembered the reflection of the trees in the water as I felt the cold around my legs. Could the trees also mean something about words? The spoken words were the real trees. The written words were merely their reflection in the creek. I'd seen the waves as pages. Pages of written words. Distorting the real trees. That was the trouble with written words. They dealt with reflections. There was treachery in writing. The country had found it. The government had turned the written word to expediency. They had cheated with their written words. Therefore they wouldn't have the power of the spoken word to use. It would become meaningless, something that couldn't be trusted. Something that couldn't make anything happen. The trees along the creek bank would not look the same to them. They would prefer their reflection. Muddied by their feet.

MARITOLE

The baby who had been born was crying.

Luthy took my arm. "It's a new voice that won't grieve for our old land in North Carolina."

I looked at Luthy, who dragged Ephum by the hand. He was throwing a fit because he wanted something she wouldn't let him have.

"Ride in the wagon, Maritole," Knobowtee said. He came to walk sometimes beside us again.

"No."

"You're thin," Tanner said.

"The wagon is for the dead," I told them, "the old and the sick and the orphans."

"And for the ones just born," Luthy added.

"Get in," Knobowtee started again. "Aren't we all orphans?"

"No. I want to walk. I feel something happen in me as I walk. Something small and strong begins to grow. A stem comes out of the ground like a squash vine. It rises in me. I have hope and strength that you can't see. I feel it inside because I can walk. I feel it because I can push a bear," I said.

Luthy finally angered that Ephum continued to cry, and she took a switch to him.

"After we build our cabins again," I said, "and plow the

fields, I will hold the memory of this trail. We'll have the new Keetoowah fire to light our hearth. We'll have our stickball games again. I don't always feel it, but somewhere deep inside me I carry a tiny piece of joy like a ball."

QUATY LEWIS

We arrived at Fort Gibson, Indian Territory, on a afternoon full of stillness. The fort was small. Only a few went in. The other detachments drew up in the woods around the fort as if it was a stockade we'd left four months ago. I felt the walls around me I couldn't see. I pushed my hands into the air to see if I could find them.

The Cherokee who survived the trail stood around not knowing what to do. We sat on the ground. We stood again. We looked at one another.

I felt the need to make cornmeal bread. I looked for twigs to make a fire. I wanted to tell my husband I was in the new territory. Some night in a dream I'd see him standing at the window of our cabin. Some night I'd listen to the wind in the pines. Only there weren't pines here. I looked around. They were oaks, a different kind of oak than we'd had in North Carolina, but they would sound the old truth of the pines.

LUTHY

As for the trail—it's over—Tanner and my boys are alive.

ANNA SCO-SO-TAH

I talk to the little bag of women. Quaty Lewis sucking her nose. Lacey Woodard. Mrs. Bushyhead nursing. Their wings sprouting behind their ears. Mrs. Young Turkey. Dead. Just lump inside fort. "Selu. Selu," she said.

Others stare at the ground. "How plow?" the men say. "With our fingers? Feet? Just speak our voice?"

I think there's no God in the afterlife. We're all loose to follow what we want. Now let them Christians chow on that.

WILLY DROWNING BEAR
Compensation Claim

1 farm (worth $677.50)
3 horses
48 stock hogs
1 acre potato patch
2 spinning wheels
1 click reel
2 weaver's sleys
1 loom
2 large pots
1 ox
1 table
1 plow
5 beehives
5 weeding hoes

ELIZABETH COOPER
Claims for Spoilation

Fields & crops, cabin, horses, saddles, harness, rifle guns, chicken, hogs, cows & calves, ducks, geese, hoes, money, gristmills, featherbeds, blankets, quilts, pots, ovens, kettles, cups & saucers, knives & forks, pails, one set blue-edged plates belonging to Elizabeth Cooper, paled gardens, sowed & planted, bacon, potatoes, beans, salt, looms, shuttles, weavers reeds, spinning wheels, thread reel, bedstead, cherrywood table, chairs, cupboard, wooden spoons, ploughs, chains, baskets, a "first-rate" fiddle, saw, shovel, & carpenter tools.

TANNER

The War Department promised subsistence for a year after the arrival, but the government contractors, Glascow and Harrison, decided to make a profit and delivered inferior meat and flour. Many died.

Three of the Georgia leaders who had signed the New Echota Treaty were killed. John Ridge was dragged from his bed by masked men and stabbed in the yard in front of his wife and children. Major Ridge, John's father, was found beside a road shot five times. Elias Boudinot was knifed in the back at his new house, his head tomahawked.

I tried to hide the details from Luthy, but I knew she'd hear them anyway.

Some of the Cherokee went back to the old territory. Some returned to the new territory again, saying the land had changed.

No one ever had news of Thomas.

But I knew there was hope for the Cherokee who'd run into the hills of North Carolina during the roundup. In the groups I heard talking. Tsali and three of his sons had been shot. Tsali had killed a white soldier who had caused his wife's death. He and his sons fled into the hills of North Carolina but had finally given themselves up. The soldiers had said the Cherokee could stay in the hills if Tsali and his sons would turn themselves in. But the soldiers shot Tsali and three of his sons. No one knew if Tsali gave himself for the sake of the others, or if he and his sons had been tricked.

"No, it was Euchella, the Cherokee chief, and the Cherokee who shot Tsali." Knobowtee would stand for the truth.

"Euchella shot Tsali in front of the soldiers because Euchella had to," I said.

"So they could keep their land in North Carolina," Luthy added.

"But Tsali had given himself up with the promise from the soldiers that the Cherokees would not be removed from the hills," Maritole said.

"In the end, I don't think the soldiers had much to do with the killing," Knobowtee said.

"Thomas will have a place," Maritole insisted, and walked away from us.

KNOBOWTEE

Act of Union, July 12, 1839

WHEREAS our Fathers have existed, as a separate and distinct Nation, in the possession and exercise of the essential . . .

attributes of sovereignty, from a period extending to antiquity,
beyond the record and memory of man.
AND WHEREAS these attributes, with the rights and franchises . . .
remain still in full force and virtue . . . it has become essential to
the general welfare that a union be formed, and a system of gov-
ernment matured, adapted to (our) present condition, and pro-
viding equally for the protection of each individual in the
enjoyment of his rights.
THEREFORE we, the people composing the Eastern and Western
Cherokee Nation, in the National Convention assembled . . . do
hereby solemnly and mutually agree to form ourselves into one
body politic under the style and title of Cherokee Nation.

"But President Van Buren didn't recognize the new nation. We're still nothing to them," I said in council, my arms sore from lifting logs for my cabin. "But we can be a nation to ourselves."

SOPHIA SAWYER

After the Ridges' death, I had gone to Fayetteville, Arkansas, to escape the suffering. In 1840, I returned to Indian Territory to visit.

I found them in huts. Mourning the trail.

"We have wept enough," I said. "Go to work and build houses and cultivate your land."

"Who should I build for?" a man asked me. "I had three sons. One died in General Scott's camp. One died on the trail. The third died here. For whom should I build my house?"

WAR CLUB

yomph

THE SOLDIERS

Most of them spoke Cherokee, and we don't know what they said on the trail or at Fort Gibson or as they started to build their farms again. We just left them there. We had horses on the trail. We didn't know walking like that.

I still see them floating like ice chunks on the Mississippi. I still see them pushing the long trail.

MARITOLE

I sat on the cabin steps with my head in my hands. Aneh sat with me. Sometimes I thought about Sergeant Williams, but when she looked at me, I swept him away.

The cabin had been built hurriedly. It leaked. The place was silent, though once I thought I heard the distant growl of a bear. Nothing of my grandparents was here. Nothing was the same but Knobowtee coming up the path.

The orphan children played in the yard. One of the girls had died, but the other girl and a boy whose father died after our arrival in the new territory were hitting stones with a stick.

Sometimes I thought about Quaty's story of the Trickster Turtle. I had heard Luthy telling it to her boys again. I told it now to the orphans. There was a turtle at the starting line in the old territory. There was a turtle at the finish line in the new. Our Cherokee nation had become two to survive.

At night the children slept against us, crying sometimes in their sleep. Knobowtee and I held them between us. Maybe someday he would touch me. Maybe someday love would come.

AUTHOR'S NOTE

In 1977 or 1978, my daughter and I drove from Tulsa to Tahlequah, Oklahoma, to see "The Trail of Tears," a dramatization about the 1838–39 march of the Cherokee from the southeast to Indian Territory.

There had been a rain that afternoon and just before the dramatization began, there were two rainbows in the sky above the amphitheater. The story and the rainbows would stay with me.

In October 1986, I went with a friend from Oklahoma to northern Georgia to find New Echota, the old Cherokee capital, which is fifty miles north of Atlanta.

It took us three stops to ask directions. No one in Calhoun, Georgia, could tell us where it was. Finally, a man told us to drive a few miles farther south and take the Chatsworth exit from Highway 75. A highway marker pointed in the direction of New Echota. It was Monday. The museum and field were closed. I could see a cabin, a courthouse, a church, and several other reconstructed buildings. Four generations removed to the territory west of the Mississippi, I felt tears at the site of the ancestors' home. Their sorrow still haunts the land.

We went back to Red Clay, Tennessee, another historical site, about fifty miles north.

After stopping twice for car repairs, we headed south again the next day. The museum was still closed. Calhoun schoolchildren were on the grounds. Finally, after we asked twice, the attendant opened the museum, and I saw a few buttons, some broken pieces of dishes, pottery shards, and other artifacts left behind after the removal. I had the same tears, the same feeling of ᏍᎤᎬᎡᎠ, home, though I don't know where my father's people came from. Besides Georgia, land belonging to the Cherokee covered parts of Tennessee, Alabama, and North and South Carolina.

I thank my friend who took me back along the route, endured my tears and our struggle to find what I wanted to see, and who drove while I first wrote the words that came from the book's central narrator, Maritole.

In the summer of 1995, I saw the two rainbows again. I was on the Rosebud Reservation in South Dakota for another research project, and there was a storm after a particularly hot July afternoon. When it stopped raining, the rainbows appeared in the evening sky, and I felt the closure of my work on *Pushing the Bear*, some seventeen or eighteen years after it began.

I would like to thank the following for valuable assistance in research:

1988 Frances C. Allen Fellowship at the D'Arcy McNickle Center for the American Indian, Newberry Library, Chicago.

1990 NEH Summer Institute Fellowship also at the Newberry, where John Aubrey showed me some of the actual letters written by the Cherokee protesting the removal. It was there, while I was looking for structure for the story, that I saw a pottery bowl, broken and glued together with some parts missing and the cracks still showing, and I knew how the story would fit together. I also thank Barbara Tedlock, who during a lecture at the Newberry asked, "Why can't we recreate culture from the fragments we have left?" It was the permission I needed to write the story.

I'm also grateful to Macalester College for a 1993 Wallace Faculty Development Fund travel grant that helped me drive back along the trail and finish my research for this manuscript.

Acknowledgment to Roger Blakely, Jim Turnure, and Robert Conley for reading the manuscript.

Gratefulness to Durbin Feeling and Bacone College.

And special thanks to Sharon Friedman, Ruth Greenstein, Walter Bode, and Theo Lieber.

I'm especially grateful to Jerry Clark at the National Archives for his comments during our discussions and the documents he provided.

I also want to thank Sylvia Taylor at the Trail of Tears State Park in Cape Girardeau, Missouri, and Mrs. Tom Garrard and the Five Civilized Tribes Museum in Muskogee, Oklahoma.

I knew this wasn't going to be a good Indian/bad white man story. You know there has to be both sides in each. I heard that once when the Osage wanted to come back to Oklahoma from Kansas, where they'd been moved and couldn't live, the Cherokee sold them some dried-up land between Tulsa and Pawhuska. But that's where the oil was.

It comes back.

Those farms General Sherman burned in the Civil War were the farms taken from the Georgia Cherokee some twenty years earlier. And maybe a fourth of their people died, too. The soldiers anyway. And maybe a little of the voice of the people.

Maybe, in the end, our acts cause little energy fields that draw their likenesses toward them.

A NOTE ON THE WRITTEN CHEROKEE LANGUAGE

In a few places in the text, certain words appear in the Cherokee for a sense of the language. They can be viewed as holes in the text so the original can show through.

Following is the alphabet of the written Cherokee language, or syllabary, used in the text of *Pushing the Bear*. Composed of eighty-five letters, the syllabary was invented in 1821 by Sequoia (George Guess), a Cherokee from Tuskegee, Tennessee. Because it was created to represent an already highly developed and regionalized oral culture, written Cherokee admits wide variations in spelling. Also, many usages included in this historical novel are archaic.

CHEROKEE ALPHABET

Dₐ	Rₑ	Tᵢ	Ꮿₒ	Oᵤ	iᵥ
Ꮜga Ꮼka	Ꮛge	Ꮙgi	Agο	Jgu	Egv
Ꮰha	Ꮅhe	Ꭿhi	Ꮧho	Ꭾhu	Ꮊhv
Wla	Ꮰle	Ꮈli	Ꮹlo	Mlu	Ꮬlv
Ꮾma	Ꮊme	Hmi	Ꮹmo	Ꮍmu	
Ꮎna Ꮏhna Ꮐnah	Ꮑne	ʰni	Zno	Ꮕnu	Ꮒnv
Ꮖqua	Ꮗque	Ꮙqui	Ꮚquo	Ꮚquu	Ꮗquv
Ꮜsa Ꮝs	4se	bsi	Ꮠso	Ꮢsu	Ꮢsv
Ꮣda Ꮤta	Ꮥde Ꮦte	Ꮧdi Ꮨti	Vdo	Sdu	Ꮩdv
Ꮬdla Ꮭtla	Ltle	Ctli	Ꮰtlo	Ꮱtlu	Ptlv
Ꮳtsa	Ꮴtse	Ꮵtsi	Ktso	Ꮷtsu	Ꮸtsv
Ꮹwa	Ꮺwe	Ꮻwi	Ꮼwo	Ꮽwu	6wv
Ꮿya	ᏸye	Ꭹyi	ᏺyo	Ꮇyu	Byv

The following poem is the story of the boxturtles and deer that
Quaty told on pages 194 and 195, with the Cherokee characters,
an English phonetic version, and a word-for-word translation.

ᎳᎩᏏ	lagsi	box turtle
ᏃᎴ	nole	and
ᎠᏫ	awi	deer
ᏚᎾᏓᏁ ᏄᏁᎢ	dunadane nunei	challenged
ᎧᏉᎩ ᏁᎢ	kaquog nei	seventh
ᎣᏧᎸ	otsualv	mountain
ᏭᏲᎷᎯᏍᏘ	wuyoluhisti	to reach
ᎳᎩᏏ	lagsi	box turtle
ᎲᎳᏁᏄᏁᎢ	hulanenunei	challenged

ᏧᎳᎩᏯ ᏍᏘᎯ	tsulagya stihi	that he would leave behind and win
ᎠᏍᎡᏃ	aseno	but
ᎱᎳᎷᎸ	dulalulv	before
ᎱᎳᏅᏖᎴ	dulanvtele	the race
ᎱᎳᏅᏖᎴ	dulanvtele	schemed
ᎳᎩᏏ	lagsi	box turtle
ᎦᎵᏉᎩᏁ	galigwogne	seventh
ᎣᏧᎠᎸ	otsualv	mountain
ᏘᎾᎴᏂᏍᎬ	tinalenisgv	beginning
ᏥᏚᏅᏍᎳᏁ	tsidunvslane	he placed along
ᎳᎩᏏ	lagsi	box turtle
ᏥᏚᏅᏍᎳᏁ	tsidunvslane	as he placed them
ᏚᏁᏤᎴᎢ	dunetselei	he told them
ᏂᎦᎷᎬᎾᏇ	nigalugvque	before he got there
ᎠᏫ	awi	deer
ᎠᏙᎯᏍᏗ	adohisdi	to holler
ᎨᏎᎢ		
ᎠᏫ	awi	deer
ᎱᏨᏍᎳ	hutsvsla	as he ran past
ᎳᎩᏏ	lagsi	box turtle
ᎾᎾ	nana	right there
ᎤᎢᏉᎶᎩ	uiquolog	in the leaves
ᏥᏭᏄᏴᎴ	tsiwnuyvle	it crawled into
ᎭᏧᏍᏗᎭ	hatsusdiha	as he ran
Ꮠ ᎣᏧᎠᎸ	sootsualv	other mountain
ᏏᏫᏂᎦᎷᎫᎾ	siwinigaluguna	before he got there
ᏘᎠᏙᎰᏍᎨ	tiadohosge	hollered
ᏄᎳᎴ	nutale	another
ᎳᎩᏏ	lagsi	box turtle
ᎢᎬᏱ	igvyi	first
ᎤᏓᏁᏄᎳᎡ	udanenulane	the challenger
ᎤᎢᏉᎶᎩ	uiquolog	in the leaves
ᏭᏄᏴᎸ	wunuyvlv	had crawled
ᎨᏒ		
ᎳᏥᎩᏰᎢ	latsigyei	was defeated
ᎠᏫ	awi	deer
ᎦᎶᏄᎮᎭ	galonuheha	cheating
ᎦᏘ	gati	with